"A raw, honest look a
of ourselves we leave behind. This powerful debut is sure to
resonate with readers who like complex family stories."

—*Library Journal*

"*Between the Devil and the Deep Blue Sea* examines the delicate
balance between identity and obligation, exploring the quiet
struggles and unspoken truths of motherhood. With pierc-
ing honesty and lyrical prose, Jessica Guerrieri illuminates
the spaces between love and resentment, sacrifice and self-
preservation, and the impossible choices women face in their
quest to hold it all together while they secretly self-destruct.
This is more than a beautiful novel—it's a mirror, a reckoning,
and ultimately a lifeline for anyone who's ever felt like they are
drowning under the weight of being everything to everyone."

—Lara Love Hardin, *New York Times* bestselling
author and Oprah's Book Club Pick

"Jessica Guerrieri's powerful debut is a deeply moving account of motherhood, addiction, and how we lose—and
find—ourselves within family. I loved getting to know Leah,
Lucas, and the entire O'Connor clan within the sweeping
backdrop of a Northern California surfing town."

—Tara Conklin, *New York Times* bestselling
author of *Community Board*

"A powerfully written page-turner about impossible choices,
motherhood and creativity, and the devastating results of using
alcohol to fill the void. I read it in a single day, riveted by Leah's
inexorable descent into addiction. A delicate and unblinking

Advance Praise for

study of addiction and recovery, but most of all, an intense portrayal of the ways we lose ourselves to motherhood and how to find the impossible balance. A beautiful book!"

—Barbara O'Neal, bestselling author
of *When We Believed in Mermaids*

"Every once in a while, a novel comes along that so completely encapsulates a piece of the human experience. Jessica Guerrieri's debut novel, *Between the Devil and the Deep Blue Sea*, does exactly that for both motherhood and alcoholism in a breathtaking story about the bonds and trauma of family, the struggle to retain a sense of self while parenting tiny humans, and the difficulties of marrying into a family with different values than the ones you were raised with. With a cast of characters so real that you'll swear you know them, this is the perfect read for fans of Celeste Ng and Liane Moriarty. Mothers of all ages will relate to Leah's desire to remember who she was before having children, as well as her perceived inability to live up to the standards of seemingly Stepford-perfect moms."

—Sara Goodman Confino, bestselling author
of *Don't Forget to Write* and *She's Up to No Good*

"*Between the Devil and the Deep Blue Sea* is a powerful and eloquent novel that plumbs the depths of the conflicts between domestic tranquility—particularly parenthood—and a growing dependence on alcohol to fuel the creative life. This book is highly recommended and impossible to put down!"

—John Lescroart, *New York Times* bestselling author

"*Between the Devil and the Deep Blue Sea* is an unflinching look at the perceived expectations of raising children and the emotional turmoil of trying to balance motherhood and identity, mirrored perfectly by the intense atmospheric imagery of the Northern California coast."

—Lindsay Currie, #1 *New York Times* bestselling
author of *The Mystery of Locked Rooms*

"Motherhood isn't necessarily every woman's dream. *Between the Devil and the Deep Blue Sea* tells the important story of a woman whose decision to marry and become a mother has been more complicated than she bargained for, leading her to feelings of self-doubt and guilt and addiction as escapism. This engaging and introspective tale expertly peels away the mysteries of addiction, painting a riveting portrait of how quietly it can start, persist, and destroy. A compelling story of vulnerability, family resentment, and second chances told in beautiful prose reminiscent of Ann Napolitano, Guerrieri's debut is not to be missed!"

—Jacqueline Friedland, *USA TODAY*
bestselling author of *Counting Backwards*

"A compelling exploration of the human experience. This novel captures the intricacies of family dynamics layered with money, status, and the weight of expectation. Each page resonates with universal reliability that draws readers deeply into its story. The interplay between characters is so vivid and profound that I was utterly absorbed, losing track of time in the process. This is, without a doubt, one of the most impressive debut novels I've encountered—a remarkable achievement. I eagerly await Guerrieri's next work, as this is only the beginning of what promises to be an extraordinary literary journey."

—Katherine Rhadan, quit lit writer
and addiction recovery advocate

"I read it in one sitting and loved it. Told in Jessica Guerrieri's inimitable voice, *Between the Devil and the Deep Blue Sea* is both real and unflinching. I was struck on every page by how painfully familiar it was, like I was reading my own story. Each chapter is both epic and powerful, causing the reader to root for Leah, while at the same time, quietly hoping that she gets the help she needs. A beautiful debut."

—Laura Cathcart Robbins, author of *Stash* and
My Life in Hiding and host of Only One in the Room podcast

Between the Devil and the Deep Blue Sea

A NOVEL

JESSICA GUERRIERI

HARPER MUSE

Between the Devil and the Deep Blue Sea

Copyright © 2025 by Jessica Guerrieri

All rights reserved. No portion of this book may be reproduced, stored in a retrieval system, or transmitted in any form or by any means—electronic, mechanical, photocopy, recording, scanning, or other—except for brief quotations in critical reviews or articles, without the prior written permission of the publisher.

Published by Harper Muse, an imprint of HarperCollins Focus LLC.

This book is a work of fiction. The characters, incidents, and dialogue are drawn from the author's imagination and are not to be construed as real. Any resemblance to actual events or persons, living or dead, is entirely coincidental.

Any internet addresses (websites, blogs, etc.) in this book are offered as a resource. They are not intended in any way to be or imply an endorsement by HarperCollins Focus LLC, nor does HarperCollins Focus LLC vouch for the content of these sites for the life of this book.

Designed by Jamie Kerner
Wave image © (MariMuz)/stock.adobe.com

Library of Congress Cataloging-in-Publication Data

Names: Guerrieri, Jessica, 1984- author.
Title: Between the devil and the deep blue sea / Jessica Guerrieri.
Description: Nashville: Harper Muse, 2025. | Summary: "Leah O'Connor is torn between the life she's currently living and the allure of a phantom life that can no longer be hers"--Provided by publisher.
Identifiers: LCCN 2024030526 (print) | LCCN 2024030527 (ebook) | ISBN 9781400345953 (paperback) | ISBN 9781400345960 (epub) | ISBN 9781400345977
Subjects: LCGFT: Novels.
Classification: LCC PS3607.U466 B48 2025 (print) | LCC PS3607.U466 (ebook) | DDC 813/.6--dc23/eng/20240917
LC record available at https://lccn.loc.gov/2024030526
LC ebook record available at https://lccn.loc.gov/2024030527

Printed in the United States of America

25 26 27 28 29 LBC 5 4 3 2 1

To the women in my life both little and big—those
Earth-side and those beaming brightly among the stars

Dear Reader,

To ensure sensitivity, I believe it is important to include potential trigger warnings for my novel. If you consider trigger warnings to be spoilers, please stop reading now. For others, please be aware that this book includes themes of alcohol abuse, miscarriage, stillbirth, and suicide.

In earnest,
Jessica

CHAPTER 1

There's a phantom life that runs parallel to the one I'm currently living, like a shadow. That version of me is childless and, therefore, untethered to the O'Connor family. I think of her whenever I'm clipping my two-year-old's toenails, and the little half-moons splinter off in different directions, and I find myself scouring the floor so I'm not stepping on discarded pieces of my youngest daughter's body when I'm barefoot at three o'clock in the morning and need to pee. I'm confident my shadow self has already circled the globe, only to have landed someplace tropical like Costa Rica—beholden to simply the movement of the sea. Sometimes I wave, but she's surfing and cannot wave back.

"Look what I found to bring to Grandma's for our shelves!" My daughter Joni's face lights up like a Christmas tree. She is my oldest, the first grandchild: a unicorn of a being, always golden from time spent on the beach. She appears more ethereal than human. Joni's very existence has made my presence tolerable to my mother-in-law, Christine. As if Lucas and I made Joni just for her.

I glance back and take note of an almost completely purple hermit crab shell resting in the palm of her hand.

"Shelves?" I ask her. It rings a bell, but I almost always mentally check out whenever Christine is involved.

"You know, we collect shells, but, like, perfect ones, for the display cases she has upstairs. She lets me arrange them by category or however I want."

I can picture it now, Christine biting the inside of her cheeks as she reluctantly doles out home decor privileges.

"Wow, lovey. That's a high honor," I say, removing a strand of hair that has caught on the corner of my mouth.

We are driving to one of the last remaining beaches that hasn't been overrun by tourists. It's a little way's walk from the road, and we have to park in a neighborhood where doing so is frowned upon for anyone who is not a resident of Half Moon Bay. I've brought along my painting supplies, though I doubt I'll be able to focus with Dottie, at age two, still heavily in the sand-eating phase.

"I told Grandma to meet us here. We are on a mission to find a whole sand dollar."

"Oh, you did? Great," I say as sincerely as I can muster. It would be nice if Christine could keep the kids occupied while I work.

Christine is already parked, standing next to her driver's side door with her beach gear in hand. I remain in the car with Reid, my eight-year-old, and Dottie, waiting to channel all the willpower I'll need for the next several hours. I watch as Christine and Joni embrace. Christine removes one of her signature scarves from around her neck and drapes it around Joni. Their movements are effortlessly in sync, which has baffled me from the beginning—a dance they started the day Joni was born.

When I arrived home from the hospital a few days after her birth, Lucas insisted we were ready for visitors. Feeling the need to busy myself, I staged a scene that only Christine would manage to believe exists inside the realm of motherhood. With soft music playing and the low morning light peeking in through dusty rose—colored curtains, I held a swaddled Joni while sitting in the rocking chair that had once belonged to Christine. She'd had someone deliver it to us with a note attached that read: *Being a mother is the greatest blessing of my life. I hope you feel the same.*

Even her kind gestures have hidden agendas.

I rocked, awaiting the sounds of feet on the stairs, and pondered how I was meant to share this tiny being with a family that resisted my every movement.

"If I had a camera, I'd take your picture," Christine had said as she stood in the doorway.

On the dry sand, I set up my easel slightly removed from our mountain of beach stuff while still placing myself within earshot of the kids. Christine and Joni have already ventured down to the water to look for shells. Only two have made the cut and are worthy of the home display. Reid has Dottie near the surf, and they are playing chase with the waves.

"My mother and I used to explore the tide pools after school along this same beach. We'd collect everything from shells to hermit crabs. Then we'd put them in vases of sea glass and use them as centerpieces at The Cove. Anything special or worthy enough would go inside the trinket boxes in our home. The same boxes I have now," Christine says to Joni, her eyes fixating on the waves. Then, drawing her focus back to her granddaughter, she adds, "The circle doesn't have to be a sphere," as she runs her finger along the edges of a sand dollar. "But there can't be any cracks." She holds it to her ear and shakes it gently. "Bonus points for teeth. The hole in the back is its mouth." She pauses. "Sand dollars were always her favorite."

Christine doesn't often talk about her mother unless she's sharing about the family restaurant they owned and operated for two generations, The Cove.

"What's your favorite sea creature, Grandma?" Joni asks.

"I've always liked the starfish. As a kid, I loved how it could be both hard and soft depending on whether it was in or out of the water. But these days, I appreciate it for the extra arms. They would have come in handy raising your uncles." If I were to paint Christine, I'd be strictly limited to muted pastels.

Christine goes to work laying out the picnic she brought for the kids while Joni takes extreme care carving out seats for her and her grandmother within the sand. She uses the excess to create a solid backing, especially for Christine's "chair," and then finally covers them completely with towels. She has positioned them side by side so she and Christine can align themselves like two little old ladies at a beauty parlor.

Their placement reminds me of the time Amy and I snuck away for pedicures on the day she lost her first pregnancy. There is something poignant about my sister-in-law's unshakable grit and being chosen as the object of her unwavering attention, though with her baby arriving so soon, I know I'll need to learn how to share her.

The sea is flat today. The waves break at the shore, and so far, Reid and Dottie have only been caught up around Dottie's midthigh. Fixing my gaze on the water plays tricks on my eyes. Each dark point that crests upward deceives me into thinking something is splashing mysteriously just at the surface—only to sink back down and pop up closer to shore. I watch one spot in particular for over a minute, convinced I see a silky brown head, only for it to disappear and never breach the surface again.

Wanting to include myself in their world, I call over to Joni, "Look! There's a seal." I point to where it was, but there are no landmarks to direct her sight. Joni lifts her head briefly but lazily rests it on Christine's shoulder, content not to indulge in what I am offering.

Joni begins biting her nails. "How did you know you liked Grandpa?" she asks in a voice that's so sweet and soft I almost don't recognize it.

Christine reaches over and pulls Joni's hand away from her mouth, chuckling a little. "Some days I'm not entirely sure I like your grandpa."

Joni lets out a laugh, and I almost do too. Christine's sense of humor is usually limited to when she indulges herself with a single glass of wine on Sundays.

"Grandpa was friends with my best friend's boyfriend. We met for a setup. That's when friends want to introduce you both to see if there's a spark."

Her response doesn't answer the question, so I am genuinely curious to see if Joni will accept it. Joni looks thoughtfully puzzled. Her eyes change shape as her lips form a thin, crooked pout that moves her nose ever so slightly to the left. It's an expression that is woven into her identity; she's been making it since birth. She puts a grape in her mouth and starts to chew slowly.

"What do you mean, spark?" Joni asks. Christine has scratched the surface of something.

"When you like someone, you can just feel it. Inside—it makes you feel warm and happy."

Joni is nodding like she understands, though, at age ten, I'm not sure she does.

Christine lowers her voice a little. "Do you feel that way about someone?"

Joni snuggles closer to Christine, placing her head back on her shoulder. I notice her whisper something directly into her grandma's ear. While my interest was initially piqued, in their secrets they have drawn the blinds down around them. Christine pulls Joni directly onto her lap as if she were a baby. Joni's four limbs cross every which way, and they are a tangled mess of sand and giggles.

On that morning of Christine's first visit when we brought Joni home, I reluctantly managed to relinquish my baby into her arms, even though it felt like the very act would tear the seams we'd spent the past nine months carefully sewing together. The hum of Christine's adoration was palpable. For a moment, the three of us were all touching at once. With Christine's unabashed tenderness, I sensed a pull, not a break, and something passed through us that told me exactly what I needed to know: Joni was her grandchild. No matter what I had done in my past, the secrets I would need to keep, this baby belonged in this family, even if I would always feel like an outsider.

I pretend to be extremely interested in my work, detailing the slickness of the seal's head that will be a focal point of the piece, which I've made too large and entirely too obvious. The bitterness of the pill I swallow as an O'Connor is that for all of Christine's many flaws, her grown sons have chosen to live only minutes from her and my father-in-law, George. By choosing this version instead of my childless shadow self, I have to bear witness to moments like my daughter whispering away her most precious secrets. I wonder how much strain our seam can sustain.

Once we have packed up the car to head home, Christine and I linger near the trunk. I can tell she's eager to say something. She has to crane her neck to catch my gaze, where she pauses as if she's locked into my orbit. Nana, my mom's mom, would say that my luminary aura draws people in. She claimed I could get a killer to reveal where all the bodies are buried. I prefer to expose confessions across a blank canvas.

It was Nana who originally helped to foster my superpower. I remember standing in her backyard, peering into the koi pond she built with her own two hands. There were seven fish, and I named them all after the seven dwarfs.

"Sleepy is extra sleepy today," I told her. The orange-and-black mammoth beast had been sulking at the bottom while his brothers wove around him.

"We all have our quiet, reflective days at the bottom of the pond," Nana explained in her infinite wisdom.

"Can we feed 'em again? I love when they nibble my fingers. It tickles," I said as my five-year-old self. I fiddled with my favorite headband that was once white but, over time, had become a dirtied beige.

"If we feed them any more, they'll outgrow their habitat, which is fine, I suppose, but I'm hoping to keep 'em in this one as long as I possibly can."

Nana dragged over a chair, and I crawled into her lap, tucking myself beneath her chin as we watched the bright colors swirl in the reflection of the water. I remember tracing the remarkable texture along the back of her hands—how her veins protruded up along the bones that connected each finger—their pillowy softness. I tried to pinch them without squeezing so I wouldn't hurt her. I wanted to lay my body between the folds of her skin and become entombed in her forever.

I painted the image of us cupped within her palms before I left Iowa for university in California. It felt important that I leave behind a piece of me, even though I had outgrown my pond. I could never outgrow my love for her.

"Thanks for being here for the kids today so I could focus on my work," I say, genuinely grateful for Christine's help at the beach.

"You know I love that child." Christine smiles, looking at Joni in the passenger seat as if she's remembering it all over again. Her favoritism has never been subtle.

"Did you want to follow us home to see Lucas?" I'm asking, but my tone carries no inflection to suggest I want her to do that.

"I need to get back to George. If I'm not there to feed him, he'll forget to eat." She looks up as if searching for something on top of my minivan, but then she shakes her head. "I'll be off."

"Hey, what did Joni whisper to . . . Ya know what, never mind." I can feel my face redden a little, so I turn, anxious to drive away. But as I step back she's stepping forward, intrusively entering my personal space.

"These things reveal themselves in their own way, in their own time," she says as if I should feel lucky to be gaining another nugget of wisdom from the Grand High Mother herself.

"Thanks for the advice, but raising daughters is nothing like raising sons."

"Yes, well." It's Christine's turn to flush.

Good, I think. Though my victory feels tainted somehow.

CHAPTER 2

t's not that I long for the other version of me, that shadow self, but I did believe that one day we'd happily merge. That somehow her momentum would still be building in the background—waiting patiently for our union.

If only I were satisfied by all the things that seem to make my mother-in-law so methodically calculated, then maybe I could meld into the O'Connor mold. Take the image of Christine's home and how it mirrors the way she presents herself to the outside world. The square footage alone is massive, but even the surrounding landscape looks like it's been hand-painted. With west-facing views of the ocean, I can envision her fingers forming a square as she dictates to the architect that the kitchen window must encapsulate the sinking of the sunset. She'd inquire in such a way that it would sound like she's asking his opinion, but she's making sure he knows who's in charge of the entire operation. She is the boss. She'd instigate just enough to ensure a battle to fill the empty hours without her grown sons to fawn over. When the home was complete in all its meticulous perfection, she'd invite the architect over for dinner, just so he'd have to eat his words.

Sunday family dinners have been a long-standing tradition with the O'Connors. My very first one will go down in history as the most memorable, given it was the setting of Lucas's and my surprise pregnancy announcement with Joni. This evening I sip my wine, keeping my eyes glued to the front door as I await Amy's arrival.

"They're here!" Joni announces.

Paul enters first, reaching behind to take Amy's hand. She's small and lovely, almost more belly than woman at this point.

"Amy! What are you drinking?" my father-in-law, George, asks before her feet even cross the threshold. He thrusts a glass of wine into her hand, and it sloshes onto her dress.

"Jeez, Dad! We went over this." Paul, in a swift motion, takes the glass from her.

She shakes out her dress; luckily, the wine was white and not red.

"What? Suddenly a pregnant woman can't drink?" George asks. "My mother had at least two martinis every night on doctor's orders. And look at me!"

"Yes, look at you." Christine appears out of nowhere, sweeping over to embrace Paul and then Amy.

Amy finds my eyes and squints, laughing without laughing. Already we're off to the races, and no one else in the room even noticed the sound of the starter pistol.

Amy keeps her hands on her stomach, likely to cover the stain but maybe to protectively shield the growing parts that will mark Christine's sixth grandchild. Her features, starting with her flowing brown hair, are warm except for her eyes— those give away her war wounds. As she removes her coat, I scan the expansive home, somehow made crowded by a single family. I spot all three of my children and scoop Dottie up in my arms, dangling her high above the heads of impeccably dressed children as I begin making guttural moaning sounds meant to imitate the African tribal music of *The Lion King*.

Amy reaches up, grinning, to accept my sacrificial offering. She pulls Dottie down onto what's left of her lap as she buries her face in Dottie's yellow curls.

"Little Dot, I've missed you," she whispers into Dottie's delicate, perfect ear. Her breath must tickle Dottie's skin, because she giggles, her whole body consumed by joy.

"Teacher Amy, sing!" Dottie commands, waiting for Amy to perform for her like she does when she's the teacher in Dottie's classroom.

"Here she is your *auntie* Amy," I correct her.

Amy shuffles Dottie off to the side and maneuvers her hands around the orb of her belly, either checking for movement or repositioning to get comfortable. Either way, she's deep in thought. I take Amy's hand, hoping Dottie and I can alleviate the weight of her worry over the baby girl she's carrying inside her. She says nothing, letting out an audible sigh as we stare into a sea of O'Connors. We both married into the same situation but under entirely different circumstances. For me, becoming an O'Connor happened by accident. For Amy, it was a welcome, purposeful change. It still feels impossible to find our footing inside such an established family. Almost immediately and without hesitation, we tethered ourselves to each other, speaking our own language of kinship.

"Hello in there, my darling," I whisper as I pretend to knock before gently resting my hand on her belly. Amy presses her lips against Dottie's cheek. I turn my attention toward the children in the room. "Hey, guys, Uncle Jack is hiding chocolate somewhere on his body. Go tickle him until he surrenders it!"

All the grandchildren, including Dottie, dash in the direction of the rest of the grown-ups. Amy recognizes the trap I've set. Despite having two kids of his own, Jack acts like a dog-bite victim in a pen of rottweilers as they circle him. Typically, I single out Christine as my target, but the night is still young.

"So," I say. I know, like me, she appreciates this moment by ourselves.

"So," she echoes.

I reach across Amy for my wineglass, which is nearing empty. I consider offering her what's left as a time machine, the memory transporting us back to all the hours we stayed up late together, drinking and talking. During those early days, safe within the bubble of our new alliance—taking turns shedding protective layers of skin until we were nothing but bones and hushed whispers—our secrets spilled like those last sips of wine.

I call out to my husband, Lucas, holding up my glass, and motion to him for more. He immediately makes his way toward us. Even after eleven years of marriage, my body hums with the vibration of want at merely the sight of him. He's aged in a way that can be gifted only through genetics, with a smile that makes him look mischievous. He's very tall, like his older brother, Paul; both are notably striking. They are considered "Irish twins," having been conceived within the same year. Christine never strays from the narrative that having three children within a few years was nothing but easy bliss. Having three myself, I recognize she's entirely full of crap.

The youngest brother, Jack, found his wife in high school and got married just out of college. Lidy, his wife, is quiet and non-threatening. She is content to exist on bland, nonconfrontational conversation topics, such as the weather or the merits of crustless sandwiches. Now and again, I'll get stranded next to her while doing the dishes or en route to the ladies' room, and forced and painful attempts at conversation will ensue. Lidy devours the version of ladylike that I've never subscribed to. Amy is a much better sport than me about O'Connor things like always having to hug each member of the family upon arrival and departure, which bookends every event with an additional twenty minutes, but I know that lately she's grown tired of playing along too. According to the unspoken O'Connor bylaws, she's a wife but not yet a mother, and those are our only two roles within this family. I often catch Christine or Lidy not even attempting to hide their confusion as to why Amy has continually malfunctioned.

"Dinner!" Christine announces to the group.

We take our designated places at the banquet table. I tried early on to sit across from Amy, as it was the best positioning for our frequent eye-roll exchanges, but Christine has assigned seats for us. The three sisters-in-law on one side, the corresponding husbands on the other, with Christine and George at opposite ends. The grandkids have had their own separate table within the massive dining room since they were babies. Having thought of everything, Christine has assigned Dory, the nanny/housekeeper, to oversee all five grandchildren. For Christine, Sunday dinners are sacred—no one, not even one of the babies, is allowed to upset the order of things.

Before the food is passed, Christine stands and leads us in a family ritual, one even more unhinged than their incessant hugging, family dinners, and obsession with birthday celebrations. I peek up to watch her movements. Even in her sixties, she is elegant and poised in a way that cannot be learned—old-world Hollywood glamour. I sip from my glass and she exhales loudly enough for me to interpret her irritation that I've delayed the consecrated proceedings—so I keep the glass to my lips a moment longer before returning it slowly to the table.

She begins as she always does, extending both hands, waiting until everyone is connected. Then she looks around, meeting each pair of eyes as if searching for someone else in all our faces. Finally, with a heavy sigh, she intones, "Let's say grace," and in unison we all respond with a single word: "Grace." We lift our heads smiling oddly, an age-old tradition that Lucas claims started in their childhood.

"How old were your kids when they started giving you sass? It's been so long that I forget these things. I feel like Dottie's ahead of the curve. Yesterday she told me, 'No way,' when I told her it was time for bed," I say, addressing the table.

"A girl who knows what she wants—wonder where she gets that from?" Lucas says, grinning as he shovels green beans onto his plate.

"I just hope she learns to express her individuality by, like, shaving her head, becoming a vegetarian, or speaking out against animals being locked in cages for our entertainment." I take a bite of bread I just picked from the basket, adding, "But boycotting nap time interferes with Mom's me time." I point to myself with my wineglass. "And that's a problem."

Christine's eyes are squinting into small slits, as if she can't quite see me despite our proximity.

"A vegetarian—what would she eat? Beans? Like some sort of homeless person?" Christine says, still standing while overseeing the pacing of how and when the food gets passed.

"The zoo is getting pretty sad. When Amy and I took Dottie last weekend, this one monkey was sitting up in a tree, not moving." Paul has stopped passing food to emphasize his concern.

"The other monkeys would just step over the poor little guy like he wasn't even there. The zookeeper came in to feed them, and he wouldn't eat." His face looks puckered as he makes big motions with his hands; his sensitivity is overkill for me, but Amy adores it. "I wonder if we should call someone." Then he turns toward Christine. "Mom, don't you know someone on the board or something?"

"I can make a call," Christine answers, noticeably tickled, though she continues to motion for Paul to keep passing. He obeys while placing his napkin on his lap.

I wink over at Amy, our code to make note of Christine's level of superiority this evening, which is bordering on a nine out of a ten-point scale—high even for her.

"What are we thinking game plan—wise? September 16 is coming up fast and furiously for the soft opening. T-minus six weeks, guys," Lucas says. "I have a list about ten feet long that I need some help with. Cough, cough, Jack, I'm lookin' at you."

"When you and Paul came up with this ridiculous idea to make Mom a restaurant, I specifically said that I can do stuff with licensing and legal, but I'm not going to be your errand boy. I am up to my ass in"—his eyes dart toward the kids' table—"poop with the firm. One of the partners is quitting, and I'm taking on his caseload until one of the other idiots steps up."

"Language, please!" Christine scolds him, eyeing Joni, who is smiling at her uncle's foul mouth. As the eldest, she's positioned closest to the grown-up table, so she's able to eavesdrop without much difficulty.

Paul, always taking his role as the oldest brother seriously, stands and makes his way over to where Christine is still orchestrating the passage of food. On his way he lightly swats his baby brother on the back of the head before tucking his mom into her seat by gently forcing her legs to bend into her chair. He lays both hands on her shoulders, and she strokes the right one before lifting her fork so we can all begin eating.

The Cove was a fine-dining restaurant that Christine's parents lost to a fire back in the '80s. As an act of taking their mama's boy tendencies to new heights, Lucas and Paul have decided to re-create the family restaurant. The entire endeavor has been driven by Lucas and copiloted by Paul. They have chosen "The Restaurant" as a placeholder name until the big reveal at the opening in six weeks.

When I first met Lucas, he was a successful venture capitalist, and Paul, until recently, was a financial planner. Paul quit his job to help Lucas full-time with The Restaurant. Working together has always been their dream. Jack has been involved in small ways here and there, but the heart of the project lies with my and Amy's husbands. We are grateful for the restaurant endeavor because, despite their long hours away, it has meant more time for us.

I prefer to drink my dinner on our evenings here, and so I push my food around on my plate until there's a noticeable lull in noise. For all the fuss the family has made over meals together, the O'Connors are notoriously fast eaters. Once, I decided to time from the moment Christine was invariably tucked into her chair to the first dish being brought to the sink, and it was only nine minutes. The real conversations are reserved for after-dinner cocktails, once Dory takes the kids upstairs.

After an unreasonably short amount of time, considering the work it must have taken Christine to prepare a meal for fourteen people including Dory, all the women pop up at once to do the dishes, a family tradition as old as the stereotypical gender roles themselves. Amy and I wash and dry so we can stand next to each other while Lidy busies herself labeling and shelving an unnerving number of leftovers. I slide up and bump Amy. My hip reaches almost half the height of her abdomen. I can rest my head on top of hers.

She grabs a dish and begins to scrape the remains of green beans into the trash. All the beans have been carefully picked out, and only the stalks remain. One of the children's plates, no doubt. Or it may have belonged to Jack, who still eats like a toddler.

I lean in, whispering so Lidy can't hear, "Not sure why Jack has to be such a dick about The Restaurant." I offer her a plate to rinse.

"Oh, was he? I missed that. I was distracted by the fact that there was mayonnaise on the table," she says, making a pretend puking sound.

"See, for me, when I was pregnant, it was hard-boiled eggs and the smell of dirty dishes." I motion downward toward the sink. The memory makes me shake with disgust. "It'd be nice if Jack wanted to take some of the pressure off our guys."

"It's too late now. He really should have gotten on board in the beginning," she says.

"Probably true," I concede. Then I add, "How did your latest appointment go?"

"Fine." Amy exhales deeply. She claims that the doctor has been saying the same thing for more than four years now. There has been no medical reason for any of their fertility struggles. When they finally did conceive, about two years ago, she lost the baby in the second trimester. Far later than anyone should have to endure a miscarriage, since her body went into natural labor and she had to birth a baby she couldn't keep. I'm sure that existing within our fertile family only adds to her insecurity and fear.

"At this point, everything should probably be fine, but they can't say for sure." She looks around for more plates nearby to scrape into the trash, then stops to place both hands on the counter as if she's suddenly overcome. I put my hand on the small of her back.

"I swear if men got pregnant, it would be priority one to end symptoms. That and abortions would be available at ATMs," I say, going back to drying.

"You're probably right." She shrugs. I know she's not in the mood to get into it.

Christine appears carrying a small decorative bag.

"I put together a selection of ginger tea for you to take home. Tames the stomach." She goes to hand it to Amy and leans in for a hug. They embrace and I watch as Amy relaxes into Christine, soothed by her touch much more than she had been by mine. Christine pulls away first and brushes past me, despite there being plenty of room between the sink and the kitchen island.

"That was nice," I say, refilling my glass once Christine is out of sight. Amy doesn't need to look at me to know I'm not being sincere.

"She does mean well most of the time. We should give her a break," Amy tells me, assuming her role as middleman.

"You think that tea is gonna come without a price?" I say, pausing to take a swig. "One ultrasound photo? Or baby-naming rights?"

"I've always liked the name Christine," she teases.

"What are we, the royals? But Leah, you know, can be spelled any number of ways," I say.

"You are too much," Amy says, smiling.

"Funny, I think I'm exactly enough."

After we finish the dishes, Dory takes the kids upstairs to

wind down with a movie, and I emerge with an expensive bottle of limoncello in one hand and a tray of sipping glasses in the other. Christine has never once told us daughters-in-law to "make ourselves at home," which means she will soon probably start locking the door to the wine cellar.

"To what are we toasting?" George turns his head to look at Christine.

Before she can answer, I hold my glass in the air and say, "To family."

"To *our* family," Christine immediately chimes in, intentionally meeting the gaze of each of her sons.

We lift our glasses high.

"Quick picture." George stands at the head of the table with his Canon camera. Everyone stops to look at him, accustomed to his request. "Say cheese!"

Christine steps around Jack and stands between Paul and Lucas. I wrap my arms around Amy, pulling her in close.

"I feel like I'm holding my breath until Amy has her baby," I tell Lucas in the car on our way home from dinner.

"Yeah . . . how did we ever get so lucky, I wonder." Lucas looks back at our kids in the rearview, all tucked safely inside our minivan.

"I hate this car," I say, tapping my finger on the window for emphasis.

"So you've told me," he says, his voice lower than usual. In the darkness it's hard to distinguish whether he's endeared by my repetition or annoyed by it, but I'm floating just above my body. I can't be bothered to care one way or another, so I continue. "I miss Bertha, my Volkswagen van. She was magnificent, ya know? I still think we coulda found a way to strap the car seats in safely."

"Airbags weren't even a thing the year she was built. We want our children to remain alive, right?"

"Ugh. Such a buzzkill." I flutter my left hand in front of his face, a maneuver that may be dangerous as he drives, but I need him to know how ridiculous I find his question.

"Big Bertha was who I was," I say, staring out into the fog. "I am not a minivan mom."

"Which is exactly why I'm driving right now and you aren't," he says, and I'm too fuzzy to read between the lines of his comment.

"Except I'm the one shuttling our kids around here, there, and everywhere, and I hate it." I groan. "I hate it."

The rest of the car ride fades away, and I'm no longer in the passenger seat of this sexless monstrosity. I'm putting muscle into maneuvering Bertha's massive haul of a steering wheel, and the freedom tastes as refreshing as the salt water from every swim in the ocean.

At home, the tediousness of the bedtime routine is made more enjoyable by my haze. I dump water over Dottie's hair in the bath, forgetting to cover her face with a towel first. She cries out in pain, squeezing her eyes tightly, and I quickly dab away the drops until she's satisfied and no longer whimpering. Lucas and I were almost on the road to full child autonomy, and then Dottie came along. I wrap her within her duckling bathrobe and place my nose behind one of her ears. There is something so appealing about a freshly bathed child, though the effort it takes to get them from point A to point Z, where they are finally tucked away in bed safely, is more daunting than training for a marathon.

Christine is constantly sharing her memories of the boys and their delightful exuberance, as if she'd sell her soul to return for only one day. She turns practically giddy recounting how strangers stopped her in the street to marvel at her strapping young boys. Now she preaches to us, saying things like *"The correct amount of parenting is like placing your hand on a spring, releasing ever so gently. Too quick and they're gone, never to be recoiled."*

"You really need to let Mom be the one to give the toast at the end of the night," Lucas says after we've finally gotten the kids down. He gets into bed, turning onto his side with his back to me.

"Huh? Now where is the fun in that?" I say, curling into an S shape around my husband, softly kissing his neck as I run my tongue gently along the length of his ear, ready to leave my body for a while.

CHAPTER 3

Dottie pokes at my lids, digging them down until there's familiar blackness. I know her by the scent of her palms.

"Reid! Can you please come grab your sister?" When I yell, my words itch. I'm certain he's somewhere nearby. As he appears in the doorway, he forms into the stamped copy of his dad—long and lanky limbs, handsome in a way that's both endearing and troublesome.

"Come on, Little Dot. Let's go watch *Bluey*," he says. A twinge of irritation is present only in the stiff flick of his wrist as he motions for her.

Dottie nods, satisfied by his request. Her arms shoot up, demanding Reid carry her out.

"Thanks, bud. I owe you." I stretch, which instantly churns the contents of my stomach. I run my open palm over my face. There's a noticeable heaviness, as if my decisions are begging to protrude through each wrinkle etched on my forehead.

Making my way toward the sound of the shower running, I recall fragments from last night in my mother-in-law's kitchen. I was probably a tad too much myself for Christine's liking; the blanket of booze always lowers my ability to buy into the O'Connor family BS. But my willingness to engage in yet another Sunday dinner should count for something.

I open the shower door, stopping to observe what years of surfing have done for my husband's body, wrapping my arms around his lower abdomen and interlacing my fingers. I place my lips on his neck. Lucas tilts his head into mine but then leaves the shower. When he turns back, I ensure he can read my confusion over his abrupt exit. I need sex to wash away the evening's sins and begin the day clean, for Lucas's sake, but also in case it all happens again tonight.

He takes the bait. "I want you back here like this. Exactly like this tonight." Now he's grinning like he's twenty-six, the age he was when we first met, when there was nothing but lust between us. "Please."

"Mm-hmm." It comes out as an exhalation of relief. I pivot and allow the water to pelt down my back.

He disappears inside our walk-in closet just as I think I hear Reid call up to me. The time I'm allotted to act in one role is finite. Wife, then mother—without any guaranteed scraps left over for myself. The need to be everything to everyone is relentless.

When I arrive downstairs, Dottie is covered in peanut butter, with Reid eating cereal beside her. Joni sits at the bay window, shoulders curled into her book, leaning so far over she could drown among the pages. Instead of moving toward them, I stand gripping the corners of the kitchen island and wait.

"Later, gators!" Lucas yells from the door before closing it.

Just like that, he escapes, and I cannot. Over coffee, I use two slices of bread to wipe the remaining peanut butter off

Dottie's elbows, smashing them together as a sandwich for breakfast.

After I've dropped off the older kids at summer camp, it's just Dottie and me back at the house. There's a neediness surrounding toddlers that I recognize in myself. We can't both want at the same time, or me ever, really, whenever it's only us two. I believe this is the rationale behind their giant eyes and mousy voices—cuteness designed to swell the heart. An evolutionary trick to keep us from abandoning them at fire stations after hour-long tantrums over accidentally peeling their banana.

"Alexa, play 'Brave' by Sara Bareilles." This song has been on in our house on repeat.

I grab a hairbrush from the dresser to use as a microphone and wait until the chorus to sing. I turn my hand into a phone and put it to my ear, using the brush to point directly at Dottie.

Delighted, she scrambles over to use the bench at the foot of the bed to fling herself on top of the covers. Once she's fully upright, her arms extend out in front, the ends of her fingers wiggling in anticipation—an unsubtle ploy to get me to join her. As I slip out of my sandals, I'm confident the rocking on the bed is going to make me dizzy. But with the spring of her curls, coiled around the fullness of her cheeks made rounder by a grin, I'm powerless to remain on the ground.

We hold hands as I attempt to match her rhythm. But she's two and has none, so we end up crashing down among the pillows. Dottie tries to stand back up. In protest, I throw the comforter over her head and use all four of my limbs to pull her into my chest. Her vibrations are a low, warm hum under my chin. The sweetness of her shampoo reminds me of college and fruit-infused cocktails.

The sensation of Dottie's entire weight trusting my body to secure her safely into me takes me back to her birth. Since it was my third delivery, I fearlessly managed to pull her out of me entirely on my own, securing her to my chest with her cord still tethering us as one. The brazenness of my action was reminiscent of the reckless abandon of my youth. My children connected to me, skin to skin, is the kind of peace I can never replicate. Though, believe me, I've tried.

Wanting to keep Dottie close, I pause the music and flip on the TV to one of her musical, colorful shows while I wait for her breathing to slow. It's the parenting equivalent of playing tennis with the net down. Just when we are riding high together, belting out a chorus about bravery, it all comes crashing down. Lately my children and I have been inside two separate glass cages.

I can feel her sink deeper into me. I'll happily accept the win, even if I'm cheating to get us here.

I align myself with a pillow propped comfortably under my neck as I gaze at an original painting I made for Lucas's and my first wedding anniversary. A re-creation of the first day we met and surfed together.

In the summer of 2011, my travels after graduating consisted of a 1974 Volkswagen van, affectionately named Big Bertha, painting supplies with a roll of raw canvas, my surfboard, and a considerable amount of money from Nana. Once I discovered the ocean at UC Santa Cruz, I knew I'd never return to my hometown in rural Iowa. I liked the drama of placing plenty of distance between who I was and who I'd become.

Eight weeks into my road trip, I found myself in Half Moon Bay, a charming town nestled into a crescent along the Northern California coastline. I was looking for Mavericks, a world-famous surf break that hosts an annual big wave competition—not that I could ever compete. Surfing was merely a source of inspiration. Foreplay before the main event.

I pulled off Highway 1 into the Cowboy Surf Shop's parking lot. It had been at least three days since my last real shower. I didn't bother to look in my rearview mirror to check the mop of blond hair on top of my head with stragglers that tickled the base of my shoulders. I threw on a hooded sweatshirt and grabbed my wallet off the passenger seat.

If the sound of waves has a scent, it's eternally encapsulated inside a surf shop: stale weed and salt water—one I'd bottle and wear around my neck. The name tag of the girl behind the counter read *Vicki*—a name that didn't suit her face. She smiled as I approached. A quiet calmness rested on her shoulders as she rummaged through inventory, and I wondered if it had anything to do with the pot smell. I couldn't help but nod in solidarity with the delicious knowing of what it feels like to escape.

A woman and a young girl I could only assume was her daughter were near the back. The child lay flat, her chest glued to a boogie board on the floor of the shop, as she pretended to ride, paddling so vigorously she knocked some shorts off the rack. Her exaggerated movements only further confirmed that she was a land mammal in a sea of ocean dwellers, out of her depth.

The only other person in the shop was a tall man in a dark tailored suit, speaking loudly into his cell phone. "Is the shipment coming in today, because I'm at the store, and it is not here." He spun around as if to investigate further, not attempting to mask his annoyance.

He stopped moving when he saw me, pointed at the phone, and then rolled his eyes as if I were in on the conversation. I kept my face neutral and shrugged. He was probably close to my age, somewhere in his twenties, and noticeably good-looking.

"You know what? I'm gonna give you the benefit of the doubt on this one. I'll check back tomorrow." Even when he'd finished talking, the hum of his presence kept a current in the air.

I foraged through the wax and grabbed a 2X extra soft.

"All set?" Vicki asked, leaving her task to ring me up. I nodded. During our transaction, I became acutely aware of being watched. As a woman in a man's world, I'd written my own script to take control over these sorts of moments. I knew that in less than one minute, he would reveal himself.

I needed to be the one to speak first. "If you make a comment about the Sex Wax in my hand, you have absolutely no shot with me."

"You mean like an innuendo? Not my style," Dark Gray Suit Guy replied, shaking his head. His grin revealed teeth that were straight and white, but not obnoxiously so. I doubted he'd ever had braces and liked him a little more.

I flipped through the stickers resting on the glass counter, placing my gum and wax near the register.

"I'm looking for one with a single wave," I said, directing my comment back to Vicki. She squinted as she tilted her head toward the ceiling. The man made his way behind the counter. He bent down and pulled up a large box from underneath.

"Can't say I've seen one like that without words or a brand, but I'm just goin' through them now," she said. "Why that one?" She started fidgeting with her necklace but stopped to ring up my items.

"I have a bunch on my van outside." I motioned with my hand toward the small window that revealed the street. "Been lookin' for something like it for a while to add to my collection." The lie formed quickly, providing its functional layer of protection.

Using a pocketknife, the tall man ripped open the box like he had experience gutting fish or animal carcasses. It felt overly violent in the way men find it necessary to display their dominance. Vicki and I both watched him, and I became mildly irritated, his presence suddenly intrusive. He reached inside the box and pulled out several smaller bags packed with decals. He filtered through them, struggling to use the tips of his large fingers to swipe past each one before bringing the container to the floor to gain more space. When he sat down, his pant leg lifted and revealed socks that conflicted with his image. They had tiny sand dollars ringed around where the sock met his ankle, something adorable that meant he, unlike the flailing child on the boogie board, could belong here.

"I think I've seen something like that before," he said, finally explaining himself. Vicki chuckled, shook her head, and then glanced back at me as if to say, *He's tryna impress you*.

"He works here?" I leaned in toward her.

"Technically, no," she replied, not trying to hush her tone. Her expression was playful. As she put her elbows on the glass and rested her face in her palms, I could sense instantly that they'd, at one point, seen each other naked.

"It's okay, really. I'm sure you have to get back to work," I offered.

Vicki pulled a joint from inside her bra, snagging a lighter from the top of the register.

"Lucas, I'm going to take ten. I'll flip the sign out front. Back in a few." Vicki pushed the bag across the counter; her exit was a subtle gesture of permission. Lucas waved, keeping his head down. I joined him on the floor.

"I like the socks." I reached out to point but did not touch them.

"You can take the man out of the beach, but you can't take the beach out of the man," he said as if it were a common expression people used. But I knew exactly what he meant. I was magnetized to the water. Even when I wasn't near it, I could feel it.

"Here!" he exclaimed, victorious, as he presented me with the spoils of his effort: the sticker displayed at my feet. I let my face remain neutral, offering him little by way of praise. His eyes, a liquid brown with flecks of yellow, remained on mine and held my gaze. He stared at me longer than I'd allowed anyone to in a long time.

He pointed toward the bag containing the wax. "When are you going out?"

"Right now. You surf?" I asked.

"I do." He paused to raise an eyebrow and added, "Is that an invitation?"

"Sure, but only if you keep those socks on," I said, appreciating the banter.

"Deal!" He nodded, clapping his hands together and then standing.

"Great! Where's your board?" I went to stand, and he took my hand to pull me up. He had several inches on me, which made him at least six three.

"These are all mine." He gestured to the ones that hung on the wall and the racks.

"You make surfboards?" I said as I eyed his suit.

"I invested in a shaper based in Southern California," he said all in one breath like he was falling into a well-scripted speech. "I'll be right back. Don't go anywhere, 'kay?" He disappeared into the back of the store.

"I'll be outside," I told him, heading toward the exit.

The bell chimed as the door shut behind me. I opened a bag of corn nuts from inside the pocket of my sweatshirt, popping a handful into my mouth. I leaned against the driver's side door, wanting to appear effortlessly casual.

Within a few minutes, Lucas emerged wearing board shorts, with a wet suit and surfboard under his arm.

"That was quick," I marveled.

"I'm like Superman, except instead of a cape, I keep my wet suit handy in case a gorgeous stranger invites me surfing." He stopped to place his hands on his hips and widened his stance.

"Gross." I turned away, scrunching my nose—selective about accepting compliments.

He placed his board on top of mine and bound them together with my bungee cords, an act that struck me as strangely intimate.

"You know where to go?" he asked as he slid into the seat next to me as if he'd done it a hundred times before.

"No, I just got here. Where do you go?" I asked, turning the key in the ignition.

"Pull out here and hang a left. Unless you were heading to Mavericks, in which case we are at very different levels."

I laughed—a genuine laugh.

"I'm Leah—I guess I skipped that part and simply invited you straight into my van."

"Lucas." He flashed me his teeth again, and I softened a bit more this time.

"You know, most guys won't sit shotgun and let a girl drive them around." I glanced back over at him, noticing he had, in fact, kept his socks on.

"My mom always drives whenever my parents go anywhere." He started humming along with the radio, tapping his hand on top of the roof. His presence was already becoming comfortable in a way that was disarming. "Up here's a sweet spot. The local break is in Montara," he said.

We headed north on Highway 1. After we pulled up to the beach access point Lucas had indicated, using his enormous fingers that matched his impressive frame, I reached behind his seat to grab my wet suit. It was overcast but not cold, typical for the end of the summer on this part of the coast. I took off my sweatshirt, already wearing my bathing suit underneath, and glanced over at Lucas, wondering if he'd use this as an excuse to check me out. He was busy removing his socks and stepping into his own wet suit. Lingering a moment, I pretended to adjust something, and still, he kept his eyes to himself and had already started to unstrap our boards. I nodded, satisfied, and grabbed my board off the rack.

The pull string on my wet suit had frayed, and it was difficult but not impossible to maneuver. As I freed my long hair from its bun, a strand caught in the zipper. I gripped the hair tie in my teeth so I could use both hands to manipulate the entanglement.

"Here. Allow me?" Lucas waited for me to step into his path, granting him the opportunity to help, even though the idea of accepting help was entirely foreign to me. I felt his fingers trace my back between my shoulder blades, running along the shape of the tattooed solitary wave under a horizon line.

I peered back over my shoulder but said nothing as his touch rippled through me.

"So more than just a bumper sticker, it would appear?" Again, he lifted his eyebrow, questioning.

"Watch me disappear," I called back, taking off toward the water, my board under my arm and the sand melting like heaven between my toes.

Lucas followed a few paces behind me until we both reached the water. A few riders were in the lineup, but not many. The act of pushing into a wave, of deliberately going against the grain, again ignited my entire body. We paddled out together side by side, gliding through the shallows toward the sunlight.

We positioned ourselves away from the main action, Lucas guiding us there, straddling our boards as we watched the break. The waves were between three and four feet tall. I let him go first, assessing his skills the way I'd watch a racehorse before placing any bets. Lucas surfed like he had nothing else to do. Beholden only to the wind. When it was my turn, the wave held together magnificently, giving me a long, graceful ride all the way in.

Lucas wiped out before I did, sinking into the unearthly realm. I closed my eyes, imagining us there together, powerless against the water's will as it hurled our bodies over the falls—the force driving us into the darkest parts of the depths. There would be seconds, sometimes only a beat too long, that would convince my mind of certain death. But somehow, with lungs exploding for air, we'd meet at the surface instead of a watery grave.

He paddled back over to where I sat on my board, scanning the horizon, and shook his head like a dog after a bath.

"Glad it was you and not me," I teased. His wipeout served as a final icebreaker, solidifying his status as a man confident enough to exist outside of the alpha role.

"Anything for you," he said, his face appearing earnest as it glistened, reflecting off the water. He reentered the lineup, seeming not to be embarrassed in the slightest as he gazed over his shoulder, already eager for his next ride. He nodded to me, knowing it was my turn. It was undeniably sexy.

After our set, we sat inside my van with our legs hanging out the back end, facing the beach. I opened the cooler, which I kept well stocked with beers, and handed one over. I had forgotten to get more ice.

"You may just be the perfect woman," he said, clinking his bottle into mine.

"Don't get too excited. This is the extent of my domestic skills." I let out a contented sigh as the beer slid down my throat. We were quiet for a minute, drinking and watching the waves. All I'd eaten that day were the corn nuts, so I felt my insides begin to tingle.

"Surfing is the only way I've found to love the ocean for exactly what she is," I found myself saying. The endorphins from the session took hold of my words. "Swimming just doesn't do it justice. I need to be aligned more closely somehow. If I'm riding a wave—it's like we're speaking." I could feel myself start to unravel, revealing a layer I'd kept hidden.

He didn't say anything, his face more pensive than content. I turned away, almost embarrassed, taking a long, slow swig from my beer.

"It's an intimacy not many people understand," he said, still not making eye contact with me.

He knew. He knew, in the way I knew, I was going to kiss

him. I was leaning in, but he was already there. I let my towel fall around my shoulders as he took my face in his hands and placed his lips on mine. Soft but deliberate. Taking command like he was already familiar with how to navigate through me. Neither of us pulled away but instead began to swallow each other whole, desperate but effortless. Time passed, and we stopped only to catch our breaths.

I awake to the sound of water running. I pat the empty side of the bed, recognizing that Dottie is no longer on me. The show is over. I can see toilet paper covering the floor inside the bathroom so the tile is no longer visible.

"Dottie," I call, and she immediately pokes her head out from around the corner. Her face is streaked with pink lipstick and black lines. I'm scared to look deeper into the bathroom for the mess I'll uncover, yet relieved to see all her appendages still attached. I have no idea how long she's played alone while I slept.

This was never really the plan. Originally, my existence involved endless travel as an artist and surfer. But then Lucas happened. Funny how someone could be the seed that grew the tree when I had no intention of putting down roots.

CHAPTER 4

My favorite spot to run is a place called the Seal Cove Cypress Tree Tunnel in Moss Beach outside of Half Moon Bay—or just the Tree Tunnel, as I felt it deserved a nickname. It's silly to get in the car and drive when I could simply walk out of my house and head a mile down the road to jog at the beach, but there is something about the way the light filters through the trees in the Tree Tunnel, as if heaven has a runway.

Running has become my physical reprieve. Besides sex and wine, it's how I'm able to feel closer to my phantom self—by exhausting my mind into quiet to dull the ache that never seems to subside. Surfing became too hard to organize with such limited time while the kids are otherwise occupied by school or all their various activities, and the window of swells so rarely aligning with my finite moments alone. Today Dory is at the house with Dottie while the big kids are still at summer camp.

I park next to the ranger station, locking my car and looking around for other people. It's mostly deserted except for a couple walking two large, shaggy dogs that appear to be a mix of poodle and another breed I don't recognize.

I insert my earbuds, syncing my playlist as I pull each leg up into a stretch and stand like a flamingo, using my car for balance. I toss my jacket onto the driver's seat, already feeling a little flushed, and take off down the path.

The trail is worn and winding. The trees huddle around one another, leaning in to create magnificent arches. Branches adjust and bend to meet the needs of other branches while supporting their weight. I make my way up and over, trees on my right and the ocean on my left. I continue this loop, up and down the cliffside, until my pulse is racing. I know exactly when to arrive in the morning before the sun consumes the sky—just when the sunlight spills out between the seams of each tree, playing peekaboo with the darkness. I run down the trail looking for the perfect combination of shadows and brightness. The gnarled arch of crooked limbs dipped in fog is almost spooky. In the distance, the coastline yawns out, teasing its existence through the trees.

As I run through cold pockets, shivers strike my shoulders and shoot down my back. After three miles, I need to stop for air. I've been sprinting away from the Tree Tunnel, not even realizing my pace until my breath comes out in little coughs. I'm a sucker for that type of adrenaline.

I stop at a bench atop the cliff and look out at the ocean. I've painted it so many times, I can see the curl of each wave, even with my eyes closed.

I startle as someone sits down beside me.

"Miles?" I ask in disbelief. It's been more than a decade, yet I'd recognize him anywhere. His grin is and always was infectious. Before I have a second to gather myself, my heart betrays me with a full-on schoolgirl flutter.

"Sorry, gorgeous, just had to say hello," he says, then adds, "Whenever you're runnin' out here, I can never catch you. Even when I'm driving the truck." Again, butterflies knock against the glass walls of my chest. I'm delighted by his admission that he's been watching me.

While aged, Miles is still ruggedly handsome. His skin looks tough and weathered. For men, that's impossibly sexy, and for women, it just means we look older.

"It's been a little while." He positions one leg on top of the other, creating a figure four as he removes his boot. I watch tiny bits of rock and dirt fall out. "Occupational hazard," he says as he shakes more out.

"Yeah, just a little bit," I say with the formation of a laugh, though it is more of a chortle, and I immediately press my lips together in indelicate submission. In his presence I feel like I could slither down between the grooves of the bench and blink up at him as nothing but a puddle on the forest floor. What is it exactly about the intoxication of young love? Or more accurately in our case, young lust? I know whatever was between us back then felt frenetic, charged to the point of an electrical storm and then an eventual short-circuiting. But seeing him here in our fully formed grown-up flesh, as he mentions the swells and an upcoming shift in weather that should bring about good surfing, I find it all too easy to go back. When he talks, he removes his cap and runs his hands through his hair. My hands have been there before too.

I close my eyes, recalling a morning, twelve years ago, we spent in bed listening to Jimi Hendrix, smoking a joint.

Miles had spun and waved his fingers up over our heads, fluttering them along with the guitar solo. The haze of the weed made his movements feel fluid, like his arms were my arms, and suddenly we were tangled up together again, with the heaviness of his body on top of mine. I remember I felt like I had to close my eyes to keep from sinking inside the bed and becoming lost.

"Whoa," I told him. *"I'm disappearing."*

Miles reached over and tapped his index finger gently on the tip of my nose. It made me laugh and laugh, until I rolled completely off the bed.

I open my eyes at the Tree Tunnel when I feel Miles's finger touch my nose in the present. I squirm and swipe it away. His boldness matches that from before. Something about his private school education, which groomed impressionable boys into famous athletes and the kind of men who'd grow up to pat their secretaries' asses as the highest form of praise.

"Years back, you mentioned Costa Rica. Did you ever make it there? To surf?" I gaze into his dark brown eyes, then look back out and feel the warmth of the sun hit my face. The mist has lifted completely, and I can feel my skin begin to glow.

"Costa Rica—of course," he says, putting his hand back down in his lap. His tone has a confident arrogance that's off-putting, as if he couldn't comprehend how dreams could suddenly be pulled out from under him.

Of course, I repeat inside my own head.

"You look just how I remember you, even though it was an entire lifetime ago," I say, a betrayal of words. "I mean, you haven't changed." Miles wasn't necessarily "the one" that could have been, but he represented a parallel life on a whole separate track. I had already known Lucas at the time, but we had yet to establish what, exactly, we were to each other. Miles kept me free in a way that Lucas was never built for. Christine had brainwashed her boys into a methodology that settling down with a family was the natural order of things. Miles surfed, smoked weed, enjoyed sex, and we arrived at the mutual understanding that these things were all that could ever be between us. The overlap with Lucas wasn't intentional. I have managed to compartmentalize Miles as part of my life before motherhood.

He says nothing back but doesn't look away. His eyes are questioning and curious, and our thighs are touching though the bench is easily big enough for two people. I can feel the flex of his shoulder when he reaches up to put his hat back on his head.

"Leah?" I hear my name and turn around to look.

Paul and Christine are about fifty feet away, approaching us on horseback. Lucas took me riding as one of our first unofficial dates. Even though I come here often, it is the first time I've ever run into anyone from the family.

Miles stands, brushing his pants, and steps back, away from me.

"Don't be a stranger," he says and then turns and walks back down the cliffside.

My face is still warm from the sun. I, too, stand and stretch my legs to get the blood flowing again—not wanting the color in my cheeks to be misinterpreted as something else.

"Fancy meeting you here!" Paul calls out to me. He looks straight out of a movie, where the strapping young lead appears as a mama's boy who loves horses. I'm fascinated by Paul's simplicity. He seems perfectly content just to exist in his happiness—like his dad, he is unassuming in the purest sense of the word.

"I love the light here," Christine says as her eyes follow Miles walking along the trail. He stops to say hello to the hikers with the dogs. "What are you up to?" she asks, attempting but failing to sound casual.

"This is one of my favorite places to run," I say, stretching my arms up overhead. "I'm surprised we've never bumped into each other here before." I can feel Christine's eyes boring into me. She is patting her horse's flank in smooth, calculated strokes. *I've done nothing wrong*, I remind myself. As a general rule, the O'Connors prefer not to socialize outside of the family bubble, so I'm almost entirely convinced that's why I'm getting her death stare. Plus, Christine's status within the community means she doesn't associate with many members of what is no longer referred to as the "working class."

I look over at Paul, who's pulled out a canteen of water from his saddlebag. No one speaks for an uncomfortable amount of time, and my ears start making a buzzing sound.

"Who—?" Christine starts to ask, but I cut her off.

"I'm on borrowed time with the kids otherwise occupied. Enjoy your ride." The last thing our already volatile relationship needs is Christine digging around inside my past. I turn to face Paul and add, "We're doing pizza after Reid's game this week. I already told Amy. You guys are welcome to join us."

With Miles halfway down the path, I'm briefly positioned between them. I've already made my decision, and I made peace with it a long time ago. Lucas is who I chose as the father of my children.

Not wanting to waste another minute of my alone time, I leave abruptly, suddenly frustrated that being an O'Connor means there isn't anywhere I can go to escape them.

After I've made it another mile, I stop to watch a family

sprawled out on the beach before me. I'm on the bluff, looking down at their elaborate setup. No matter the weather here,
tourist families commit themselves completely if they decide
on a beach day. They bring the blankets, sand toys, towels,
and a giant cooler for snacks. Children require such an unreasonable amount of stuff for "fun."

My pulse starts to slow as I reach around to hold on to my
ankle and pull my leg into a quad stretch. There is a mom, a
dad, a little boy who's about four, and a girl around Dottie's age
down below. Before having kids, I never would have been able
to identify any specific ages of kids, nor did I care to possess
that particular party trick. My brain, which was once filled with
artistic creativity, is now overrun with useless child-rearing
knowledge, and I feel older without having become any wiser.

I fixate on the mom, seamlessly unpacking objects at everyone's request. The toddler sticks her tongue out to taste the
sand that has stuck to her fingers.

"No, yuck!" the mother says, jetting out her tongue and
making a face of disgust—somehow teaching her daughter
without getting angry or irritated at the hassle of it all.

I miss my own family. The five of us could be down there,
alongside these strangers, creating our version of this image—
intentionally putting in the effort required to make lasting
memories.

I shake my head, removing the vision, realizing nothing
about what they are doing is compatible with the life I have. I'd
start by resenting Lucas for not knowing me well enough to
remember that a beach day with everyone places all the burden
of work squarely on my shoulders. The chaos and the cleanup
are rarely worth the price of admission.

I'd spend the day attempting to dull the ache, wishing I

could be happier or at least better somehow. I'd be powerless
to stop thoughts of Christine and how she managed to make
beach trips with three children a weekly occurrence. Just
thinking about her makes my insides tingle, like my limbs are
tethered to four horses and she's holding the starter pistol,
eagerly waiting to make them run.

"Why do you let her get to you so much?" Amy asked one day
when I'd had enough.

I couldn't answer her then, and I can't now. My fixation
with Christine and how she mothers, who she is, has been
going on since our very first introduction. I don't think I
would know how to stop it at this point even if I wanted to.

Do I want to? I wonder.

The little girl puts an entire fistful of wet brown sand in
her mouth this time, and her mother's tone grows slightly
sterner. The wind is picking up, and I can't make out what
she's said, but I watch the features of her face pinch and release in frustration without becoming overwhelmed. She has
a towel and is patting down her daughter's tongue.

The dad is busy with his son, building a sandcastle, unfazed and unaware. The mom reaches into the cooler for a cup.
It's one of the biodegradable ones that cost more than a new set
of paintbrushes. She shows her daughter how to take a sip and
then spit it out. This makes the girl giggle, delighted that her
mom is doing something seemingly naughty. They take turns
drinking and then spitting it out. The mom leans over and
kisses her daughter. Sand sticks to both their lips. She doesn't
even bother to wipe it off.

My own mother, Debra, loved me best during these ages,
what Nana lovingly referred to as "the kitten stage." The fleeting
segment of time consists of total and complete nurturing, where

an infant or toddler's survival requires a certain level of care. Nana said Mom thrived then because she felt endlessly influential. Later on, as I began to develop what my mom called "a mind of my own," she took my growth as an affront to her past efforts—all the times she licked my fur and placed food at my feet. As if by wanting my autonomy, I was somehow ungrateful for her role in helping me become a full-grown cat.

I stand and my movement causes the woman to look up in my direction. I want to smile back at her, but instead, I turn and run like something is chasing me.

I wander over to the Moss Beach Distillery, the only upscale restaurant in our area that will rival what the guys are creating. It's not yet ready to open for lunch. I try to think about what it will be like to exist inside a new space like this one with the O'Connors. It's something that will belong to us all while still being based on a history that originated with Christine. Yet another thing that will revolve around her.

The wind whips at my ears as they sting with exposure. I put my hood up over my head and wander onto the deserted back patio. I feel like a criminal being out here. The owners know who we are and the competition we will bring, but our community is so quaint and polite that somehow no feathers have been ruffled. I can't say I'd be so forgiving if a rival artist popped up next to my studio in town. But that's the family I married into, all softness and sunshine from the outside.

When Joni had just entered her toddler years, we left her with Christine for the afternoon and met Paul and Amy here so we could have our first of many double dates. It was still early in their relationship, and Lucas and I prided ourselves on our superior wingman skills, especially since I had served as their original matchmaker.

"Already bringing out the big guns," I said to Paul, nodding toward the distillery sign. "Lookin' to get some, Paul?" I teased. He has always been too easy a target for me, so I never really poke too hard.

"Well, I guess not anymore," Paul replied, nudging me gently on our walk to the table. Unfazed by our banter, Amy trotted beside me and hooked her arm with mine.

"I like your bracelets," Amy commented. I always had the colorful bands with intricately woven beads stacked halfway up my forearm.

"Thanks. I used to buy them at street markets in Santa Cruz. My attempts never to fully succumb to the adulting process."

"I know what you mean. I still eat peanut butter out of the jar for dinner sometimes," Amy said.

She understood. It's impossible to rationalize aging as it happens. In my mind I'm still twenty and *responsibility* is a four-letter word.

"Does Lucas get annual physicals?"

I practically spat out the cocktail we had ordered at the bar while we waited for our table outside to be ready. Leaving us alone, Paul and Lucas had wandered over to say hi to some friends of their parents whom they didn't want to subject us to.

"Ha! Not that I'm aware of. I have limited points of reference in that area, but based on my own dad, my mom would have to be the one to pick up his blood pressure medication or, like, he just wouldn't take it. They argued about it all the time."

"Yeah, see, I brought it up with Paul just, like, casually one day after my routine trip to the gyno, and he assured me annual medical appointments are not the same for guys. But that can't be true." She paused and looked over at the guys, who were still chatting up the older couple in the back corner of the restaurant. "I bet Christine set up all those appointments for them growing up. Maybe she even still does." Amy made a face like she'd stepped in dog poop.

I laughed. "Oh, for sure."

"Stuff like that makes me nervous. I've been on my own for forever, and that level of parental involvement is just wild to me."

"Just you wait, girlfriend."

The guys made their way back and we settled around our table. It was slightly overcast, which left the beach we overlooked almost empty except for a few families. We were close enough to hear the waves without having to shout over the sound.

After our orders were taken, Amy remarked, "I've always wanted to come here!" She removed her scarf and draped it delicately on the table. "I hear it's haunted."

The busboy overheard Amy and jumped at the opportunity to tell us about the "Blue Lady" as he tended to our waters.

"So, during Prohibition, the San Mateo coast was the perfect spot for rum running, bootlegging, and speakeasies." He picked up each of our glasses, filling them precisely to one inch from the top. "This building was originally constructed in nineteen twenty-seven by a successful restaurateur, Frank Torres. Rumor had it, a woman always dressed in blue was having an affair with a musician, and they'd meet at that spot." He gestured with his chin toward the bar inside the restaurant. "One night, the lovers were found stabbed on this beach." He held up the pitcher to signal where some kids were playing, which felt grossly unsettling. "He survived, but she died and haunts this restaurant still—wanting to reunite with her long-lost love." The waiter left to tend to another table.

I watched Amy's enchantment. Her eyes were wide with intrigue. Lucas snorted laughter into his napkin. He's always been much too practical to believe in ghost stories.

"The moral of the story: Don't be a liar and a cheater," he said, dipping his calamari into the tartar sauce, but only after he used it to point at each of us at the table.

My stomach had dropped a little, and I took a large gulp of my cocktail. "I've seen her in the bathroom. We'll have to go later when we need to talk about these two," I told Amy, eager to change the subject.

"This place is good. But it's a little too upscale for the clientele in the area. We need another spot in our town that's considered fine dining but, like, not snobby," Lucas said as he took another bite of the appetizer.

"I still say we go after the restaurant idea," Paul said as he sat more upright in his chair. "I can't believe you opted to do surfboards before The Restaurant."

"I'm still in if you are. But this one is going to be 'the project,'" he said, using air quotes to emphasize its extreme importance. "We will have to get it exactly right." Lucas's pupils were getting more dilated by the second. When he gets excited about something, it monopolizes his entire focus. I turned back toward Amy to clarify what they meant.

"So, Lucas has an idea to re-create the family restaurant. Have you guys gotten there yet in your O'Connor family history tutorial?" I gestured with my glass between Paul and Amy.

"Your family has a restaurant? That's cool!" Again, Amy's

eyes shone with fascination, and I couldn't quite determine if she was genuinely interested or just playing along because she liked Paul.

"*Had*. It burned down in a fire like thirty years ago," Lucas cut in.

"That's a shame," Amy lamented. "But how incredible you want to open another one!"

I knew an undertaking of that magnitude would essentially widow us both, so I wasn't quick to match her sentiments. Amy clearly had more than the enthusiasm required to be an O'Connor. It irritated Christine that I couldn't simply play along as the unconditionally supportive housewife. Only with the aid of a steady buzz could I stomach her unhealthy competition for my husband's attention.

"Oh, we are resurrecting The Cove. For sure. It's just a matter of when." Unblinking, Lucas nodded at his brother, who was bobbing his head in agreement, only much more slowly.

"Ugh!" I said, motioning toward the waiter. I required more alcohol if I was expected to match their excitement. "I'm going to need another drink."

Back at home, the decibel level within the house is almost always set to vibrate. I forgot just how loud a two-year-old can be since there is a significant age gap between Dottie and the older kids. Her volume resides somewhere between loud and extremely loud at any hour of the day or night. We are all scattered around the living room with Lucas still at The Restaurant.

"Mom, can I get an Apple Watch?" Reid asks.

I wait for Joni to chime in that she's older and doesn't yet have an Apple Watch, but instead, she awaits my response as if she were the one to ask the question.

"I'm trying to avoid that whole cell phone thing for as long as humanly possible. Can we pretend that we all aren't basically turning into robots? When I wanted to get ahold of my friends, we would bike over to each other's houses."

"Okay, can I bike to Tommy's house?"

"It's dark outside. So no. Good try, though," I say.

I scroll through social media accounts until I find Miles, which isn't difficult—his profile isn't set to private. After sifting through mostly surfing pictures, I find what I'm looking for: a wedding anniversary appreciation post to his wife, "Kat," and a picture of his boys on surfboards. I zoom in to try to see their resemblance to Miles, but they are in wet suits and too far away.

Dottie tips the sippy cup that is somehow now missing its lid all over the wooden farm animal puzzle with giant pieces she's been working on, and milk begins to drip onto the rug beneath the dining room table.

"Do you think I could go over to Grandma's tomorrow? She told me at the beach that she got us kits to make friend-ship bracelets, and I want to make some for my friends before school starts up again," Joni says, completely oblivious to the inconvenient timing of her request.

It's the everything-all-at-once phenomenon I've come to dread about this time of night. Already the invisible load of motherhood is immense, but there's something particularly enraging when all three children simultaneously require my attention. The volume of questions and their exaggerated level of urgency, especially when Lucas is at the restaurant, makes me want to stand, throw my head back, and scream like I'm receiving an exorcism. Instead of screaming, I walk to the kitchen island and pour what's left in the wine bottle into my glass that's been on the counter since before dinner. As I allow myself a full swallow, I grab the paper towels and spray bottle to clean Dottie's spilled milk. She's already moved on to another area of the living room, where she is dumping out every single toy from the basket I sorted just after my run.

Later that night, I ask Amy to come over. We always unload together after Sunday dinners with the O'Connors—recalibrate back to regularly scheduled programming.

I'm still a little stunned that I saw Miles, so I'm not ready to mention it.

When she lets herself in, she pulls a pint of ice cream out of her bag and says, "So I tried to work up the courage to visit Isla today, but instead, I stopped at the store to get Ben & Jerry's because that sounded better."

"Ohhh, that does sound better," I say, making my way over to grab two spoons from the drawer. "We need to eat fast, though. If my kids come downstairs and catch us, you know those little monsters will try to hog it all."

"I love how lovingly you speak about your children." Amy grins as she pulls open the lid. Peanut Butter World was an excellent call.

"Whoever thought to put chocolate and peanut butter together is essentially my hero," I say, taking a giant scoop after Amy has had her first bite.

"I feel like you and me are like chocolate and peanut butter. At first it might have seemed like an unlikely duo, but now and forever it's a match made in heaven."

"You're adorable with your food metaphors," I say, licking the remainder of the chocolate off the spoon. "You are definitely the chocolate in our scenario, consistently wonderful. I'm the peanut butter—always nutty, and a little sticky at times."

"Can't argue with that."

"Hey, do you want me to go with you? To see Isla?" I reach for the blue container between us and root around until I find a hunk of peanut butter.

"No digging. You get what you get and then pass it over," she says as she pulls it out of my hands. "That would be good. Thanks."

I know she needs me there when she goes out to the trailer. Besides Paul, I am the only person who could tag along. According to what Amy has told the rest of the O'Connors, Isla, Amy's mother, is dead.

CHAPTER 5

The following day, I stop to pick up a coffee from my favorite spot downtown. It's where Amy worked as a waitress when she first moved to Half Moon Bay and *"the location of our meet-cute."* Both mine and Amy's and Amy and Paul's, which is exactly the line I used for my toast at their wedding.

That day Lucas and I had Joni in the stroller, while Paul trailed behind us. Amy glanced up from the register, and I remember being consciously aware of what the image of us must look like. As a painter, I'm always able to freeze time in a way that others overlook.

I knelt next to the stroller to offer Joni a stuffie from the backpack I pulled off my shoulder, which she promptly proceeded to throw on the ground.

"Leah, order for me, would you? We're going to check in with everyone," Lucas said.

I gave Amy our order, and she remarked how lovely Joni was. The guys had hung back and were debating getting coffee to bring back to "the house," which was a reference to Christine and George's home and where the family would often congregate.

"Joni, can you wave hi?" I inquired. Joni didn't move. "She's being shy today." I laughed a little.

Amy covered her eyes, playing peekaboo. Joni's face lit up with delight.

"Do you have any kids?" I asked.

"No, but I just got my credentials to be a preschool teacher. I love kids." I felt immediately absolved of my mom guilt. Some women are good with kids as a genetic trait—Nana had it, but it skipped my mom and me completely.

Amy snuck in one more round of peekaboo with Joni before she noticed other people observing me. While I had grown accustomed to looks and stares, I found it amusing to witness other people's reactions to my impact on strangers.

"A woman who's more than six feet tall is a sight to behold," Nana would always say. Nana's remarks about my appearance were subtle compared to my mother's. From her, I heard things like *"It's important to always be observed as the most beautiful woman in any room."*

"Which preschool? I need to send Joni somewhere soon so I can get back to work."

"I'm still looking for a position somewhere," she whispered softly. "I only just got here a few months ago."

"You're dangerously pretty to be a preschool teacher. Single?" I asked. She blushed as if she was not accustomed to anyone commenting on her beauty.

"Ha! Thank you. Yes, newly single," she said.

I ruffled Joni's hair and snagged a banana from the basket by the tip jar, peeling back the layers and handing her the bare fruit. She let out a scream as if I'd slapped her with it.

"What?" I asked, my face starting to warm.

"Oh, she probably wanted to peel it herself." Amy opened a fresh banana but left the skin intact for Joni to pull down, which immediately seemed to appease her.

"You know," I said, my eyebrows raised and looking back toward the men. "My brother-in-law is also single. He's a catch if you're into the whole mama's boy thing."

"Who's a mama's boy, now?" Lucas said, finally joining the conversation.

"Um, you. But I was talking about Paul," I teased and went in for a kiss that likely was too passionate to happen in public. When I pulled away, Amy was pretending to busy herself with the pens near the register.

"I'm trying to convince her to go out with your brother," I said. "Now we just need him to stop taking orders on the phone so they can start fallin' in love already."

Amy told me later that my energy was contagious but that she could tell straightaway that I was undeniably trouble. She also said that besides her mom, she'd never met anyone who said whatever was on their mind. But unlike with Isla, my words felt laced with good intentions.

Paul approached and apologized for his rudeness.

"Mom kept trying to convince us to just come to the house for coffee," Paul explained to us.

Christine always insisted on doing everything. Why buy pj's for the grandkids when she could sew them herself? Why would we pick up coffee when she could grind fresh beans at home? I ignored his comment and plowed forward with my plan. "So, Amy," I said, noting her name from her name tag. "This is Paul, and that's my husband, Lucas. Paul, this is your future wife, Amy."

"How long was I on the phone for?" Paul extended his hand toward Amy. "Nice to meet you, future-wife Amy." I could instantly tell he was taken by her.

Embarrassed, she reached out and shook Paul's hand and then immediately pulled it back to run her fingers through her ponytail. Paul revealed his straight white teeth. His lip curled up a little on one side, an expression that reminded me of Elvis.

Sensing their chemistry, I grabbed a pen from the register and scribbled down Paul's number. "Paul's free any night but tonight because it's Sunday. Sundays are reserved for the *sacred family dinner* . . . No, that's not made up; boy, that sounds made up." I looked toward Lucas, who was shaking his head but had learned to go along with my ideas.

"Paul, I will call you if you'd like," Amy said, later confiding that she felt momentarily brave from channeling my energy and confidence.

I wrote down my number, too, taking Amy's open hand and curling her fingers around the crumpled paper. "This is my number; I'm Leah. If this does work out"—I moved my finger between Paul and Amy—"I'm going to need a partner in crime. Their boys' club is off-limits to me on account of my vagina," I said, while pointing in the direction of it with the hand that wasn't gripping the stroller.

"Did you just say *vagina* in a coffee shop?" Amy tilted her head to the side, likely noticing the line that had started to grow behind us.

"Oh, I definitely said *vagina* in a coffee shop. I'd say *vagina* in church if we ever went. I'm hoping it's the next word this little girl picks up. Feminism, am I right? Can never start 'em too young." I pushed the stroller back and forth, even though Joni had yet to make a fuss.

"Okay, honey, that's enough outa you for a Sunday morning. Nice to meet you, Amy. My wife is totally nuts, but my brother is as solid as it gets," Lucas said as he placed some cash on the counter for all the to-go coffees. He put his hand on top of mine, and together we wheeled Joni away.

I stepped to the side and turned around to mouth, *Call him* and *Call me*, using my thumb and pinky finger to form a pretend phone at my ear.

"Yes, please call me," Paul said.

"I will." Amy handed him the change, and he put it directly into the tip jar. Years later, Amy recalled, "I couldn't help but watch you all walk away and ache for what you had . . . the embodiment of family."

"I'm leaving to see Isla. You still up for coming?" Amy says, launching right in when I answer her call. We always skip the formalities.

I glance down at my watch and see I still have at least an hour to spare before I have to get the big kids. Lucas has taken Dottie over to his parents'.

"Yeah, 'course."

Amy meets me in the coffee shop parking lot and I hand her a decaf. She looks especially lovely, which I know is not an accident. It takes me a moment to remember the last time we went to Pacifica. Typically, Amy will bring me along when she stops by The Nursery, the plant store Isla co-owns with Rita, who became a pseudo–foster mom to Amy during the end of her adolescence. We chose the nickname The Restaurant in secret homage to the simplicity of The Nursery's name. A little inside joke for Amy and me to fall back on whenever Christine starts spinning her wheels about the boys and "The Restaurant."

"I'm trying to remember, when did we last do this?" Very rarely, we'll go see Isla at the trailer where Amy grew up.

"It has been a while. Months, maybe." She shrugs. "But I just came from Dr. Lee's, so I'm feeling brave. One last time before the baby comes," she says. According to what Amy has shared with me from her work in therapy with Dr. Lee, "in order to gain autonomy" Amy has "created a boundary surrounding Isla" where she can visit her on her terms.

As long as I can paint, I'll never need therapy. Amy's creative outlet has always been children, which is why she doesn't deserve the hand she's been dealt on the road to motherhood.

"Is there something in particular you are hoping to get out of the visit?" I ask.

"Zero expectations, really. Hopefully she's sober, but you never know," she says.

The silence in the car grows louder suddenly as my eyes dart over to the construction happening along this part of Highway 1. The erosion on the cliffside has earned the name "Devil's Slide," resulting in dangerous mudslides after heavy rains.

There was an ongoing battle between environmentalists and Caltrans about whether the city should build a tunnel or an overpass. Ultimately the tunnel won out, but that meant the temporary lane has been pushed out as close to the beach as it can possibly go. With a tiny sneeze or swerve to avoid debris, a car could veer off and simply slip right out into the sea.

What a way to go out, though.

After exiting the freeway, we find the dirt path that leads to the trailer. I'm grateful my family is all the way back in the Midwest. I have no interest in conjuring up childhood feelings that pinch in a place just beneath that protective layer I must always maintain.

The trailer park itself is fine, but its proximity—mere steps—to the beach is what Amy says Isla was always prideful about. They couldn't afford a mansion on the cliffs, but this location couldn't be better.

I see Isla sitting outside the double-wide, resting her feet up on the firepit. She has a fire going, and the smoke is billowing out like she's been burning garbage instead of actual firewood. It's the only way we've seen her the handful of times we've come by this past year. Sitting here, like this, cloaked in a thick blanket.

Isla's eyes, like Amy's, are deep brown, almost black, and are fixed on the flames at her feet. They have the same dark hair; Isla's is draping down her shoulders, full and flowing. "Mermaid hair" as Joni calls it whenever she's allowed to brush out Amy's locks after Sunday dinners.

Their resemblance is uncanny. More akin to sisters since Isla was only fifteen when she was pregnant with Amy, sixteen when Amy was born. Isla turns her head toward the crunch of gravel and then returns her gaze to the flames. Amy turns off the engine but keeps her hands resting on the wheel.

"In and out," I say, doing my best to reassure her. "I'll be here the whole time."

Some of the paneling on Isla's trailer is displaced, though the windows are all still intact. The thing that makes her particular plot stand out in the line of mobile homes is the garden of succulents and flowers she has built up around her little lot.

"Hey," Amy says as we tentatively approach the fire.

"Hey, yourselves," Isla says, squinting up at us despite the lack of sun. The heat has gone to her cheeks, and she seems more radiant somehow.

I grab two plastic chairs leaning against the trailer, dragging them to where Amy and I can be positioned on the opposite side of the firepit, but not so close that the heat will melt them.

"You look good," Amy says, clearly attempting to offer her mother an olive branch.

"You look like hell," she says, unsmiling.

"Just tired, that's all." Amy frowns, folding her hands across her lap.

It's the dance they always do, talking about her pregnancy but not really talking about it. During their short visits, they don't bring attention to anything of substance. Why we even bother to trek out all this way, I don't know, but sometimes the nature of Amy and me is simply to show up for each other, with or without understanding.

"It looks exhausting," she says as she eyes Amy's ankles, which I'll admit look swollen.

"Wasn't it for you?" Amy asks, opening the doorway between them a crack. I can't help but hold my breath.

She snorts, sucking in air through her nostrils. "At fifteen, I could have run a damn marathon while I was pregnant. I tell you, those Egyptians had it right, having kids at twelve." She lifts her arms in exaggeration, the smoke parting between her hands. "Your body is like a well-oiled machine when you're young, and everything just bounces back. Old women should not have babies. Now that's exhausting!"

"So thirty-one is considered old now?" I ask, officially joining the conversation, staring at the backs of my hands for signs of age spots.

I know they never discuss pregnancy because the simplicity of how Amy was conceived mocks her painful attempts at conception. Amy is the product of drunken teenage lust. Her father and his family from the East Coast were in town for a funeral. According to Isla, Amy's dad and his brother decided to escape their family's scheduled sorrow and join her mom's crew of—what Amy and I assume were—misfit friends for a beach party.

"Jake something. Or Jamie. Definitely a J name," Amy was told of her father's identity. This is the extent of her knowledge on the subject, and she has never expected Isla to share more. Amy says a blank slate is easier to work with. He doesn't even know she exists.

"Mm-hmm," Amy breathes out. I've observed that Amy needs to remain quiet whenever Isla gets all worked up over nothing. Speaking but not saying anything.

"What have you been up to?" I ask.

"I met someone," Isla says, smiling.

For a moment, I think we could all have a normal conversation, so I try to keep it going. "Oh yeah? What's he like?"

"He is charming. Inspired." Her eyes are dancing with the reflection of the flames. "Pretty for a man—he looks a lot like Paul, actually, but I guess he has a common face."

Isla has seen Paul only a handful of times, but Amy has given her a framed five-by-seven-inch photo from their wedding. Isla wasn't invited, nor had Amy even mentioned her and Paul's engagement. The picture hit two birds with one stone: it included everyone from the O'Connor family, and it showed Isla what Amy was a part of now, despite her.

"Your boyfriend looks like Paul? That's disturbing on so many levels," I respond, almost laughing. "Are things going well?" I'm feeling slightly hopeful for Amy that this could be the beginning of something promising.

"No, on our last night together, he admitted he was married with kids out of state. The good ones always are." She stops to wave the smoke out of her face before continuing. "He was looking for a muse for his next short story—a writer. I can't fault him. We do what we need to do for art."

Isla considers her green thumb her creative gift to the world, so she's perpetually drawn to artist types, which is why I think she tolerates me always serving as Amy's chaperone. She does have a magical touch with plants; I'll grant her that. Amy once said the irony of it all is that her mother did the absolute bare minimum required to keep her daughter, a human, alive while her garden thrived. Amy was left alone, green with envy.

"And by *do*, you mean *you*. He needed to *do you*?" I catch myself joking.

"That man is somebody's husband. He has a wife." Amy is having none of it.

Isla doesn't reply. No one speaks again for more than a minute. I watch the wind whipping through Isla's hair—the way it clings to her olive skin, weathered, but more delicate than damaged, from a lifetime out in the sun.

"You're managing all right at The Nursery? You sober?" Amy inquires, scratching at a small white stain on her black leggings.

"Yes to both," she says, saluting her as if Amy were a commanding officer in the military.

"This isn't a joke. Rita says you've been sick." Amy stiffens in her chair.

"I'm sober. I'm good this time—Scout's honor." Isla looks her version of sincere.

Amy stands; it's time to go.

"I'm glad you girls could come by," Isla says, still sitting with her feet up.

"Mind if I use your bathroom before we hit the road?" I'm

sure it feels strange for Amy to ask about entering a place she used to call home.

"Knock yourself out." Isla starts humming loudly.

Amy disappears within the trailer.

"You know I'm keeping a secret from her," Isla tells me in a low, eerie whisper.

"Oh yeah? What's that?" I ask. It isn't unusual for Isla to speak in ominous riddles.

She shakes her hair, and the ripple of curls bounces around her face. "Not just yet. I'll tell you soon enough, and then you can decide what to do with the information."

"Great. Can't wait," I answer, frowning. I hope Amy hurries; I want to get out of here. We don't say anything else as we silently stare into the flames.

Amy emerges from the doorway, holding tightly to the railing. Her wedding ring dings along the piping, and I can tell she's struggling to find her balance. I rush over to help her down while Isla remains seated.

"Good?" Isla asks. I see her eyes moving toward Amy's bag. Maybe Isla has already guessed what Amy's done. She makes a point to steal Isla's journals when we come, which she claims is her only channel into her mother's head.

The inside of the car feels damp and cold as Amy heaves herself into the driver's seat. I'm envious of her regular-size sedan. I watch Isla in my side-view mirror all the way to the end of the dirt road. She's still sitting there when we pull out onto the highway.

One night, in between Amy's last miscarriage and when she became pregnant with this baby, the guys were working late, and my kids were inside watching a movie. Amy and I sat outside, finishing off a bottle of our favorite red. She revealed her rationale behind keeping her two worlds separate. "I see no point in trying to explain my mother to Christine and the rest of Paul's family. It's my turn . . . ," she began. I sat rapt, mid-swallow, wanting to see where she'd take her thought. "I need something that is only mine. I don't want to share the O'Connors with Isla. She hasn't earned that. *I've* earned my own life." Even with her voice cracking, I could tell she believed every word.

"You make the O'Connors sound like we've won the marriage lottery or something," I said dismissively.

"That's how I feel. I know you have your stuff with Christine, but she's Mother Teresa compared to Isla."

I couldn't help but shake my head in disagreement, though I knew to leave it alone in that moment.

"And what if Christine and Isla just happen upon each other out on Main Street one day? What then?"

"Well . . ." She paused. "That would be a drop in the ocean compared to what could happen if I willingly let my mother into my new life."

Back in the parking lot of the coffee shop, Amy pulls out the notebook she stole from the trailer. "I want to hear the whole story about her breakup. There's something she's not saying."

"You little thief."

She flips it open, but all the pages are blank except for a single sentence: *Not this time, Amy.*

I am tempted to tell Amy what Isla said to me. I won't, though, not yet. I don't know any of the important details, and with Amy as pregnant and anxious as she already is, it will only create more worry. Which I desperately want to subtract from her life, not add. And I know a little something about being the keeper of secrets. That even the knowledge of their very existence can be enough to haunt a woman forever.

CHAPTER 6

Most days I feel continually blindsided by my family's vortex of need. Since I'm at the center, everything happens *to* me while somehow simultaneously happening *around* me. Lucas and the restaurant, the kids' incessant calls for action. By the time I'm able to do anything for myself, I'm more than halfway to exhaustion or completely deflated.

Reid was my holdout this morning when, typically, he's the easiest kid to get out the door. Something about his friend borrowing his favorite hat, which he now needed.

"Can you wear your baseball cap from your team?" I asked, exasperated by his hang-up on clothing, an issue we managed to sidestep with him entirely until this morning.

He looked at me like I'd grown another head.

I've finally thrown away the last of the matchless socks, and with the kids occupied at preschool and camps, I'm just sitting down to paint at the studio. The problem with being a mom and self-employed as an artist is that I have only scheduled blocks of time to create, and that needs to happen whether or not I'm feeling particularly inspired.

My cell rings on the counter.

"Hey."

"Hey, it's me." Lucas sounds breathy and mildly annoyed.

"What's up?"

"I left a manila folder on the kitchen island. Could you bring it by The Restaurant in the next twenty minutes or so?" I exhale forcefully into the receiver. "I'm sorry. I need it for our next meeting, and I don't have time to come grab it."

"Fine, yeah. I was just about to finally get to work, but I'll go back home and bring it by."

"Thanks, babe. You're the best."

"I know."

After my stop at home, the drive over to The Restaurant has more traffic than usual, and it's not exactly on my way downtown. Anytime the weather is good here, people from over the hill line 92 in bumper-to-bumper traffic, and it clogs our single main intersection. The monotony of moving my foot from the gas to the brake pedal and back again causes my mind to drift back into the pockets of the past. Deep channels that could just have easily led me in an entirely different direction.

About six months after my arrival in Half Moon Bay back in 2011, I told Lucas I was going out of town to some sort of artists' retreat. He should have gathered that I was lying or inquired further because actual artist retreats, like Burning Man, are essentially glorified orgies. I could have told him what I was doing, but I didn't feel like I owed him the truth at that point.

My friend Beth from college owned a small, semi-renovated church. She rented out the space for friends and independent contractors to finance her art career, which was nonexistent. Her parents were wealthy and had bought up a bunch of old historic property in the area. She was the only friend I knew who ended up in the Bay Area, and her building was near a Planned Parenthood.

When I arrived, Beth came out to greet me. She was short and stout with a large, wide smile. We hugged, though sort of awkwardly, since we were never close friends. She reminded me of a sponge, attempting to soak up artistic inspiration through me and others within the art program. But raw, natural talent cannot be faked—either you've got it or you don't.

"Hey, thanks for this," I said, throwing my flip-flops on the ground in front of me and stepping into them. I always drove barefoot back then. I slung my backpack over my shoulder and gathered the shopping bag from the passenger seat.

"Yeah, not a problem. Can I help you?" She went to reach for the plastic grocery bag in my hand.

"Oh, no thanks. I've got it," I said as I pulled the bag with the pregnancy test and vodka in closer to me. I wasn't up for her cheerfulness.

"I kept the bell tower room open for you tonight. It's pretty cool." She nodded toward the building, so I stopped to peek out over my sunglasses. The redbrick church rose before us. At the top was a massive bronze bell. When I turned back toward her, she was grinning, showing all her unusually large teeth, which took over her entire mouth and made her look almost cartoonish.

"Thanks," I said as I looked back up at the tower.

"It's a little bit of a hike but totally worth it," she said, opening the door. I could tell she was examining me, comparing our bodies postcollege. It's something all women do without even thinking. I pitied her lack of confidence.

We ascended the stairs in silence. I appreciated Beth's inability to climb and chitchat between labored breaths. When

we reached the top, she unlocked the door with an antique-
looking key and then handed it over to me.

She turned her head in my direction and asked, "You're
stayin' for two nights, yeah?"

"Yeah," I repeated as I looked around.

There was a twin bed and a writing desk with a lamp and a
phone plugged into the wall. In the middle of the room, a long
rope hung from the ceiling, encircled by a railing. I tilted my
head back to look inside the giant bell.

"Wow, this is amazing!" I said, unable to contain my
disbelief.

Beth clapped her hands together and drew in a breath.
"Isn't it something?"

I could tell she was dying to share with me the entire history of this building, but at that moment, I felt overcome with
exhaustion.

"Thank you. This is great, really. But, uh, I have an early
appointment tomorrow, so I think I'm gonna lay down for a bit,"
I said as I walked her back to the door.

She nodded, clearly disappointed I didn't want to spend
more time together.

"I can bring breakfast by whenever you'd like," Beth told me
just before she crossed the threshold of the doorframe. Then
she added, "Oh, and we ask our guests to refrain from ringing
the bell after eight o'clock at night if you could." I couldn't help
but laugh. I imagined myself drunk at midnight, trying to
resist pulling on the rope. "Door open or closed?"

"Closed, thanks."

I waited until I heard her on the stairs before turning the
lock. I ran my fingers along the exposed brick, appreciating the
texture, then took my art supplies out of my backpack. I wanted

to paint, but the pull and nagging sensation of the plastic bag's contents wouldn't let me focus.

I took out the pregnancy test. I was late, so I already knew what it would say. I had taken one other test in my life in high school, back when I was hooking up with Trent Jacobs every Tuesday and Thursday behind the gym after his soccer practice. Our circles didn't exactly mix, so we were never seen together publicly. It seemed the cheerleaders or social elite were a bunch of prudes. I didn't mind messing around in secret because I didn't need Trent for anything other than sex.

I was one of those in-between popular kids. I could nod hello to almost anyone in the halls, and we would acknowledge each other. I spent most lunch periods with one or two friends before sneaking away to the art room.

The art teacher, Madame Tessier, was easily my favorite person on campus. She was originally from France, and there wasn't a single day she didn't reek of cigarette smoke. She'd give me the keys to her tiny hatchback and ask me to go grab the packs she kept stored on her dashboard. Then she'd prop herself up on a stool and stick her hand out the open window while unsuccessfully attempting to blow the smoke directly outside.

Her hair was a silvery brown and went down her back in an intricate braid. She'd always have exclusively female musicians playing on a boom box she kept at the center of the room. When she'd sway along from her stool, I'd watch her braid take on a life of its own, a snake's S curving its way down her spine. I'd stay after school for as long as she would let me.

Madame Tessier was brutally honest when it came to my work. "What are you so scared of?" she'd say in her sultry French accent. "Don't be afraid to show them things that will make them feel something!"

She'd tell me wild, inappropriate stories about her time living as a nomad across Europe. Describing in detail the time she posed nude along the Seine for her lover, Julien. When she said his name, it came out as more of a growl than a word.

Mom met Madame Tessier during back-to-school night, and they took an instant disliking to each other. Madame Tessier never officially said anything, but when they met, her nose scrunched the way it would whenever I tried to fake a project I wasn't inspired by. Mom told me that a black crocheted lace shawl was a "poor choice" for an event that was meant to impress families.

"It's meant to showcase our work, not what the teachers are wearing," I explained to her on the drive home, my breath steaming up the passenger side window.

The following morning, I shared my mom's comment with Madame Tessier.

Smiling, unbothered, she said, "Art, at its best, forces us to examine ourselves. Some people are not up for the exposure. You'll see that life will try to take you one way . . ." Joni Mitchell's husky voice tolled in the background. "There will be times when it feels like the . . . *rainures*—the grooves—in the road have been put in place because you were meant to follow them. Everyone around you will fall into place since they've just come to accept that they are ordinary." Then she pointed at my work almost as if she were angry. "You, Leah, are not ordinary. *Tu n'es pas ordinaire!*" She slid between English and French, trying to convince me in as many ways as she could.

I don't think I really understood what she meant until the moment I stood in the bell tower holding a positive pregnancy test. The lines weren't faint; they were the road markers of a highway headed straight for *l'ordinaire*.

I reached behind me until my hand found the bed, and lay down. My breath caught in my lungs, and it felt like I was pinned under a wave, knocked flat on my back—the daylight mocking me from above.

My parents were youngish when they had me. They were adults, but newly so, and they needed all the help they could get from Nana. I spent the majority of my childhood with Nana at her house. I guess my upbringing and my parents' inability to parent me in any real way were meant to serve as their version of the "birds and the bees" conversation. Nana tried once as I covered my face with my hands, but I was already having sex with Trent at that point.

When I arrived in Half Moon Bay, I was twenty-three. Lucas and I would stay up late, drinking and talking. In the mornings we'd sleep in and opt for sex instead of surfing— sometimes both. On a couple of nights, I found my way into Miles's bed.

Thinking back, I knew there was one morning after a night of dancing when I woke up realizing I'd forgotten to take my birth control for several days in a row. I popped three pills in my mouth, and then later, while I was out surfing, I emptied the entire contents of my stomach next to my board. Food particles and important babyproofing hormones floated on the surface of the water. I paddled away, knowing the seagulls would descend upon me soon enough. I should have insisted on condoms.

I heaved myself off the bed and made my way to the center of the room. Holding on to the railing, I reached out to touch the rope's coarse thickness with the tips of my fingers before gripping it with both hands and pulling it downward in one swift motion. It was heavier than I expected. I pulled it again, and nothing happened. Unsatisfied, I yanked with all my might, and the bell tolled. I repeated my motions over and over until my arms shook and pulsed with fatigue.

The momentary relief of exhaustion quickly dissipated, and I returned to treading water in my mind. All my thoughts bunched together, causing a crowded discomfort I desperately wanted to ignore. I took out the only thing I'd ever found to dull the noise when it all became too loud. I brought the bottle to my mouth and drank. Satisfied, I placed it next to the stick marked with the proof of life inside my body.

"How perfectly ordinary," I said exactly as Madame Tessier would have—mimicking her accent and the cadence of her voice. I instantly regretted not getting cigarettes.

I picked up the bottle again, took a swig, and chased it with another.

When all my edges went soft, I thought of Lucas and his willingness to care about me, despite my hesitance. His commitment to family, especially the way he talked about his mom. I still hadn't met any of them—I had refused all invitations to do so. It felt wrong to accept while I was still sleeping with someone else.

I lay down on the bed and closed my eyes. The loneliness suddenly felt like too much to bear.

On the drive over Lucas had texted, *I'll be at my parents' tonight, but call me when you can, because I already know I'll miss you.*

I had thought this impossible after only one night. But in my blurriness, neediness no longer felt like the worst thing.

Lucas answered after several rings, and he sounded winded. "Leah?"

"Hey, yeah, it's me. What are you up to?" I asked, studying the markings along the rim of the bell.

He would love this place, I thought.

"Oh, Mom and I were just having a Joni Mitchell sing-off. Man, that woman's voice scratches at your insides," he said.

I laughed. "Is that a good thing?"

"Totally. My mom is a closet Mitchell fan. We gave her two and a half glasses of wine, and now suddenly she knows every lyric to 'Both Sides Now.'" He paused and then added, "When you meet her, you will realize how hilarious this actually is. So not her."

"Joni Mitchell, huh?" I took this as a sign that the baby was his.

That night I dreamed I was lying directly under a rope hanging down from the ceiling. It was braided exactly like Madame Tessier's hair. The end was made into a noose that would sway and shift next to my head. I kept trying to wiggle myself out of the way to avoid getting caught, but my body felt like it was being weighed down, my limbs like lead. Suddenly the rope was around my neck. I shifted my gaze upward. Lucas was hovering above, manipulating the noose. Finally, the entire ceiling dropped away, and only he remained, still holding tightly to the rope.

I tried to scream, but my voice sounded like it was underwater. It wasn't my own.

"Look again!" he shouted down at me. "Look again!"

I can't! I wanted to say. *I'm trapped. This is going to be the end of me.*

"Look again." This time when he pointed, the rope had disappeared. Somehow I'd curled into a crescent on the floor and sensed a warmth inside the nook between my pelvis and chest. I looked down, and it was a baby girl. She was familiar in the way a memory can surface but never fully appear. A stranger, and yet she felt like a part of me I recognized.

I came to, probably still slightly buzzed. A wash of shame crept through me. Everything felt wrong.

It was still early, so I wrote a note for Beth and left it with the remainder of the alcohol on the desk. I walked past the rope one last time. I yanked down, prepared for the strength it took to make the bell ring. It tolled, immediately sobering me.

The entrance to Planned Parenthood was littered with picketers. When I made the appointment, they said I could call and get an escort to the door when I arrived. I told them that wouldn't be necessary.

"Abortion is murder! Let your baby live!" A middle-aged man broke off from the mob, shouting as I walked toward the double doors.

How presumptuous to assume I was coming in for an abortion.

"Let your baby live!" he repeated, loud enough for me to need to cover my ears. My shoulder intentionally knocked into his. I refused to break eye contact and lifted both middle fingers inches from his bulbous, protruding nose.

I imagined the poor fragile women who had walked before me; some of them may have been bullied into changing their minds—not because it was what they wanted but because of men like him who needed to control women. He stepped backward, silent, unaccustomed to any kind of pushback. For the first time that morning, I felt better.

A volunteer from the clinic was suddenly next to me. She wrapped her arm around my shoulder, having to stand on her tiptoes to do so. She waved her key card at the front door, and we were in, the shouting replaced by an eerie quiet.

"I'd ask if you're okay, but you clearly had them handled,"

she said. She looked to be about my age, maybe younger. Her eyes were empathetic without being pitying.

"I mean, I'd respect the right to protest if it were women out there, but men don't exactly have a dog in this fight," I said, immediately thinking about Lucas.

They called me back about twenty minutes after I checked in, just long enough to make me question every decision I'd ever made in my entire life. Inside the room, I shivered in the thin paper gown. The doctor and nurse came in together, gloved and looking ominous.

I lay back on the table, staring up at a poster taped to the ceiling—rows of sandcastles along the shore with little buckets and shovels. Children were notably absent from the image. I brought my fingers to my mouth, aggressively searching for a jagged edge of fingernail I could chew on.

The doctor was using medical terminology I wasn't able to focus on. All I could see were the abandoned toys over my head.

"M'kay," I said, not sure which question, if any, I was answering.

"You'll feel my hand here and then a little pressure," the doctor said. That part I felt.

A screen next to my head flickered on, producing an image in black and white. Suddenly the silence was flooded with sound. It reminded me of being at the trough of an enormous wave, the moment when I need to abandon my board and dive headfirst, separating the curtain of water with my own body. Upon entrance, the powerful churning produces a cacophony of noise. Then came the sound of a rapid pulse, beating out of sync with the static.

"What's that?" I asked, knowing but requiring verbal confirmation.

"That's the heartbeat. You are measuring at about ten weeks or so. Does that sound right?" the doctor asked.

None of this sounds right.

I looked back up at the shovels and buckets, the heartbeat putting me there with Lucas and a sound that could somehow transform into a baby.

"Stop," I told them.

The noise disappeared as the doctor removed the probe. He and the nurse both sat poised, unmoving, waiting for me to decide on something that felt impossible either way.

"I'd like to leave." My voice came out stronger than I felt.

"Sure. Would you like to discuss prenatal care? I can come back in, and we can talk more after you're dressed," the doctor said.

"Um, I don't know. Can I have a second?" I asked, suddenly wishing I wasn't there alone.

I left the clinic with prenatal vitamins I was advised not to take on an empty stomach. *How do they go down with a hangover?* I wanted to ask but, of course, didn't.

The entire drive home, I acknowledged every element of my decision. I knew I'd never go back to Iowa; my parents would visit us out here, probably twice a year, and maybe Nana would come more often. I didn't know all the questionable corners of who Lucas was, but I understood enough to know he'd make a great dad. Maybe this version of my life was what I was meant to find all along.

Mom was young when she had me, though she'd made it abundantly clear that she always wanted different for me. Funny how we are doomed to reenact our parents' choices, but in a way that's uniquely our own, so we can convince ourselves that it's different somehow. The initial decision not to keep the baby was in many ways a middle finger to my mom's attempt at the impossible standard she'd painted for me.

Don't get pregnant, but don't have an abortion.

But she never took a keen enough interest in my teen years to extrapolate that I was having a decent amount of sex. I could tell my normal amount of teenage-girl angst terrified her in a way that pushed me further away, and yet Nana ensured I could still remain safely tethered to the ground, without drifting off into oblivion.

I pulled up to Lucas's condo and stood outside his front door for a moment. I hadn't been gone for even twenty-four hours, but I'd missed the smell of the coast. A deep inhale provided me with the courage needed to cross the threshold. I let myself in. Lucas was in the kitchen drinking coffee at the table. He had the newspaper sprawled out in front of him. A scene too quaint to feel real.

Would this image fit us? Me and my child, who, after my dream, I just knew had to be a girl. He peeked up from what I assumed was the business section. His eyes on me were both warm and confused.

"You're here? What happened to your retreat?" He stood and walked over to me; a section of the paper floated to the floor as the air shifted in the room. He held me, and I let my head rest right under his chin. He was the first man to fit like this.

"Can we go for a walk?" I needed to taste the air inside my lungs again.

He poured us coffee, trying to read me as he did, but I turned away, not allowing him to decipher anything from my body language. He grabbed two blankets from the back of his couch, handing me one of the mugs. He tried to wrap a blanket around my shoulders, but I folded it over my arm. We made our way to a bench on the path that looked out over the water. Neither one of us sat down.

The surfers were out in droves. It was a damp, foggy morning, but clear enough to be able to watch. I longed to be out there with them.

"Let's just stay here for a second." For all my hurry in getting back, I now wanted to wait. I remained standing, setting the blanket and my coffee down on the bench. Seeming puzzled, Lucas set down his coffee too.

Of the dozen or so surfers in the lineup, I could spot only one girl. I kept my eyes on her the entire time. She caught a wave but then was thrown. I held my breath and found the mirrored pulse beneath the wave and on that paper-lined examination table.

I just needed to tell him. If I said it, it could be real.

Comfortable within the silence, Lucas pulled me closer, wrapping me inside the cocoon of his blanket.

"I'm pregnant." The words fell out of my mouth as I breathed them into his neck.

He gently pushed my arms back and moved his big hand into the small of my back. He didn't speak but stared into my eyes.

"Oh yeah?" His breathing sped up. "Okay, okay." He bobbed his head back and forth like he was saying yes, although I hadn't asked a question.

"I'm scared. I don't know what I'm doing." It wasn't what I wanted to say, but sometimes the truth can betray us. Lucas was shaking his head now, less confident. "This isn't what I wanted," I said as I started to feel tears prick my eyes.

He let me go, taking a few steps away from me. The blanket fell, becoming a lifeless puddle on the ground between us. "You don't want to keep it?"

My legs felt numb, and my mouth was suddenly dry. "I didn't, no. I was sure this was a mistake." I wanted to tell him about my dream and appointment, but I also wanted to keep that just for me. I was already sharing so much of myself.

"So, you didn't want to—but you do now?" he asked, confused but maintaining patience.

"What do you want?" I asked. He looked a little pale.

"If it were up to just me . . ." He paused, shifting his weight from one leg to the other. "I would say, let's go for it. I mean, my mom is going to kill me."

I snorted, feeling lighter despite the heaviness. "I guess this is one way to meet your family. I probably should have met them earlier." I bent to pick up the blanket and hugged it tightly to my chest as a sick, nervous feeling started to sink in. "Now they're gonna think I got pregnant on purpose to trap you and steal all your surfboard money."

"Oh, they will definitely think that." He leaned over and kissed me directly on the nose. "Except they already know I'm insanely crazy about you." Then he flashed me the same smile that made me sleep with him in the first place: the one that revealed Lucas's ineffable charm and his ability to assuage any of my doubts. He always, in every circumstance, primed himself to carry enough for two. While I was too young to understand it at the time, it's what separates the boys from the men. Miles never stood a chance. "You still haven't said you want to keep it." His eyes hadn't broken contact with mine. "Are we doing this?"

I watched his face; his eyebrows were slowly creeping up his forehead. We stood across from each other, our bodies like two lines in the sand. I channeled the sensation of warmth, a feeling that wasn't a betrayal but something I could trust. Something that was.

I made a decision that became ours.

"We are doing this," I said, trying to match his enthusiasm.

Over the past few years, I've seen The Restaurant in various stages of development. Its evolution reminds me of the layers I swipe onto the canvas—how the thickness protrudes outward as it takes on a life of its own. Inside The Restaurant, Lucas is rushing around, his arms up overhead. Paul has his fingers knotted below his waist, poised and professional. The inner workings of their dynamic revealed in a snapshot of time.

"Babe, oh thank goodness. You're a lifesaver." Lucas exhales, almost tripping over a chair to greet me in the entryway.

"You okay there, sailor?" His clumsiness is unusual. He is more stressed out than I realized.

"He's fine. Everything's good. This next meeting is a big one," Paul says, translating.

Lucas leans in and gently kisses my lips, squeezing my hand and pulling the folder from the other.

I know better than to comment on their progress. Paul would be the only one who would hear it, and right now, Lucas is the only one who needs to. So instead, I whisper into my husband's ear, "I promise to help you de-stress tonight by any means necessary."

He grins, and instantly his body softens. Sometimes I envy the predictability of what makes him tick. Nothing in me feels that simple anymore.

CHAPTER 7

Amy and I are meeting for brunch downtown. She's already sitting at a table outside on a call when I arrive. I make my way in and order breakfast at the counter as well as a mimosa and coffee to bring back to the table. The morning fog has lifted, and the sun is breaking through the clouds.

I sit down and close my eyes, turning my face in the direction of the light, allowing the warmth to sink into my skin as Amy says into her phone, "Hey, it's me. It's Amy." I gaze out toward the parking lot when a motorcycle engine rips through the quiet. "Yeah, good. You? Okay, then. It's all right, though? Is it Isla?" Her tone has shifted toward nervousness.

Amy jolts a little, moving her hand to her stomach. The baby has probably done a somersault. I remember the forceful kicks in the third trimester were always so jarring. I reach over, hoping to feel my niece's movements.

"No, I really don't. I'm sorry." She ends the call and shoves her phone deep within her purse. "Sorry," she says to me. "I was checking to see if Isla made it to The Nursery today. Something was off when we saw her, and Rita just confirmed it for me without going into details, but I need to let it go. I can't . . ." She shakes her head. Even when Isla and Christine are not physically present, they still have the ability to suck all the oxygen out of the room.

Amy shrugs, moving my hand to a place where I feel a distinctive thump. "There, you feel that one?"

"Well, hello to you, too, baby girl!" I say toward her belly.

"Hey, did you guys get pet fish?" Amy asks as she sips from her ice water.

"*Got* fish, yes. We went through two rounds, and they all lasted exactly six days in total. Oh no, did Dottie tell you about it at school?" I say, scrunching up my nose.

"She did, but I'd love to hear the actual version of events because hers sounded like 'fish potty.'"

The waiter comes to deliver our breakfast.

"I like Dottie's better, actually." I pause to sip my mimosa. The orange bubbles froth around the corners of my mouth, and I wipe them away with my hand. "So I thought, cool, we live near the beach, and a dog would for sure tip me over the insanity scale, so let's start slow. I took Dottie to the pet store, and we picked out two of those fish that are like twenty-five cents that people feed to other pets."

"Feeder fish, yeah," Amy adds.

"Right, feeder fish. The guy at the register asked if we would be keeping them as pets—super quick on the uptake, this guy. So he explained, and I quote, 'If you bring back the fish carcasses'—Carcassi? Plural? Dunno—'within thirty days, you can get two new ones free of charge.' End quote."

Amy puts her fork down mid-bite to chuckle while covering her mouth full of food. "Please tell me you didn't actually do that."

"Of course I did! Have we met? I took it as a challenge. I would have returned the bodies a second time, but Lucas flushed them before I could explain about the return policy. Hence the potty reference. I think we are done with pets for a while," I say, exhaling, finally lifting my bagel to my mouth to take a bite.

"What are you wearing to the opening? Have you decided yet?" I ask.

"Literally whatever I can squeeze into at this point. It's sort of cruel that I have to find a nice dress I will only ever wear this one time," she says, frowning in protest.

"Just keep the tags on and return it. No one will know."

"Uh, I'll know and I'm a preschool teacher. Isn't that stealing?"

I roll my eyes and sip from my mimosa. The warmth of the bubbles travels up my nose, almost tickling my brain. I laugh, waving my hand from side to side. "It's fine. But in case they arrest you, just to stick it to them, you could try to squeeze out the baby in the back of the cop car."

"You are a terrible influence."

"I've never claimed not to be." I smirk.

Amy tells me several stories about Dottie from Discovery Day—one perk of our small town is that Amy has been the preschool teacher of all three of my kids.

Six years ago, Amy and I were sitting on the benches in the outdoor area of her preschool. Amy had just finished teaching for the day, while Joni and Reid were on the play structure outside her classroom. Everyone else had gone home, and we were sipping the coffee I brought for us. Paul and Amy's engagement party was scheduled for the next day at Christine's house.

"Lidy and Christine already gave me explicit instructions," Amy said. "Dress up and get a manicure."

"Ugh, they would say that. Which one? Sounds like Lidy. You know what, never mind." I rolled my eyes and sipped my coffee, watching as Reid attempted to climb up the slide.

"Slides are for coming down, Reid," Amy called over to him.

"You are such a preschool teacher," I said, teasing. She was so easy to love.

"You know Christine wishes my career was something more impressive," Amy said, disappointment causing her shoulders to droop toward her plate.

"Oh please. One of the first questions she ever asked me was, 'What exactly do you do with a fine arts degree?'"

"I think she thinks teaching is more of a hobby and that I'm just biding my time before I can get pregnant and become a stay-at-home mom like Lidy." Amy's lips were anchored into a fully formed frown. "That isn't the plan, though. I love teaching. I'm proud of myself for getting here."

"As you should be!" I beamed at her. "Christine believes that there is only one correct path, and it is the one that aligns with her own experience." Before I can squeeze in one more juicy layer of gossip ripping Christine to shreds, Amy has moved on.

"I wanted to ask you something. I was going to put it in a card or organize a parade, but I knew you would hate that, and then I'd run the risk of you saying no." Amy was smiling like she had a secret she was dying to share. "Will you please be my matron of honor? In the wedding?"

"*Matron* of honor? Oh wow, that makes me sound old," I said, but then I took her hands in mine and added, "Of course. Yes, of course!"

She rocketed herself into the air, only letting go of me to

clap her hands together. Her childish glee spread through me, and despite myself, I sprang up along with her. Reid looked over at us and started to clap and jump as well. Amy let go of my hands and ran over to where he was standing, lifted him up, and began spinning round and round. Joni climbed off the monkey bars and joined in. The three of them spun together, effortlessly happy.

"Your mommy is my ma-tron of hon-or! Ma-tron of hon-or!" Amy was singing it now.

"The more you say it, the older I feel!" I shouted over at them. "If either of them pukes, you are cleaning it up."

Amy stopped spinning and set Reid on the ground, holding him tightly until he was no longer dizzy. Joni had already returned to the playground.

Amy made her way back over to the bench. "So, should we discuss place settings now or later?" she asked. I knew she was joking without even needing to look at her.

"My acceptance of this position has more to do with the bachelorette party. Or making sure your boob doesn't accidentally pop out of your dress on the day. And much less to do with the girly details," I explained. Amy nodded and waved her hand around like none of that was new information before picking up her coffee.

Joni and Reid wandered over and climbed up on the bench and into my lap. Both of my (no longer) babies, filling up all the space near my heart.

"I've never really told you the full story about my mom, and it kind of seems like something a matron of honor should know."

"Oh yeah?" I reached into my bag to hand the kids some snacks and off they went. "Please tell me something dark and twisted so that I feel less like an unbelievable asshole for all of the skeletons I keep in my closet." I said it casually like it was a joke, because at this point Amy didn't know anything about Miles. That didn't come until later.

"It was never meant to be a big secret. It couldn't be, really, because I only moved to the next town over. But now that she is sort of back in my life, I'm not entirely sure how to keep the charade up with Christine and the rest of the O'Connors. Or if I even want to." Amy sighed as she geared up to further clarify. "My mother isn't actually dead."

I waited, not sure what else I should do. She looked up at me, ready to share more. She described a shadowy childhood. Right around the word *alcoholic*, I sort of went numb. It was hard for me to imagine sweet little Amy suffering as a child. I marveled at her resiliency. Suddenly even the minimum I was given from my own parents felt like more than enough.

"I feel like Christine would judge me if she knew the extent of my upbringing. She would have an opinion, and even though Isla was a neglectful mother, that's for me to say—no one else. Like, she was a mess, but she was my mess. You know?"

"Oh, she would most definitely be judgmental about it all!" The ability to recognize the cracks among the O'Connors' perfection was quickly becoming the glue that bonded Amy and me together.

Amy went on to explain how she'd been back and forth to Pacifica a few times since the engagement, almost as a middle finger to her mom that she was happy now despite her.

"I sort of felt that way when my parents came when Joni was born. Not that our childhoods were even in the same league," I told her sincerely. "There's just something about making those first major decisions for yourself that marks the ending of past ties we were supposed to break free from. Enjoy it while it lasts, though, since you're about to become an O'Connor. Consider this secret your last piece of independence."

Amy looked puzzled for a moment, not yet quite grasping the concept of the "royal *we*" she'd have to grow accustomed to. The endearing warmth of the family's unity dissolves as soon as Christine catches wind of anything that could disrupt their perfect facade.

Back at breakfast, Amy has been waiting patiently for me to spill the thing I wasn't ready to share until right now. That's the thing about Amy—she has the patience of a preschool teacher.

"I saw Miles at the Tree Tunnel," I say finally. The wind starts to whip my hair around my face, so I set my coffee on the table and sweep it all up into a messy bun. "He's a park ranger there now, apparently. He came and sat with me when I was resting on a bench. Paul and Christine were out riding and saw us sitting together."

"Miles, Miles? Like Sexy Surfer Boy Miles? Potentially, but we don't talk about it"—she lowers her voice to a whisper—"Joni's maybe real father, Miles?" Amy has stopped using her knife to swipe avocado across her toast. She waits for me to answer before she continues spreading.

"No! Lucas is Joni's real father. Anyway, Christine's judgy little eyes when she saw us . . ." I drift off.

"Wait. What were you doing?" She licks the avocado that's slid onto her finger.

"Nothing! Literally nothing. We were just talking while sitting on a bench. He must have been transferred recently from a different state beach. I've never seen him there before and I go all the time. I swear I didn't know."

I'm sure my defensiveness sounds excessive, but I shouldn't have to explain myself to Amy.

"Okay . . . well then . . . it should be fine." Her words are long and drawn out.

"He leaned in a little too much. It probably didn't look great," I admit, mumbling the last part into my coffee mug.

"What are you doing, Leah? Really? From now on, you should probably avoid where he works—seeing him can only lead to dangerous consequences." She puts her utensils down and places both palms on the table. I finish the remainder of my mimosa.

"Just like you could tell Christine that your mom actually lives in Pacifica." The second I've said it, I wish I could take it back. The words between us have the power both to wound and to heal in an almost symbiotic capacity.

She throws her hands up as if to surrender. "Whoa, where did that come from? You sounded like Isla just now."

I bat my hand in the air, hoping to wave off the comment.

"Sorry. I'm sorry, okay? That wasn't nice," I say, wanting to sound remorseful. Amy knows that I'm guilty of word vomit when I feel backed into a corner.

I signal to the waiter for another mimosa.

"You need to go inside and get it," Amy says. "When I worked at the coffee shop, I used to hate it when people couldn't be bothered to walk the twenty feet to the register."

I'm a little stunned. This isn't us, the last few back-and-forth snide, underhanded comments. I push off from the table with one hand, curling the champagne flute into my other palm.

When I return, I want to be done bickering. She is the closest thing I have ever had to a sibling.

"When are you coming into the studio for me to paint you in your gloriously preggo state?" I ask.

"You already have enough pictures of whales; why do you

need another?" she says, sticking out her tongue, officially ending our fight.

"Ha ha," I scoff but refuse to let her off that easy. "You are a vision. Truly. It will be fun to have for your nursery. It's my gift to you. Come on . . . please."

"Fine, but I'm keeping all my clothes on."

"Nonsense, Moby Dick! You know I prefer nudes."

I come home and am surprised to find Lucas standing in the kitchen with Dottie, who is eating turkey slices while sitting atop the kitchen island. Lucas is making a sandwich and singing James Taylor, adorably off-key. He stops squeezing mustard to look up but continues singing. Now that Paul and Lucas are both exclusively working on The Restaurant, they keep odd but typically long hours.

"What are you doing up there, Little Miss Queen of the Castle?" I make my way over and pretend to snag a slice of turkey but go in for a nibble on Dottie's neck instead. She squeals with delight. Bills and mail are strewn across the granite countertop. I'll need to sit down and sort them out later. We are lucky that we never have to worry about money. Lucas's ventures have always paid off, and even if they hadn't, his parents would never let us starve. I adapted quickly to the O'Connor way of life: a remarkable level of wealth that further exploded after George made smart investments in the stock market. Amy was slow to adjust. I could read her guilt at breakfast that she'd been brazen enough to add avocado to her toast, a splurge she'd previously deemed incompatible with a preschool teacher's measly salary.

"What are you doing home?" I say, walking over to give him a kiss.

"We had a break between inspections and then more inspections, and I didn't want to leave this one at my parents' for too long." He holds up the dry side of the bread. "Eating this before I go back for more inspections." He looks tired.

"I ran into an old friend at the Tree Tunnel on Tuesday and then saw Christine and Paul riding. Let's do pizza after Reid's game," I say, plowing forward, changing the subject. Only Amy knows all my secrets. Together we understand that there are some things we are meant to carry ourselves. Whenever we share with men, we also become responsible for shouldering their pain. Pain barreling like a snowball picking up ice, growing in size as it plummets downhill.

"Sounds good." He doesn't even bat an eye.

"You all done?" I ask Dottie, bringing her over to the sink to wash the crevices between her fingers that seem to attract stickiness. Then I let her trot ahead of me, patting her diapered butt as she maneuvers the stairs before locking the gate behind us. She runs to her room, no doubt about to destroy it, while I make my way into our bathroom, putting both hands on the sink before taking some deep breaths. I sit down inside our bedroom closet. I have some pillows propped up along the floor, a little sanctuary I made for myself on the very first night we moved in. I don't ever allow the kids in here. It's a place where I can return to being a woman and not a mother. I pull up the video monitoring app on my phone so I can watch Dottie in her room. She's pulling clothes out of her dirty laundry hamper but stops once she finds one of her favorite stuffed animals.

Lucas pokes his head in and asks, "Want some company?" He's standing motionless, awaiting my reply.

I nod, feeling grateful for him, for the fact he knows me well enough to ask.

"I'm going with Amy when she gets waxed around thirty-seven weeks. I'm thinking I'll go full Brazilian." I make a face so he can appreciate my sacrifice.

"Which one is the Brazilian again?" he asks, his voice dropping about an octave lower.

"All of it gone." I mimic ripping a strip of wax in a swift, upward motion.

"And why does she need to wax her lady parts while pregnant?"

"I warned her that everyone will be all up in her business down there during the delivery. She thought there would be some modesty involved like in the movies where they at least fling a sheet over your legs and the doctor ducks underneath. Ha! Remember when the custodian came in to empty the trash while I was around seven centimeters with Reid?" I say, pausing to witness the smile spread across Lucas's lips before continuing. "I know how freaked out she is in general . . . At least her pubic hair is something small she can have control over right now. I figured I'd get one for moral support. Plus, I'm sure you won't mind." I wink.

"If you want a hairless labia majora and labia minora in solidarity with your sister-in-law, I will support you." He grins.

I laugh, a little bit of spit catching in my throat as I let out a small cough. "Are you researching technical terms now?"

"I grew up in a house of almost exclusively male genitalia. Before Joni was born, I had to read up on the importance of proper butt-wiping techniques for baby girls."

"You're the cutest." I put my head on his shoulder. "It's front to back." I show him using the opposite motion I did for the waxing strip.

"Yes! See, you have the parts, so you know these things. I just shake it off and go on my merry way."

I move my head onto the softest part of his chest until I can hear his heart beating, and we stay like this. Before the kids, Lucas and I could keep up, match each other round for round— meet inside the silly banter and exist there together. We've drifted from this place recently, or maybe not so recently. It's hard to tell with the way time has blurred.

We both stare into my phone, watching Dottie lining up her stuffed animals around the child-size pink table and chairs.

"Remember how clueless we were in the very beginning when we first had Joni?"

"Still feel pretty clueless most days." Lucas chuckles. "My mom said she had a blast at the beach with you and the kids. Thanks for inviting her." It feels like Lucas and I are always playing catch-up when it comes to filling each other in. The beach trip was already a week ago, but it's the first time we have discussed something that wasn't directly related to the kids' schedules or The Restaurant.

I don't correct him. "Joni was so happy to have her there" is the most I can offer.

In the hospital when Joni was born, Christine was a version of herself that I could love. If only she could be that way all the time. She arrived there breathless, sweeping in all showered and glamorous, admitting she left George circling around looking for parking. Nana and my mom and dad had just left for the hotel where they'd stay for a few days before heading back to Iowa. I'd made sure they were the first to meet the baby.

Desperate for sleep after laboring for twenty-eight hours, I was surprised when Christine said she would hold the baby while I rested. I was too exhausted to argue, which may have marked the first time that happened in our history together. Before dozing off, I watched Christine with my daughter. She spoke in hushed tones, just loud enough that I could still make out what she was saying. She whispered sweetly in full sentences, as if Joni were capable of conversation—faces so close, their cheeks were touching.

"You, my girl, are exactly who I've been waiting for. I wish you could have known her. I wish. I wish." Christine was crying softly. I wanted to hear more but was too delirious to escape the pull of sleep.

I awoke panicked that I had rolled over onto Joni, drenched in a thick layer of sweat. Christine was still cradling my baby in her arms, seemingly unfazed by the sound of her cries. I worried something was wrong.

"She just needs to nurse. That's what a hungry baby sounds like," Christine said, standing up and walking Joni cautiously over to my bed. Normally she'd delight in holding knowledge over my head, but her reassuring words felt like a welcome hug.

I could hear Lucas in the hallway. His voice was elevated to a level of enthusiasm that could be heard inside our room.

Dazed and anxious, I regarded the thought of nursing as another frontier in vulnerability, especially attempting it for the first time in front of my mother-in-law. As if reading my mind, Christine offered, "I'll give you some privacy. Why don't you get comfortable with the pillows?"

"I . . . um, okay. Where should the pillows go? I need a nurse to help with this, I think," I said, wincing in pain as I attempted to sit farther up in bed. "Seriously, is this hell? No one prepares you for . . . Ouch!" I couldn't help but cry out. "How am I supposed to do any of this?"

"You can do it—I know you can," she said. Then, as if catching herself, she added, "I'll go bring Lucas back in here." I felt a weighted relief at her kindness. My defenses were down and my energy was depleted. "You're right, though. There's really no way to prepare for being a mother. The hard parts are, well, hard. But the trade-off . . . ," she said, handing me Joni. "You'll see."

Back within the closet, Lucas starts in on something else. "I'm so anxious that we'll miss some important detail at The Restaurant. There is so much history to cover." His breath blows my hair down in front of my face, and he sweeps it away. The roughness of his fingertips grazes my cheek.

"I'm confident you guys will knock it out of the park. I don't think I ever heard the full story of how it burned down," I say, keeping my head resting on his chest. Every time the topic has come up, Christine has been quick to change the subject.

"Mom doesn't like talking about it. Not because anyone did anything wrong; it's more that she prefers to leave the past in the past. There was a fire in the kitchen and the sprinkler system failed. With the insurance money, they had the option to rebuild or retire, and so my grandparents chose the latter. But my mom loved that place. It was the original location of Sunday family dinners and how that all started."

"This is all making sense now," I say, nodding. Christine doesn't like things that could reflect poorly on the family, accident or not. Lucas has always trod lightly when it comes to sharing stories with me about Christine. He tolerates that we aren't exactly warm and fuzzy toward each other but prefers to remain Switzerland whenever tempers between us flare.

"I hope, at the very least, you will be naming a dessert after me." My sacrifice of carrying the primary load of the children and household while Lucas's attention has been with the restaurant should most definitely count for something.

"Baby, you know my favorite way to eat dessert is off your naked body, and we can't put that on the menu. I would never share you with anyone."

He licks my cheek, wanting me to giggle and affectionately retaliate somehow. But I don't.

CHAPTER 8

Reid is obsessed with baseball, so much so that he insisted on playing in a summer league. His lankiness means he's a little awkward while running the bases. But height makes him a good pick for first base, with a long stretch to catch balls thrown to him from the infield. Of course, Lucas is thrilled, although the restaurant has taken him away from the field far more than he'd like.

Somehow, against my will, we've morphed into those die-hard sports parents. The kind that forfeit most of their precious weekend just to sit around barbecuing hot dogs between doubleheaders. The team moms take turns bringing snacks while the dads openly pass around red Solo cups filled with beer or wine. There is a universal understanding among adults that alcohol makes it easier to sit through the tediousness of certain parts of parenting. The expression "mommy wine time" has been casually adopted within the context of motherhood and has only continued to catch on among groups of mom friends.

Initially, I drank along with the others and managed that way for a while. But something about this summer season has made the wine and beer not quite enough to get by on. I'm not trying to be sneaky about anything, but it has been easier to get buzzed alone beforehand. That way I can smile and nod along, half listening to the other parents' stories as we are all strapped inside the endless merry-go-round. We speak in nonthreatening, ambiguous terms because none of us really cares all that much. Every so often someone is a little too honest: "We are getting divorced," they say, or "My husband's mother died." After politely inquiring further, we grow impatient, wondering how much longer we should stand there miming concern over other people's hurt when we are already buried in our own.

Baseball caused some friction within the O'Connors since socializing outside our big family seemed like a waste to Christine, who has intentionally created her very own little self-sufficient commune. She's always been a staple in the community, the PTA, or with anything she deems important. She functions as more of a political dignitary, where she keeps everyone except the family safely at arm's length. She likes to be seen but never really approached. Once Christine learned the games would never compete with Sunday dinners, she showed up on opening day and hasn't missed one since.

I know she enjoys the extra time sitting in the stands with Joni. They sequester themselves off to the side, away from the rest of us. Most of the time, I can appreciate their closeness. As a child back in Iowa, both my parents worked, so Nana would always be the one who attended my art shows. It wasn't that my mom and dad didn't participate in my childhood; they were just still young and, therefore, still growing up themselves.

"Did you want us to come?" my mom asked me one night before my fourth-grade art collection showing.

It's such a strange thing to ask a child. Joni would know

how to respond, but Reid, if given a choice, would feel torn—
wanting to find a way to please all parties involved.

I was thrilled that Nana could come to several of Reid's
games last season when she was in town, driving through with
her RV and latest boyfriend, Ricky. At least she could provide a
small, albeit loud, representation from my side of things.

When I called Amy to ask for a ride to today's game, I could
tell she was onto me. She knows it wasn't just the mimosas with
brunch. After Lucas left, I continued to sulk by treating myself
to more wine from the fridge. Luckily, I'm in too deep to care.
I will promise her to be good tomorrow, and that should appease her for a while. Maybe I'll actually consider stopping for
a while this time, although I doubt it's really that serious. The
heat from the sun warms us on the bleachers, and I'm hit with
a wave of happiness I haven't felt for some time.

Everything will be fine. Everything is fine.

Christine and Joni are huddled together, giggling like they
do. And just as quickly as contentment filled me, I'm suddenly
drained of it. I wish I had brought a container of something
and look around to see if there are any red cups floating around
in the bleachers. Strangely, there are none, even though it's an
evening game. I wonder if it was my turn. Was I the one who
was supposed to bring the mommy juice this time?

Joni's giggle ripples through the crowd, and she's leaning
her head on Christine's shoulder as Christine strokes her silky
blond hair. When all else fails, I think about Joni's heart beating
the day I almost decided it wouldn't. A lighthouse and a siren
song that led me here—into the life that I can both cherish and
resent, sometimes in equal parts. The splintering off from my
phantom life that belonged only to me.

Normally Amy is chatty when she comes with me to the

games, but she's been quiet since the car ride. I am sure she's uncomfortable with the weight of her belly as her legs stretch out, just barely resting on the step in front of us, whereas mine are dangling off the ledge. Sitting next to Amy this way on the bleachers, I'm reminded of the last time we got pedicures together. Years ago now, but I know the memory still stings for us both.

We opted for a salon just outside town, cocooning ourselves away from the rest of the O'Connors or anyone else who could rob us of our precious time together. Amy was pregnant with Elijah; they were referring to him by name already. She was just shy of halfway into her second trimester. I was pregnant with Dottie.

Amy's infectious joy over her pregnancy was helping to ease my mind about our whimsical decision to have a third. I'd told no one, not even her, that I feared this baby was my way of staying relevant inside my own life. I'd already committed to motherhood at that point; getting pregnant with Dottie felt like that final drink in the middle of a blackout. The fact that I'd be even with Christine in the child department was what ultimately convinced me it was a good idea.

"Anything sexual is so awkward!" Amy had said as she adjusted her hips in her chair. "I don't think of this process"— she waved a hand around her midsection—"as sexual, despite how it all started." She laughed for a moment and added, "You know, with sex."

"Ha! Does Paul still want to? Lucas is all about it anytime— nothing stops him," I said, shrugging.

"I've been so sick—it's not even really on the table. Hopefully that will fade soon like they say it does."

"I hope after we meet that little one," I said, pointing toward

her nonexistent bump, "you guys can get back to a place where
sex is fun."

"You mean with all the free time we'll have with a newborn?" She grinned again. "We can't all be *Lucas and Leah*."
Amy stopped to look at her nails. "You know, I'll never forgive
you for that one camping trip. I assumed, since you were, like, a
million weeks pregnant with Reid, our tent would've been safe
next to yours." She snorted. "Fool me once. If someone asked
me to go camping right now, I'd literally slap them in the face.
You are a much better sport than I am." She looked over at me,
grinning.

The lady appeared with a bottle of champagne and orange
juice.

"Just the juice, please," Amy said.

I thought for a minute. I hadn't been drinking, but something about my final pregnancy felt different. Alcohol no longer
sounded repulsive like it had with Joni or Reid. I sensed a crack
in that protective barrier. Within the chaos of already having
two children, I craved the escape—to bask in the place where
worry and meddling mothers-in-law couldn't find me. Plus,
unlike during my previous pregnancy, the European mentality
of "half a glass here or there never hurt anyone" was quickly
becoming the socially acceptable norm.

"I'll have the tiniest splash of champagne in mine," I said,
feeling Amy's eyes on me. "Before you even look at me, girl, I
have two kids at home. I deserve a little break."

She opened her mouth to speak but took a sip of OJ instead.

Okay, seriously, just this little bit and then done. That's all. My
internal pep talk was meant to serve as my reminder.

"How's Christine been with you lately? Overbearing?" I
asked Amy, wanting to change the subject.

Amy shook her head. "She's been popping over to bring us little gifts for the baby. Thoughtful."

"Overbearing." I took a sip. "Trust me—if she thought I wouldn't narc her out for kidnapping, she'd have Joni halfway to Mexico by now." Amy leaned her head all the way back in the massage chair as she rolled her eyes at me. "Roll your eyes now, but you haven't had the full Christine experience yet. Just you wait."

"Gotta pee." Amy stood and stepped into her flip-flops to shuffle toward the bathroom, disappearing around the corner. The manicurist came by with the bottles again, seeing my glass nearly empty. I pulled my jacket onto my lap as I heard the door to the restroom close.

"More?" the woman asked, holding up both bottles.

"Yes, both, please."

She poured too slowly. My fingers hummed with anticipation and fear that Amy could come back any minute and I'd have to explain myself again. With the woman's back to me, I downed the entire glass to precisely the point it was before. Champagne was easily my favorite buzz.

Just this, that's it, I thought, closing my eyes as I waited.

"All set?" Amy stood in front of me, holding her purse. I envied how she didn't even look pregnant at all.

"Yep!" I said, clapping my hands, realizing my enthusiasm may have been overkill.

In the car after our pedicures, I tried to stay quiet, letting Amy tell me about the latest saga of Isla as she drove me back to my house.

Once we arrived, Amy leaned over and kissed me on the cheek. "This was so nice. Let's do it again soon. As many times as possible before the babies come."

I squeezed her hand and nodded, shutting the car door, noticing Lucas's truck still missing from the driveway. Anxiously, I pulled out my phone. He answered but sounded far away, noticeably in the car. "Hey, baby, we decided to take Joni Belle and Reid into San Francisco. You're on speakerphone. I'm in the car with my mom."

"Okay, so I won't try to seduce you like I normally do, then," I said, imagining the look of horror on Christine's face.

"Ha! Please don't. We won't be back until later. How was the hand and foot polishing?" Lucas asked.

"Mani-pedis," I corrected him. Sometimes it was glaringly evident that he grew up with only brothers. "Exactly what we needed."

Inside, I knew I would find a bottle of something. The thought formed the moment I learned my family was out in the world, driving away from me.

Just today, and that's all.

I remember it was the following glass that brought on the relief. The one that hit exactly as I needed it to. I felt it make its way into my blood—lighting up all the places that had gone dull, reminding me just how much I loved everything and everyone. It was inside that space that I could recall why I chose Joni, Lucas, Reid, and now Dottie. I could remember that I was buried somewhere underneath. Even Christine and her unrelenting condescension could be forgiven within the glow. I pushed her out of my thoughts, not granting her permission to steal my bliss. Everywhere else, she had managed to be so thoroughly entangled—especially when it came to Joni. But not here.

I knew to hide the evidence, putting the bottle in our neighbors' recycling. They kept it on the side of their house. I crept around, tipping the bin to the side so it could slide in and not clank among the other glass in case they were nearby. An act that struck me as hilarious.

I had made it upstairs, leaving my bag and all its contents on the kitchen table. I brushed my teeth and gargled with mouthwash. After undressing and slipping between the sheets, I felt grateful for the imminent medicated sleep.

When I awoke, Lucas was speaking. The light in the room had shifted into the low hues of the evening. He sounded upset. *He knows*, I thought.

I stretched and turned onto my side, feigning a yawn. Pregnancy is justifiably tiring.

"I just got off the phone with Paul." He sat on the tiny space near the edge of the bed and rested his hand on my back as if he needed it for balance. "Amy's in the hospital."

I shot up, knocking him back and forcing him to stand up. "What? Why?"

"She tried calling you . . . She lost the baby." He looked pained in a way I hadn't seen before. Lucas was looking forward to experiencing fatherhood with Paul. It was the only thing remaining they had yet to share.

"No." I brought my hand to my mouth.

I'd left my phone downstairs. I'd intentionally left my phone downstairs so I wouldn't be caught. So no one could find me where I was hiding. I needed to form these thoughts more completely, but I couldn't. I didn't want to. If I leaned any further inward to examine myself, I'd sink into the blackness and be lost.

Lucas handed me my phone. Eleven missed calls from Amy. I swallowed the sour taste that was caked in a thin layer along my tongue. I called her back, but it went straight to voicemail. I tried again and again.

I waited for the beep, "Am, I just talked to Lucas. I am so, so sorry. I will try you again. I fell asleep. I was exhausted, you know preg—" I hung up.

Shit. Shit.

I saw Lucas watching me in our bathroom mirror, his eyes squinting. He wrapped a long string of floss around both his fingers and opened his mouth wide. Our sister-in-law—my best friend—and his brother had just lost their baby, and he was actually flossing his teeth. The detachment men are capable of is unbelievable—how I envied him. I tried my luck to keep things casual and got pregnant with Joni. It turns out there are no half measures in motherhood.

I found myself tiptoeing around Amy for months afterward. She finally confronted me, and I apologized for my absence. I wouldn't allow her to inquire further. Amy is my only compass in the storm that rages on with Christine. I wouldn't survive without her. Sometimes, it seems, family is who we are lucky enough to locate and piece together among the wreckage. We needed each other more than she needed to hear the truth about where I was the night she miscarried.

The roar of the game brings me back. Amy holds my arm as we are up and clapping for one of Reid's hits. He's striding around the bases with such speed that I can almost detect a whizzing sound in my ear.

"Go, Reidy!" I call out, clapping as he makes it all the way to third base. A triple with two RBIs.

Amy is tugging at me slightly, likely to steady herself within all the excitement.

In the car after the game, Amy is driving us downtown to meet everyone for pizza. I love these rare golden opportunities whenever it's just us without kids in the car. I tell Amy about a conversation I had recently with Nana and all her travel adventures with Ricky. I can hear myself rambling on and on, almost like someone else is talking and my lips are just serving as a mouthpiece.

"I can picture her dancing at a dive bar, wearing some sort of kitten heel with red lipstick and showing a little too much cleavage for someone her age. Ugh. I want to be them, though," I say, slapping my hand on the dashboard. "Seriously, imagine the freedom they have." I glance out the window, and the fast-moving images start to blur together. "We should blow off food with the family and go dancing. No, let's go to the beach—I want to go for a swim!"

"Okay, champ, let's get some pizza into you first, though," Amy says, using her teacher's voice without looking in my direction.

"You don't need to treat me like a child. I know you hate it when I've had a few. I'm sorry your mom was a total asshole, but I'm not a meanie like her. I'm fun. I mean, I'm fun, right?"

She waits a few seconds, could be more because it feels like longer, then says, "Yeah, you're pretty fun."

"Pretty fun, she says! Ha! Naked polar bear swim it is." I clap my hands together.

She signals as we turn into the parking lot of the pizzeria.

"Party pooper!" I shout, pushing my head back into the headrest.

The car is in Park and she's not getting out, so I look over at her, half expecting her to say we should blow this Popsicle stand.

"Sometimes I worry about getting lost inside the shadow you cast," Amy says, though she's looking past me now, out my window. "I've lived in that place before, but never again. I won't do it again."

"You know when you talk in metaphors, it's a real downer . . ." I sigh. I hate that we aren't going to the beach.

"The thing about shadows, I've learned, is that sometimes someone just needs another person to help them find their light."

And suddenly I'm all alone in the car.

When we get home, I request that Lucas be in charge of bedtime upstairs.

"What are you going to do?" His tone borders too heavily on the accusatory for my liking.

"What do you mean, what am I going to do?" My own temperature is rising to match his. The thundering clatter overhead ultimately draws him away. I'm grateful for the fortunate timing of our children's neediness. I have no interest in getting into it with Lucas tonight.

Lucas and I work best when we allow each other our own separate spaces. He has the restaurant and I have my art. At home with three kids, we often need to divide and conquer; rarely is there an opportunity for one of us to tap out, though lately I know I've been requesting reprieve more and more. But this sensation of detachment, of feeling like I'm on the outside looking in on my own family, has been getting stronger.

I make my way onto the deck. I wish Amy was out on the deck with me, but she made a whole thing about dropping me off after pizza and how I should go straight up to bed. Instead, I keep drinking because the glass has become an extension of my hand.

The air outside feels like I'm being wrapped in a blanket that's still damp. The unease of Joni and Christine, Miles, and Isla's secrecy has been lulled.

I am all too familiar with unease as my normal resting state. Since birth I have been mis-wired. The receptors that should have been loaded with serotonin and dopamine on Saturday cartoon-and-pancake mornings from my childhood were replaced with the sensation of being submerged inside a glass cage with a slow leak that dripped just enough water for me to know I'd drown someday, just not necessarily that day.

That was until I discovered all the ways to leave myself, if only temporarily. Painting, sex, and then surfing. And finally, my children. My god, my children. No one was more surprised than me when it turned out my children were the answer to all my problems: my escapism of choice. With one whiff of the top of their heads, the relief flooded me, a gelatinous goo that was both warm and amniotic in its purity. It all worked so well for a while. I was able to assume the identity of all things maternal. But it was hard. I longed for an Easy Button to push until I came into a mothers' group where I was given permission to view alcohol as the great stress reliever. The panacea for all the aches and growing pains of surviving the day-to-day grind of leaky diapers, sleep regressions, tantrums, and doctor visits. I joyfully joined in, thinking it would serve as the cherry on top of an already delicious sundae. While everyone else around me seemed able to find exactly the right balance, stopping after one glass of wine while our children crashed into one another inside the inflatable bounce house for yet another child's birthday party, I found myself craving more. I envied other mothers' ability to find a playful balance: mom and woman living in tandem. I've tried to observe or pry out their secret at book club, on playdates, or over wine. How they blend it all together, seemingly so seamlessly. While I have always been all or nothing.

Christine is and always will be Paul, Lucas, and Jack's mother, and that's enough for her. But being a mother is not enough for me. Amy doesn't yet understand what it means to truly lose yourself at the mercy of your children, and she would be the only person I'd want to confide in, though I'm terrified of losing her to the Christine Method of Motherhood. That they will somehow leave me in the dust.

I drop my hands, wanting to scratch and pick at myself, wishing I could somehow shed my discomfort. But I'm connected to the glass, and so it goes up to my lips.

CHAPTER 9

G randma!" I hear Joni shout as all my children emerge from the house. I managed to skip out on the last family dinner when Dottie complained of a tummy ache and I happily offered to stay home with her. The summer has ended, and I'm stuck in the worst parts of the daily grind. I'm trailing far behind, holding a large mug of coffee, irritated that I have to endure an ambush by my mother-in-law this early in the morning. The kids take turns giving Christine a half hug with the arm that's not carrying a backpack or lunch box.

"Morning, kids! Leah, can I talk to you?" she asks as I turn my back to her to lock the front door.

"Kids, get in the van. We're going to be late." Because I have run out of hands, I am biting onto a bill I'll need to mail and therefore say this through my teeth.

She waits until they are loaded and the sliding doors are closed before she finally asks her question. "Who was that man you were talking to at the Tree Tunnel?"

I drop my bag at my feet so I can pause to take a sip of coffee. I wonder if it's too late for us to move to Costa Rica.

"Seriously? Just a friend from way back when," I say, shift-ing my gaze from Christine to the van. "Any other questions, *Christine*?"

I'm certain the way I say her name will be enough to get her off my back. Amy calls her "Mom," which has always struck me as ludicrous. I was there when Amy proposed the idea just be-fore a Sunday dinner, a week before Amy and Paul's wedding. The three of us took our glasses out to the gazebo that serves as the entryway into Christine's garden.

We were each an arm's length apart, forming a kind of triangle inside the wooden circle of the gazebo floor.

"I'm not sure how to ask," Amy said, tucking her hair be-hind her ear, though it immediately came undone due to its immense volume. "I was hoping that after Paul and I are married . . . I was wondering if I could call you Mom?"

I glanced at Christine, genuinely curious how she would react, sure that Amy was equally nervous, which was why I was there serving as a buffer.

The pause was notable, and I watched Amy waiting pa-tiently, nervously fiddling with her engagement ring, spinning it around and around her finger. I recognized the gravity of her question and what it represented: a seemingly motherless child asking aloud for one to call her own.

"I would be honored," Christine said, moving to embrace Amy. I had to turn away as they hugged. The intimacy of it was overwhelming. I drank from my glass while they remained still, our bodies no longer forming a triangle but a new shape entirely.

The car alarm sounds and brings me back to standing on my front porch, face-to-face with Christine. I think I accidentally locked the kids in and one of them must have tried to open the door. I quickly tap the button to quiet the alarm. Dottie's probably upset. The frustration of the situation makes my tone sound more threatening than I intend. "Leave it alone, Christine. I mean it."

"I didn't like what I saw. The way you were interacting. If you hurt Lucas and those kids by engaging in something outside of your marriage, I swear I'll . . ." The irony that Christine believes I'm currently having an affair with Miles is almost laughable, though it only further solidifies her opinion of me. But suddenly this power over Christine is too intoxicating to resist. "What? You'll what? It's our life, not yours." I've allowed Lucas to believe a version of interconnectedness with the O'Connors because he needs that. Christine has designed them that way—a house of cards where none can be removed from the middle, or they will all tumble. Except we've built an entirely separate structure—one Lucas, out of love for his mother, refuses to draw any attention to, which is why we live just down the road, attend dinners, and I can tolerate it. But only because of the existence of Amy.

Right now I'm happy to point out our separate structures. How, if forced to, Lucas would choose us—me and the kids. She should know better than to push me.

"Back off," I say, breaking into a jog. My legs are shaky, but I somehow make it into the driver's seat.

"Why were you running away from Grandma?" Joni asks, looking puzzled.

"I was not *running away* from Grandma. I just don't want us to be late, that's all."

What is it about children's ability to put us back into our

right place? To see the truth in a way that strips away all the nonsensical theatrics adults are forced to perform.

"You were definitely running," she says.

It's my day to volunteer in Dottie's classroom. I'd never dream of being *that* parent in any classroom other than Amy's. The children are circled around the reading rug, and I'm at the back table cutting out shapes the kids will paste into autumn scenes along with any leaves they find later on their nature walk. She's reading one of Dottie's favorites, and Dottie has been in a mood all day.

"Let's be sure to keep our hands out of our noses and folded in our laps," Amy tells the kids in the singsong voice she reserves exclusively for them. "Ronan, I like how quiet your hands are!"

Dottie is flopped down on her tummy, a position that's discouraged during story time to avoid kids' little limbs kicking their neighbors, but I think Amy is giving Dottie a special pass on my account and because Dottie seems uncharacteristically tired.

"I want a cookie!" Peter, a precocious little redhead, calls out from the floor.

Amy intentionally ignores the interruption and continues reading. She looks up so we can exchange a glance in appreciation of the irony that's lost among these young minds—if she were to answer Peter, the floodgates would open just as they had for the boy with the mouse in *If You Give a Mouse a Cookie*. The class would probably be derailed discussing dessert for the rest of the day.

Even from within her own misery after losing Elijah, Amy

was determined to connect with Dottie. I had hoped maybe she could funnel all her love into this baby. If only these things could be that simple.

Dottie and I were upstairs in the rocking chair that once belonged to Christine when Amy appeared, watching us from the doorframe. I hadn't expected her to come. It seemed incomprehensible that someone could be capable of separating their feelings into properly labeled compartments: happy for you, devastated for me.

"Oh." Her voice was already catching in her throat.

"You're here." My eyes misted at just the sight of her.

"Of course I'm here," she said, wiping away her tears. "I'm here to hold my niece." She walked over to us. I stood up slowly, grimacing in pain. "No, sit," she told me, taking my forearm to guide me back down. I resisted and stood up.

"I have to pee, and it's a whole thing with a squirt bottle and numbing spray. I should be back in four hours—'cause I may fall asleep on the toilet."

I crinkled my forehead, indicating that Amy could hold the baby if she wanted to. It was an impossible position for us both. Amy nodded.

We transferred the baby into her arms, and the three of us were momentarily connected before she took my place in the rocking chair. Her eyes fixed on Dottie's perfect pink skin. The lightness of exhaustion blanketed Dottie's whole face as if sleep were her singular concern in all the universe, until she started making a tiny sucking sound. I wiggled a pacifier into her mouth and touched her lightly on the nose.

Before I stepped into the bathroom, I paused to make an announcement from the doorway. "Amy, I'd like you to meet your niece, Dorothy Amy O'Connor. Dottie, meet the bravest

woman you'll ever have the honor of calling your aunt." I didn't
linger long after I spoke, but when my eyes caught Amy's, I did
my damnedest to make them void of pity.

After school, I invite Amy back to my house, offering to make
us lunch. Dottie falls asleep on my bed the moment I bring her
upstairs. I feel her forehead to make sure she's not warm, but
she feels normal. Amy has followed me upstairs and she curls
up next to Dottie. I don't blame her; there's something intoxicating about being intertwined with a sleepy child.

I escape into my bathroom to change my clothes. I don't
know how Amy gets used to the smell of Elmer's glue that seems
to have followed us back to the house.

I pause to gaze out the bathroom window, watching the
fog continually roll in, and am reminded of a moment just
before Amy and Paul's wedding, during the sweetest spot of
our relationship when nothing had yet come between us. We
sat together alone, out on my deck, unable to see anything
beyond the railing due to the fog.

"What do you mean you've been going on walks with her
every morning?" I asked, incredulous at the idea of serving
more than my required sentence of time over Sunday dinners
with Christine. Just the thought made my brain want to swell
out of my ears.

"We discuss wedding details, and I get my steps in." Amy
shrugged, her big eyes blinking rapidly.

I shook my head. "Please tell me you and Christine wear
matching joggers and sweatbands. Never mind—that will be
my gift for your bachelorette party instead of crotchless pant-

ies for the honeymoon. Ugh, Paul may actually get more turned on by the idea of you matching with his mother."

Amy swatted at my knee so hard I almost spilled my glass. "Gross." She stuck out her tongue, which was stained a deep, swampy purple.

I made the mistake of asking what it was exactly that they talked about on their "walks."

"Lots of stuff," Amy said like they were suddenly thick as thieves. "You should just try talking to her sometime. She's got a lot of insight. The other day she told me a story about menopause."

"Menopause?" I was positive I had misheard her.

"Menopause," she repeated as if it were a perfectly normal conversation for a mother-in-law to be having with her daughter-in-law. "Yeah, it sounds weird, but there was more to it. How she was caught off guard at age forty-nine with the finality of her body shutting down the opportunity to have any more children—specifically a little girl. She swore it should have been a relief since the boys were grown, and three is a large number by most people's standards, but removing the possibility, taking it off the table completely, closing the portal . . . She said it wasn't until Joni that she was able to experience all the preciousness that comes with muted pink ruffles and high-pitched giggles."

"She said that?" I asked in disbelief. I hated not only the idea of their private conversations but also how they could involve my daughter. Though some part of me felt relieved that even the Great Christine believed something was missing from her experience. Christine has no phantom self in which she dreams up another version where she chose something different. Instead, in every reality and season, she's able to funnel her hopes and aspirations into her boys and never needs to have anything left over for herself.

"Plus, it's fun to hear stories about the boys when they were little. I didn't know Lucas didn't speak until he was three, did you? And Jack sounded like a little monster. I finally got her to say out loud that Paul has always been her favorite."

"She finally admitted it, huh?" For all of Christine's attempts at motherly perfection, this was a clear violation. While her affection was obvious for all her sons, it appeared her affection for them was ranked in birth order, though I never had any real proof.

"Mommy?" A two-year-old Reid had toddled out onto the deck, his face crumpled with sleep. I checked the monitor, surprised I hadn't heard his movements before, and realized it had been on mute this whole time.

"Hi, my guy." I stood to direct him back to his bed, petting the top of his mop of blond hair. "I'm really regretting transitioning him from his crib. I miss the containment of children being in baby jail. Be right back," I whispered to Amy.

After lying down with him until his breathing slowed, I returned to the deck with an open bottle in my hand.

Amy continued speaking as if I had never left. "I will say we got into it a little bit the other day over the wedding flowers. I told her I will have sunflowers or nothing. She tried to get me to pick something 'more coastal' and less 'farm chic.'" She paused to use her fingers dramatically as air quotes. "But I wasn't hearing it."

"Sunflowers are your thing. Everyone knows that."

"Exactly," Amy said, smiling. "I can't really explain to her without oversharing. But I shouldn't have to justify any decisions for my wedding. Yes, we are having it at their house, but still."

I remained silent, buzzing with vindication.

Amy continued, "I have been incredibly flexible because, really, I don't care about most things related to the wedding. But there was something about when sunflowers would first arrive at The Nursery—it marked the beginning of the summer months when Isla somehow shifted and became more human. More attuned to me. Like she lifted her head up from the pillow after a period of hibernation and remembered I was there. She'd bring me little bunches every day and we'd line the trailer's every window with them and watch 'em turn in the direction of the sun."

Amy paused, searching out into the fog. I sensed it was my turn to speak again.

"As your matron of honor, I'd be more than happy to say something to Christine."

"Ha!" Amy laughed, swiping at the corner of her eye. "Oh, I am sure you would be. No, I need to practice standing my ground with her—if I'm going to become an official O'Connor, like you."

Dottie is still fast asleep on my bed and I make my way downstairs to find Amy standing in the doorway of the open slider that leads out onto the deck, pensively searching the haze outside. Just by her stance and how she's rotating her hand in concentric circles along the periphery of her entire belly, I know she's thinking about Elijah. She clears her throat. "There are parts of marriage no one prepares you for. When we said our wedding vows, 'in sickness and in health,' it all sounded so idealistic and hopeful. There's this underlying assumption that we could only ever be handed something entirely fixable. Something that will be gift wrapped with a guaranteed solution."

The pained calls from a row of seagulls perched along the railing draw my focus away from Amy.

She takes a deep breath. "I'd seen Paul break his arm falling off a horse. I stupidly thought physical discomfort would be as bad as it would ever get for us. But Paul's face in the hospital after Elijah is something I must consciously block out or I would never get out of bed. It was the only time I've ever witnessed him fall apart."

She is crying now, and I want to rush over to hold her, but I'm scared to look in and witness the pain in her eyes. How I wish we were sitting out with the gulls on the deck, in simpler times, sipping our wine and sharing stories much softer than these.

She continues speaking, though I'm desperate for her to go quiet again. "Afterward, I pushed him away, almost urging him to run as far from me as possible because look what happened when we tried to be happy—when we tried to create something together. The loss filled me with an emptiness that spread through my whole being. It seeped into the marrow of my bones."

I wish she would stop. I try dropping a spoon on the floor just to swallow up the noise of her words. I'm unable to shoulder any of her pain, though I'm desperate to while I'm wading within my own distractions. Something is pulling me away from getting close enough to understand why she is telling me all this again.

But she continues, "In the beginning, I tried to cry my baby back into existence. I thought maybe if I dried out my body completely, I could sprout him right there on the floor of his nursery. Paul tried to talk to me, to grieve with me, but he couldn't possibly understand because his loss was that of an idea. Mine was physical. Elijah was part of me one day and then gone the next. I kept hearing how it wasn't my fault; these things happen. Why my baby? Shouldn't people have to carry only a certain amount of grief in a single lifetime? Surely after my traumatic childhood, this part should have come simply."

The wall clock is ticking too loudly. While it's another sound that I wish would devour our discomfort, I find myself walking over to pull it off the wall so I can remove the batteries. I'm sure its noise is bothering Amy as well.

I urgently want to crawl into a small space to contain a fear that feels bigger than me. I'm useless to her and she can sense it, but still she speaks.

"I got used to the predictability of waking up in dread and soul-crushing disappointment. Existing with love but no place to put it. Now I'm putting it all into her, but I'm so scared to. What if my body is failing me again?"

Suddenly there's a look of panic on Amy's face. She winces as if something is pushing from within.

"What? Braxton-Hicks?" I ask.

She shakes her head. "I don't know, I never had those with Elijah. This feels— Oh." She stops to push on her belly. The color is draining from her face.

"You're in your own head now. It's okay. Everything is okay. I'm going to make you some tea. Everything feels intense this late in the game. That's totally normal."

"I don't know. I don't trust it." Again she winces in discomfort. "I feel like a pulling around my stomach." She is patting and rubbing as if to counterbalance the sensation. She stops moving, waiting, although I can tell she doesn't trust it won't return.

"How far are you now?" I ask, hoping to relieve her mind somehow.

"As of today, I'm thirty-five weeks, another inconsequential milestone"—she shakes her head—"especially when I know how quickly everything can change." It is unclear if she needs space, but I'm desperate to help, so I place my hands on hers on her belly.

"It's fine, my girls. It's all fine," I say. We look down watchfully, though neither of us is entirely convinced. I move toward the stove to make some tea because I need to do something else with my hands. Amy needs several minutes to gather herself and arrive at her own conclusion that everything will be fine.

I can tell the alarming sensation returns, because again Amy's squatting awkwardly and pressing just beneath her belly button. I know it's just Braxton-Hicks; I'm certain of it, but I also know she's worked herself into a state that isn't helping matters.

"I'm going to call Christine. I mean, is that okay? I'm going to call her," Amy says, reaching for her phone within her bag that's hanging on the back of her chair.

Stunned, I manage to stutter out, "Sure, y-yeah, of course." But it's not okay. I'm here. What will Christine do?

"Do you want Paul?" He, at least, I can understand.

"No, I can't see that look on his face again. Mom, hi," she says into the phone. "I'm here at Leah's. Um, can you come over?" She's nodding, indicating Christine must be saying yes on the other side of the phone.

I recognize it's not unusual for Amy to be calling. They still check in regularly during the week before Sunday dinners. Over time I've sensed that Amy's ability to serve as my ally against Christine has slowly been crumbling away like the dunes along the bluffs they walk together. Amy ends the call, makes her way into the kitchen, and uses the table to shift some of her weight around. "I can't help but think about Isla and how terrifying it would be to experience this at sixteen."

Out the window, the color of the sky is gray and lifeless, a dreariness I'm tired of.

I think of a story I know will cheer her up.

"Remember how, after Elijah, I'd drive you up and down the coast searching for pockets of sunshine? When I first got here, I couldn't understand why everyone was so obsessed with the fog. I was sure it was a code word for something much more interesting, but the longer I've been here, the more I've subscribed to its majesty." I pause to make sure I've captured her attention, which I have, so I continue, "I love how our entire city can be blanketed underneath. Remember that time I drove you and it was so thick that when we stepped out of the car, I pretended I could scoop it in my hands and blow it at you like bubbles in the bath? You weren't having any of it, so I ducked down behind you, putting my arms around your middle like you were my life-size doll, and then told you to blow as hard as you could."

She nods. A glint of a smile urges me to go on even though she already knows the ending.

"And then, like magic, the light dropped down in front of us."

Just as the beam behind Amy's smile ignites, reimagining our small miracle, Christine lets herself in using her key, which Lucas gave her for emergencies only. Christine drops her things to the floor, an act entirely out of character for such a meticulous person. As she comes toward us, she has her arms outstretched toward Amy, and Amy has hers out, too, inviting her in in a way that's unfamiliar to me. Without speaking, Christine lets Amy sob into her shoulder right there in my kitchen. The veil has descended, separating us into our respective corners: them and me.

"I'll just go check on Dottie upstairs," I say, unsure why I find the need to do so in a whisper.

Neither acknowledges me, and I watch from the stairway as Christine alternates patting and rubbing Amy's back. I wait to ascend the stairs another moment, desperate to hear what Christine is able to offer Amy that wasn't enough coming from me.

When Christine speaks, her voice is shaky. "I want motherhood for you, Amy, so very much. I know you have been a mom this entire time, but you've only ever experienced the unimaginable part. The part that hurts so much it feels like you won't survive it." She pauses and adds, "I know that pain."

I wait for her to say more, but she doesn't. Amy appears comforted as her coloring returns. They look more connected than two people tied together through marriage.

CHAPTER 10

After Christine convinced Amy that an emergency appointment to see her doctor wasn't necessary and she was in fact having Braxton-Hicks contractions, as I had said all along, they left my house together.

I desperately need to leave the house. I want to go for a run, but the stroller doesn't fare well along the Tree Tunnel path, and I'm hoping that I can run into Miles again.

Dottie is singing "Brave" as I pull in. I see Miles near the station, shoveling mulch onto the path. Still, it's like seeing a ghost. We met for the first time in the summer of 2011, my first summer in Half Moon Bay. I had just come out of a set when someone paddled up next to me. "That was impressive," a voice called out from over my right shoulder.

I shrugged without answering. I didn't like to talk out on the water. It felt a little bit like flirting in church. Everything about my sets that morning had been ideal. There is something about being out there and placing my very being at the mercy of the ocean.

"I haven't seen you out here before. I'm Miles," he said, paddling a little closer.

"Leah. I just got here a few weeks ago," I said, not taking my eyes from the bump just barely discernible on the horizon.

"You look like a California girl, but that accent isn't ours." He's about as California as they come, right down to his long, golden-streaked hair that may as well have been pulled from the sunlight reflecting off the waves.

"Iowa," I said.

I nodded to Miles that he could take the next ride even though I was ahead of him in the lineup. Unspoken rules between surfers are sacred. I watched him gliding, cutting through the wave with precision. I fixed my gaze, wanting to witness what I was missing for myself—only turning my head when he spun off his board.

I rode the next one to the shore. I'd improved drastically since surfing almost every day with Lucas, though I would never give him the satisfaction of knowing that. After using my van as a changing station to get out of my cold wet suit, I returned to the shore. It was gloriously warm, so I had on my bathing suit top and a towel draped over my legs. I loved the sensation of the sun's heat on my bare shoulders.

I marveled at how the water moved, lured by the magic of its endless push and pull. If our bodies are made up of something like 60 percent water, could that be what draws us to the shore? I was in no rush to get anywhere or do anything. My only plan was to paint later that afternoon.

Miles appeared in front of me, his outline with his board temporarily blocking the light.

"Can I sit?" He pointed at the sand next to me. I appreciated that he didn't assume his presence was necessary. In my experience, the weakest men need to find ways to assert their dominance and reveal themselves quickly. I allowed Miles the opportunity to show his hand.

"Suit yourself," I said with a nod. He situated himself close, but not so much so that any part of us could accidentally graze. He, too, had stripped down and was in a hoodie; the waistband of what I assumed to be fitted swim shorts peeked out over a striped, oversize beach towel.

"How long you here for?" he asked, our gazes fixed toward the water.

I'd learned through Lucas that Half Moon Bay is primarily a tourist town—with people coming and going often, it's evident to the locals when someone is a visitor. Something stirred in me, a twinge of discomfort. An unfamiliar sense of wanting to belong.

"Dunno yet." I shrugged as I watched him watch my breasts rise and fall.

"Are you around long enough to have dinner with me?" he asked.

Immediately I thought of Lucas. At that point, I was sure he wanted to be exclusive, although we hadn't had "the talk." My dating history was long and complicated, but Miles looked cute and harmless enough. The whole point of my coastal exploration was to explore, after all.

"Sure. Why not?"

He grinned as he wiped at the droplets of water that had fallen from his hair into his eyes.

"Somewhere on Main Street?" he asked.

Again, I thought of Lucas.

"I'd love to try somewhere outside town," I said as I stood to go.

He reached out his arms so I could help him get up, a maneuver that made me like him more. I yanked upward, using my strength, and for a moment he was so close that I could smell gum on his breath. I stepped back.

As we walked toward the cars, the light trickled in between clouds. We solidified our plans in Montara, a safe-enough distance up the coast.

When I met Miles at the restaurant that night, I already knew we would sleep together. I was looking for an easy way to create more space between Lucas and me. My freedom felt like so much of my identity; I didn't know another way except maybe to run.

After dinner, I found myself standing outside Miles's place. He pulled me into his arms and I rested on his neck. I tried to tuck my head down to align myself lower, not wanting to identify any similarities between Miles and Lucas, but that maneuver made me lose my balance; he practically carried me through the front door. I had admired the power he possessed as he cut through the water on his board. His massive wing-span could completely consume my body, and I was drunk on the idea of being made to feel small.

We kissed in the entry hall. He had just enough stubble to scratch my cheek. I was surprised his fair hair could produce something so sharp. The roughness sent tingles down my spine. He took hold of my face in his hands and then pulled away to look at me. The wine from dinner made me brave. I drank more than I should have to wash away any lingering guilt I was harboring related to Lucas. I bit my lip as an unnecessary act of seduction.

"Are you always this sexy?" He put his index finger on my mouth where my teeth had been.

"Come on," I said. "Show me where you sleep."

The morning after was the day we got stoned and listened to Jimi Hendrix in bed. When he gently tapped my nose, and I disappeared inside the haze.

"Hey, hey," I call out to him now at the Tree Tunnel. He stops, lifting the shovel high over his head in hello. The fall months in Half Moon Bay are my favorite, with the warmer afternoons and early evenings. I would live in shorts and a tank top if I could get away with it here, but the fog almost always requires layers, no matter the season. I button up Dottie's sweater but don't bother with my own. After loading her in the hiking backpack, I make my way over to where Miles is working. His uniform stretches across his broad shoulders that once made me feel dainty. Time hasn't changed his body.

"Lucky me. To what do I owe the pleasure? And who do we have here?" He cocks his head to the side.

"This is Little Dot," I say, turning my body sideways just a little before quickly swinging her back.

I want to ask him about his kids, but I notice he's looking at my long, bare legs that make up more than 50 percent of my body.

Eager to move the topic away from anything potentially dangerous, I say, "This is my turf. Since when did you start working this park?"

"They transferred me over a few months back. It's closer to my house, less of a commute. Can't beat the view," he says without removing his eyes from me. Then he scoffs, adding, "Your turf, you say? You're not a townie; you're a transplant. A Midwest transplant no less!"

"Hey, you mistook me for a Californian when we first met."

"Well, they don't really grow them like you anywhere."

Somehow today the power has shifted back in my favor. I know he's flirting; it isn't subtle, and his attention is a welcome respite. Something so different from the nuances that are always so predictable these days.

"Need a hand?" I pick up the extra shovel that's in the back of his John Deere utility vehicle. "I never get a chance to work my arms." Again, he takes an opportunity to examine me.

"So no surfing then?"

I shake my head. "It's been too long. What about you?"

"Every morning. Or every other, depending," he says as if it's no big deal.

I heave a huge pile onto the area he's landscaping and do another and another, funneling every feeling into the movements of manual labor. Of course, dads can surf every day because somehow the family, work, and pleasure balancing act never seems to apply to them in the same way it does to moms. I don't want to compare our family lives, though; having Dottie here is already enough of a disruption to this alternate universe I'm temporarily allowed to visit.

"Whoa, slow down there. I get paid no matter what. One of the main perks of working for the state."

"Our tax dollars well spent," I say, recognizing that it could sound as if I'm flirting now too. "You still smoke?" Suddenly, adding a joint to our interaction sounds like the cherry on top of the ice cream sundae.

"A little. Never on the job, though." He stops shoveling to watch me.

"No, of course not." I give him a grin and look up through my long lashes, blinking.

It's his turn to shake his head. "I'm serious. We can't lose our benefits."

I know the *we* isn't meant to be off-putting. Still, I can't help but interpret it as a means of him establishing his decade-long existence without me. I doubt I was more than a blip on his radar, but his impression on me was more than a little impactful. It does feel good, though, to be standing here with my third child strapped to my back so that it's plain as day I've moved on too. I could keep working while we talk—such a dangerous genie to be let out of the bottle. There's something thrilling about standing before someone who once held so much power over me.

Dottie hasn't made so much as a peep. She's always happy as long as she's attached to my body somewhere in some form. I throw the shovel back in the tractor.

"We should get moving before we lose the sunshine."

"Always a pleasure," he says.

I nod at him before taking off down the path.

By the time Lucas gets home, I'm well on my way to being more than a little tipsy.

"Let me tell you how much I hate picking out furniture for a ladies' lounge," he says, blocking my view of the TV in our bedroom. "Also, what's the deal with a powder room? Why would anyone want to hang out in a room next to a bathroom?"

"That's a lotta questions," I say, cocking my head to the side, hoping he will take the hint and move out of the way. "Powder rooms are a representation of a much larger problem. All part of the continued oppression of women to maintain the patriarchy. 'Course men would create an entire room meant for women to apply more makeup." I fan my face like I'm a debutante.

"Duly noted," he says.

"Listen, I just need to sit here in silence and watch my garbage television in peace." I've recorded my Bravo shows, and *Vanderpump Rules* has gotten really juicy again. Someone is shouting about something and I have to keep pausing it so I don't miss any important context. Reality TV is like a banana bag of bliss that shoots directly into my veins. I can turn it on and turn off everything else around me.

The "hike" wasn't enough. I need another distraction from being outshone by Christine. I'm slowly and systematically being replaced . . . Will it be that way when the baby comes? Amy calling up Christine about every case of the sniffles like I'm some amateur who is just bumbling around in the dark? I, too, have three kids, for crying out loud. All I do is answer their demands for attention and food.

I glance up and notice Lucas looks hurt. I should just listen or half listen like I usually do, but my concern over Amy is all-consuming.

"Look, the kids just went down, and I'm really tired." I tilt my head back so it's resting on the pillow. My neck jets up toward the ceiling. I want to get to the good part of my show, the portion they showed in the preview, when a couple fights over the way the main girl was flirting with a random guy at the bar. The boyfriend's possessiveness is kind of hot. I wonder if sex would be a quicker means to get back to my show.

Lucas begins to unbutton his collared shirt and moves toward the hamper in the closet. His silence is a bad sign.

"What's going on with you?" he asks, still maneuvering his fingers through the buttons. The wineglass next to me needs refilling, and I stand to walk down to the kitchen.

"I know you just want to talk, but I need, like, twenty minutes of mind-numbing TV, please. Then you can tell me all about menu fonts and we can discuss at length why gossipy women need a place to sit before they shit." I make it to the doorway. In my head, I am already pouring my glass and drinking it. I can almost feel it sliding down my throat, erasing our conversation.

"Nah, that's not how it will go, actually," Lucas says. His shirt is all the way off and gripped tightly in his fist. The way he is squeezing, I can see his pectoral muscles hardening. "You're gonna go down and get more wine. You'll do that and then disappear. Become a ghost in our house." He is standing less than a foot from me in only his underwear. My heart beats faster. The slipperiness of his words isn't something I have the strength to hold up and use against him. "Don't think I haven't been noticing something is going on with you. I've been looking online when you're passed out asleep." His sentence catches in his throat like he is going to cry.

"What, like watching porn?" I laugh, forming a sentence that can distract him enough to stop what is happening. To keep him from taking this further, which he has never done before.

But his expression doesn't waver. "No. Like, I think it's a problem. It isn't okay for our kids to see you drinking like this." His eyes move down the hall, acknowledging each of their closed bedroom doors.

Fury rises in my throat. The audacity of him questioning my actions when he's been checked out at The Restaurant all this year and half of last—the reason I'm so oversaturated by my time with the kids that a glass or two has turned into a bottle. I need it to keep the rough edges blurry enough that I can wake up tomorrow and do it all again . . . by myself!

"Our kids are asleep! They are safe in bed because I put them there while you were at The Restaurant. *Again*." My confidence is building. I know I can outmaneuver whatever he is attempting to get at.

"Don't do that. This isn't about me, and you know it," Lucas says, shaking his head. The motion makes me suddenly despise him. His frustration over me not paying attention to him is one thing, but shaming me into submission is quite another.

Joni appears in her doorway. She has a book in her hand, and she's peeling the corners of the binding away with her fingertips.

"Why are you talking so loud?" she asks, the size of her eyes doubling by the second.

"Sorry, Joni B. Go back to bed. We'll talk softer," Lucas says as he throws a white T-shirt over his head and pulls on a pair of flannel pajama pants. "Here, I'll walk you back." He reaches out and uses his large hand to cup the small of her back, guiding her down the hallway toward her room. "What's your book about?"

Relief floods my body. I take Joni and Lucas's exit as my opportunity to descend the stairs. I'm the one who's allowed to call him out on his behavior; it's rarely the other way around. He's lovingly accepted me for all my flaws and treated me as if I walk on water. If there was a way I could get him to understand, I would, but I can't even follow the logic myself. There isn't any way for me to explain to Lucas that my decisions at this time of night are already a foregone conclusion. My actions are predetermined. I don't want to be opening the fridge, but I am. It's unclear how I emptied this latest wine bottle. But I did.

CHAPTER 11

've spent the past couple of days on my very best behavior, which feels odd to need to do in my own marriage inside my own life. I've gone out of my way to pack lunches for Lucas so he can remain focused without having to stop working to eat. I make sure I'm attentive and present when he gets home. I wish I could lean harder on Amy, but things feel weird between us.

I've tried to bury myself in work, but forcing creativity is impossible. The last successful collection I created was titled *The Fluidity of Sexuality*, but that was years ago. I did a modern-day take on Georgia O'Keeffe's flowers as female genitalia but with coastal scenes. I was tickled to watch my mother-in-law squirm in discomfort at even the postcards I sent out advertising the show. I made sure there was always one front and center on her fridge whenever we were at their house. There was nothing more wonderful than witnessing her palpable distress whenever she'd need to pull things out of the refrigerator and she'd come face-to-face with the crest of a wave meant to mirror the hood of a woman's clitoris.

I always believed my art was heading toward something bigger, and for some reason the allure of the West Coast felt like my mecca. In high school, I applied to schools in California, convinced by Madame Tessier that all my dreams would be possible based on my talent. Out-of-state tuition was considerable, but she said she'd help me find scholarships. She left a UC Santa Cruz brochure on my desk one day after school. The second I opened it and saw the beach summoning me, I knew I belonged there.

Nana and I drove Big Bertha to UCSC and my parents met us there via plane. She spent the entire 1,965-mile trek grinning like a lunatic.

"I always knew you were a California girl," she said, her gray hair catching in her mouth with the window rolled all the way down. She started singing the Beach Boys song as she pretended to hold a microphone. I studied her commitment to the lyrics. The way her enunciation matched theirs.

Once she got to the chorus, it was my turn, and I took my hands off the wheel to steal the mic away. Nana reached over to steer until I got through the last refrain. I wished I could bottle the happiness contained within the walls of my chest—find a way to encapsulate the unencumbered euphoria that existed on the drive with her that day.

I should be avoiding the Tree Tunnel, but the dangerous thrill of seeing Miles combined with my runner's high has kept me going back almost every day this week. There's a risk associated with Miles's presence—like standing on the edge of a cliff knowing I won't jump. A reminder of my uncertainty about the many choices I've made. By visiting that spot, I'm not an O'Connor wife or mom to three kids. I'm harmlessly waving over at my shadow self.

As I walk along the path leading out our front door, my feet are freezing. I'm wearing a long, oversize men's button-up

dress shirt and no pants. In one hand I'm awkwardly maneuvering a heavy bag of trash, hoping nothing will leak out onto
my bare toes. We have too many boxes of junk blocking our side
door, so I have to go all the way around the front to reach our
outdoor bins. I see Christine's car parked in our driveway and
she's just sitting there watching me. I continue on my mission,
heaving the bag as it rattles, and glass clinks together, indicating there was nothing below to cushion the fall.

I walk back to the front door just as I hear her car door slam.

"Leah," she calls out, knowing me well enough to understand that I would have just gone back into the house without
ever acknowledging that I noticed her there.

I turn. "Hey, Lucas isn't here," I say, resting my hand on
my hip.

"I came to talk to you." The pins and needles of her voice
prick without penetrating. "Are you here alone?"

I regard her with a single eyebrow raised, teetering on the
edge of disbelief. The audacity of her question is offensive even
by Christine's standards.

"The kids are here if that's what you're asking." I arch my
toes, almost digging them into the driveway to keep from
snarling my teeth. She believes she's clever, that she's caught
me doing something I shouldn't be.

She folds her arms; the sun has gone down, sucking out
all the warmth from the air. I know neither of us wants to be
standing outside anymore.

"I need to know who that man was you were with the other
day," she demands. I fidget back and forth, shifting my weight
from one leg to the other. I can't seem to steady myself. I could
just answer her and end this game we've been playing with each
other, but somehow that feels more dangerous.

"What are you getting at 'ere, exactly?" My words come out a little slurry. If this is her attempt at socializing with me outside of Sunday dinners . . . I only wish Amy were here to witness how horribly she treats me.

When Lucas and I got engaged several months into my unplanned pregnancy with Joni, he insisted on telling his parents first. He swore the proposal had been preplanned, but the look on Christine's face when we arrived at the house told a different story. It was no secret Christine was uncomfortable with the order in which we did things, but I had thought that making everything legal would somehow appeal to her traditionalism.

After they had toasted with champagne and I with apple cider, Lucas and George went in the backyard, which left Christine and me alone in the kitchen. I attempted to spin the ring around my finger, but my body was more swollen than I was used to. I readjusted it, admiring the sparkle it cast in the light from the kitchen window.

Christine took note of my movements. *"My fingers swelled in pregnancy. It would be a shame to have Lucas resize it just because you're pregnant."*

Suddenly headlights blind our eyeline as Lucas pulls up the driveway where Christine and I awkwardly stand. He gets out of his truck, and we are silent, waiting for him to rescue us both.

"Hey, Mom, you coming or going?" Lucas leans in and kisses his mom first and then walks over to greet me. Before she can reply, he continues, "Come back inside; stay for a drink." I watch Christine, daring her to say something that might upset Lucas.

"I'd love to come in and say hello to the kids," she says, beaming because suddenly we are all about to present as one big happy family. Lucas hooks his arm in hers and leads her toward the house as I stagger a little way behind.

Once we're inside the kitchen, Joni's face illuminates into a grin.

"Grandma!" Joni is sitting at the table, dropping small cut-up pieces of fruit onto Dottie's high chair tray. She makes her way over, and Christine kneels to embrace her, burying her face in Joni's hair as her fingers cut through its silkiness.

"Wine?" Lucas asks, maneuvering around the island, reading the label of a bottle already open on the counter.

"I'll take red if you have it," she says.

"Red coming right up. I have one that we are sampling for you to try. Needs your approval."

I despise the casualness with which he asks her. Like her palate is that discernible, as if she'd know the difference between a $50 bottle and one that's $7.99 on sale at Safeway.

Joni wanders over to Lucas, and they break into their elaborate handshake that ends with a drumroll on the counter.

I lift the bottle of white and drain the remainder into my empty glass next to it.

"What were you up to today, Mom?" Lucas asks as he reaches over to pass her a glass of red.

"You know I'm always busy—odd things here and there." She lets out a heavy sigh and continues, "Never feels as fulfilling as when you kids were younger, though." Then she imbibes a small sip. Thankfully Lucas poured it slightly too full for her to swirl it around her glass; otherwise I'm certain I'd be sick over her pretentiousness. "Mmm, you know how I love a full-bodied red." She places it down and I count the seconds until she picks it back up again. But she leaves it there.

"Tell me about what's happening with The Restaurant." Her

eyes widen with interest. The Restaurant is meant to be a love letter from her boys, which is no secret, and the smugness of her smile may, in fact, be what ultimately turns my stomach.

"We are getting so close. Did you order your dancing shoes?" Lucas asks his mother.

"For what?" I inquire, confused.

Lucas pauses, eyeing me carefully. "We're getting a band for the soft opening."

I nod like that jogged my memory. Of course, I should know all the details before Christine about my husband's restaurant because I'm his wife and she's his mother.

"I told you we were getting Dory's nephew's jazz band in from the city." Lucas stands, hovering near Christine. Their shadows meld to become a singular sentinel of suspicion.

Lately I cannot seem to fit all the pieces together of what's been said and shared. It's as if I am recalling scenes from a dream and it's up to me to decide what happened in my real life or while I was sleeping.

"Dory is just so tickled about it," Christine says.

"She's not coming to the opening though, right? We need her to stay with the kids," I clarify.

"Of course she's coming to the opening! She's practically family!" Christine responds before Lucas can.

"Okay, well then, you're in charge of finding a sitter," I explain to Lucas, more than a little irritated at this point. "I already had her locked in for all the cousins to be together that night. Still no kids, right? Adults only?"

"Yes, the one on Saturday evening is adults only, and then we'll open it up to families for the following weekend before the main open," he answers, looking back and forth between me and Christine.

"Good luck finding a sitter, since our whole town will have snagged them already." I give him an exaggerated look of exasperation.

"I mean, if Dory's watching everyone's kids . . . I dunno, we'll figure it out," he says to his mom as if she's been juggling any of these logistics.

"You mean I will," I say, sipping from my glass.

They chatter on about the music again and I stop listening. I'm dazed, observing Joni wiping Dottie's mouth as Dottie sits in her high chair.

"Have you eaten?" Christine asks Lucas.

"We had some bites at the restaurant. I'll grab something out of the fridge later."

I recognize it as a dig at me. I'm supposed to have an apron on and a hot meal prepared. Lucas just shrugs a little, refusing to acknowledge what's happening here.

It's almost nine o'clock and Christine is still at our house. I've been hiding out in Joni's bed until I hear her car leave the driveway. I cannot take another minute of her undermining me in front of Lucas. The whole thing has me seething and stewing about every life choice I made that brought me into the O'Connor family.

"Hey, Mom?" Joni's voice is quiet and tentative.

"Mm-hmm?"

"There is this girl in my class . . ." Joni's words are long and drawn out. I've stopped listening because I've just survived a diatribe in which she discussed at length the plot of her latest book about a mythical kingdom of fairies and the roles they need to play in order to protect themselves from evil trolls.

Christine is the evil troll, attempting to pull everyone to her side. My luminescent fairy is Amy. I don't want to lose my eye-rolling partner. Amy is the only person who makes me feel less crazy. I can't be considered the black sheep in a family of pretend perfection. I'm terrified to read the writing on the wall.

"Yeah? Tell me about her." I'm suddenly so sleepy I can't possibly stay awake for another minute. She continues to speak, but the blackness sets in.

CHAPTER 12

Normally Amy can take Dottie home after the short preschool day, but she's not available today and I need to get to the studio. I'm way behind on my current collection.

I'm surprising Lucas at The Restaurant, hoping he can keep Dottie occupied for a few hours. The manager, Scott, greets Dottie and me at the door. He's a short, stylish, openly gay man Lucas recruited from another restaurant in San Francisco. He and his partner were thrilled to move back to the coast, having grown up in La Jolla down in Southern California.

"How's everything?" I ask, though I'm anxious to cut and run as quickly as possible. Just being in here, I feel like thousands of Christine's intricate scarves are suffocating me.

"Busy but good. He's in the back office," Scott says, eyeing Dottie like she may be infected with something contagious. I know The Restaurant has been a child-free zone lately during crunch time, but I'm not in the business of making other people feel more comfortable.

I take both of Dottie's hands so she won't touch anything and walk her around behind the bar toward the office. Paul and

Lucas are seated at their desks facing each other. They both look up. Paul grins, standing to scoop Dottic into his arms.

We don't get the same greeting from Lucas. "What are you doing here?" His tone is thick with irritation.

"I need to get into the studio this afternoon."

Lucas combs his hand through his hair. There's a lingering pause as no one, not even Dottie, says a word.

"Little Dot, have you ever tried bubbly water?" Paul makes his voice go up an entire octave to add a layer of excitement to his question. "Let's go find you some while Mommy and Daddy have a little chat." Paul walks out with Dottie still in his arms.

"I wish you would have called first. I seriously cannot have her here right now," Lucas says, pushing forcefully away from his desk as he stands.

"Okay, well, I cannot have her at my studio, so what do you want me to do?" My eyebrows furrow together so closely that my vision starts to blur. "What, because I'm the mother and despite us both working full-time, it somehow always falls on me? I never agreed to that."

Lucas exhales loudly. We've had about a million versions of this same argument over the years.

There's a crash in the dining room, and I can hear Dottie start to whimper. Paul's voice echoes from behind the bar. "She's fine. Everything's fine!"

"We are literally days from the opening now. Days," Lucas says. Which isn't accurate. They have more than three weeks.

"But it's been this way for *years*. Why does your work always take priority over mine?"

"Can we please not get into this now?" he says, touching the point directly where his nose begins between his eyes.

"Okay, when should we get into it? When can I pencil you in?" I pretend to hold a notepad in the palm of my hand just because I know it will piss him off.

"Well, not tonight, because by the time I get home you won't be coherent enough to carry on a productive conversation."

It feels like he's struck me, and I touch the skin on my cheek to see if it's warm. Paul appears in the doorway, cradling a visibly upset Dottie as if she were a baby.

"Sorry to interrupt. I tried all my uncle magic. I even tried juggling those plastic cups. No luck today, I'm afraid. She must sense the intensity in here." I suddenly feel like I'm being ganged up on. Paul will generally stay out of it, but his dig suggests I'm somehow in the wrong for bringing Dottie here. Too many girls in the boys' club.

Lucas is vibrating at a level of agitation I've never seen before. "I'll just call my mom, and she can come get Dottie," he says, pulling his phone off his desk.

"No. Don't do that," I snap. I'd rather bring Dottie to the studio than listen to Christine drone on and on about having to come to our rescue. Even though I'm furious over Lucas's ludicrous accusation, I need to get back into his good graces. "I'll just take her with me." I pull Dottie out of Paul's arms. I know he's uncomfortable, but I want to tell him to get used to it. He will soon discover for himself that being married with children isn't always unicorns and rainbows as his mother would have him believe.

Inside my studio, Dottie is attempting to dance along with Elmo on the iPad. Her little butt protrudes backward, creating a ninety-degree angle. I laugh to myself but turn away, wanting to make sure I capitalize on her distraction.

I've finished the painting I started when Christine crashed our party at the beach. The seal-in-the-water print is much too obvious. I had meant to make it more of an optical illusion: Is it there or is it not there? But by the time I finished, I might as well have painted a giant red arrow saying, *Look here! Aren't I clever?*

My latest plein air painting is of a surfers' lineup captured in the morning light. After school drop-offs, I've been bringing my coffee and sitting in my car to watch. I can't bear to stand outside with the other tourists. It is impossible not to feel bitter, being on this side of the divide, when I know what it feels like to be out there. I pretend it is enough to re-create the scene with my paintbrush—but it's contrived, like a man depicting childbirth.

"Mama, up." Dottie has abandoned the tablet and toddles over to me with her arms over her head.

"Okay, lovebug," I say, giving in to her.

She extends her arms, wanting to take my paintbrush. I carry her to the cabinet and pull out the washable kind of paint that won't destroy her clothes. I locate her smock and catch our reflection in the mirror in front of us. I take a picture to send to Lucas.

I think she wants to be an artist! I type and then hit Send.

A minute later, he responds with a smiley face emoji. I shouldn't use the kids in this way to make things right between us, but I need him to remember that I'm a good mom so I can remember it too. It's my way of getting us to move past what's been said without having to say anything at all.

Dottie walks over to the paper I have laid out for her on

the floor. I am already dreading the mess she will make. For a moment, we are painting in tandem. She is appeased, if only temporarily, and I am doing it all: working, mothering, living. What should be a wash of satisfaction followed by a surge of happiness is replaced by a need for more. Better. Why can't the momentary bliss satisfy me? Like the last flame before it transforms to an ember, I can only exist in the waiting—the space that knows the flicker will die out.

I remember one night early in our relationship; Lucas and I sat on the floor in this very spot of the studio. I'd had the keys for less than a week. The compulsion to rent a spot had surprised me, but I'd officially run out of space with all that I was creating in Half Moon Bay.

Lucas and I had Chinese takeout spread out like a picnic. A bottle of wine and two glasses were sitting between us.

"Hey." Lucas pointed at me with his chopstick.

"Hey," I said, not looking up.

"I want you to meet my family this weekend," he said, swirling his noodles around the chopsticks before taking in a huge bite. I waited to respond. I had a mouthful of veggies and rice and they suddenly tasted dry. I coughed a little. "Is that a yes?" he asked. This time I lifted my eyes to meet his gaze.

"I . . ." I felt a lump rising to the top of my throat. I put down the box of Chinese food I was holding. "I need to explain something." At that point, I had been sleeping with Miles, and the idea of meeting Lucas's parents would only further solidify my actions as a betrayal.

"Okay, that sounds scary." He put down his food too.

"It's not meant to be scary. I guess I just want to be honest," I said. I knew, to the naked eye, it would seem like we were at the beginning of a relationship. "I don't think that's a good idea . . . meeting your family." I paused, trying to choose the right words without giving anything away. "I like that we are keeping it casual." I didn't phrase it as a question because I wasn't looking for an answer.

"Casual," he repeated as if half laughing and half spitting out the word. My face began to warm, and I knew the alcohol was doing its job.

Take me out of here, I thought, speaking only to the wine. I picked up my glass, trying to disappear within a long, slow sip.

"Casual," I said again. Lucas had stopped moving entirely. Instead, he was watching my every movement, which made me want to perform for him as if I were onstage. "I'm happy here and inspired. But meeting your parents sounds like the start of a quaint little life I'm not sure I want to be mine. At least not today."

"What makes you so scared of my family?"

"I'm not scared of your family."

He paused before pressing me further. "Okay, what makes you so scared of the idea of family in general?"

His statement stung like an open-palm slap on bare, cold skin. "You don't get it. I'm used to being alone. I like being alone." Even though I said it, I wasn't sure I meant it. "I love Nana and my parents; we have our own thing going on and it works for us." Lucas had told me all about the O'Connors at that point. I thought it was adorable that any family would want to remain that close to one another long into adulthood. The close-knit raising of the second and third generation was something out of sweet little children's books—a work of fiction. The fact that I had moved on and far away wasn't a testament to some dysfunctional upbringing; it was totally normal to want to flee the nest. But the look on his face made me feel like some sort of freak, which only agitated me further—better anger than sadness, though—a risky thing that meant I was giving too much of myself away.

"Not everyone had what you had growing up. We can't all be happy, well-adjusted breeders—then the world would be void of any art," I rationalized, suddenly perfectly content with my explanation of everything. "So, thanks very much for the offer. I'm sure your family is lovely, but you don't need the likes of me in the mix messing with your cookie-cutter perfection."

Lucas returned to spinning his noodles around his chopsticks. My defensiveness was excessive. I knew it. He knew it. But I had yet to meet Christine, and I was already convinced that the only way for a woman to have it all was for her to exist as an island. I didn't want anyone to show me otherwise.

"Do you hate me?" I asked, looking into his big brown eyes, finding the yellow specks and using them to recenter myself.

"The opposite; I love you, Leah. I'm in love with you." He drew in a large breath and continued, "I hear what you're saying, and yeah, that sucks. But I know you."

I took my gaze away and looked at the walls of the studio. I'd made more art here than during all my travels combined. *Love?* I drew in a breath. Standing, I walked to the cabinet and pulled down another bottle of wine. Neither of us spoke as he sat watching me open it. I waited him out.

Leave me alone, I wanted to whisper under my breath, quiet enough so I could take it back in case I didn't mean it.

I'd always been able to maintain a safe-enough distance between myself and most people—create a protective barrier from all of life's what-ifs. Even when I was younger, I wasn't interested in allowing others inside.

"Pick you up Sunday? Or the following one? We do it every

week," he said, steamrolling over everything I had just pro-
claimed.

I snorted; it was no longer cute. He was hogging possession of
the ball while offering up his family as the shiny piece of jewelry.

"Did you not hear me? I don't want this. Any of this," I said,
using his own words and gestures against him by creating an
imaginary circle around us with my glass. I watched as red
droplets sloshed over the side and fell to the floor, red beads
on top of old, dried paint splatters. It created a remarkably
beautiful texture.

See, I wanted to say, *this is what I love—the simplicity of colors
on the ground.*

"I think you do want this," he said, and then he gestured
toward my art. "Look what you have done here. You don't think
I see these?" He stood, pausing next to one I painted at the Tree
Tunnel. The focal point was a single tree standing alone inside
the arch of the other cypresses. "You don't think it has anything to do with us?" After a beat, he added, "I see you in ways I
don't think you can see yourself."

Even in the short time I'd known him, I recognized Lucas
could pitch a line and sell a product. What if that was all he was
trying to do with us?

"You think those are about you?" I said, suddenly furious
that he wanted to take credit for my creations.

He made his way back over to me, bent down on both knees,
and wrapped his arms around my back until the weight of him
came crashing down on top of me. Our faces were inches apart,
our bodies forcefully toppled together. He leaned in passion-
ately, kissing me deeper and more intensely than that first kiss
after surfing. He was confident, even though I had given him
no reason to trust me.

I kissed him back because it felt easier than continuing to say words back and forth. I pulled his shirt over his head, panicked, my fingers fumbling. Between the wine and our exchange, I wanted to climb out of my body and bury myself in his. He pulled up my skirt, letting it bunch around my thighs. I shuffled to remove my underwear. They slid down my legs, and I let gravity drop them to the floor. He kept his eyes on mine as his fingers traced the length of my leg. He moved slowly, the sense of urgency suddenly gone.

I leaned over, pushing him backward all the way to the floor. Once he was horizontal, I took off his pants. I admired his body in front of me, in complete undress compared to my almost covered state. The power I had at that moment was intoxicating.

I swung my leg over him, feeling his body react beneath me. He sat up, making a V as he pulled off my shirt. He kissed my shoulders and around the bottom of my neck. How easily I could disappear in him if I wanted to.

I found his mouth with mine again, tasting his last sip of wine, wanting to swallow it up for myself. Once he left, I could kill the bottle alone. He could fill the places inside me that were empty, and the wine would finish the job.

He pulled away and outlined the shape of my lips with his finger. "I love you," he said again, searching my eyes for anything to give me away.

"Stop talking," I said without smiling.

That night on the floor of my studio, we may have accidentally created the very thing I had fought so hard against: a family of our own.

I shake my head and return my eyes to the canvas. Normally I finish a piece on location; re-creating from memory defeats the purpose of a plein air, but I recognize it needs brightness. More yellows. This one may actually be my first in a while that works. I return to the cabinets, pulling out gold hues and warm tones. I turn around just as Dottie's brush meets my painting.

"No, no, no. Dottie, no!" I am shouting as I run toward her.

She's flapping her arms up and down, splattering even more red droplets across the canvas. I yank the brush from her hand a little too roughly, and she starts to whimper. She falls back, landing on her bottom. She is a little stunned at first but then erupts into a full-blown wail. It isn't her pained cry, like when she gave herself a black eye from tripping into the coffee table, but one of fear, more like the time at the zoo when two female lions were fighting right up next to the glass. Their ferociousness was on full display, and for the first time, it became impossible to see them as anything other than what they were: caged wild animals.

I cannot immediately console her because I am so angry. Angry that I had to bring her to the studio today. That my art isn't what it once was. Just minutes before, I had it all. Wasn't my desire to be selfish meant to disappear completely when I became a mother? Isn't that the way it works? Why can't I take a page from Christine's book of how to become Martha freaking Stewart? Pretend that the emptiness isn't all-consuming. Pretend my thoughts aren't ugly and awful.

I look down at Dottie. Her bottom lip is quivering, consuming her face. I should scoop her in my arms and tell her, *Everything is forgiven. No harm done. An accident. Mommy's fault.* But I can't. I resent Lucas. I want to return to our argument and scream, *I told you so! These were precisely the people I was trying to stop us from becoming that night on the floor of my studio.* But instead, I can only squat down so I'm at eye level with my youngest daughter. I use her little body to steady myself. My compressed reflection mocks me in the floor-to-ceiling mirror directly behind her. I have made myself so much smaller.

I want to be sorry. I know I am meant to be the bigger person. What kind of mother behaves this way? Dottie's needs come before mine; there is no room for selfishness here. She tries to lean into me, but instead, I stand, leaving her to whimper while I tend to the mess.

The bell chimes, announcing a customer's arrival. I look up to see Christine in the doorway. Dottie runs over crying, and Christine drops to her knees to pick her up. Dottie is sniffling and pointing to the painting she ruined. I can't get away from them; it seems the O'Connors are always close by, lurking in the wings—especially in my darkest moments.

"That's okay, love," she says, rocking her back and forth in her arms. "It's okay."

"No, no!" Dottie shouts, repeating my loud, stern tone.

Christine pulls a Fruit Roll-Up out of her bag because of course she carries those with her everywhere for the grand-children. Dottie is immediately happy again and plops down to unravel it—like a long, retractable tongue—shoveling little pieces into her mouth.

"I was just on my way to pick up something for Jack's birth-day celebration, and I saw you in here." She stands, wandering around my studio like she's looking for something. I want to point out that the exit is exactly the way she came in, but be-fore I can, she says, "I overheard your conversation last night during bedtime on my way out of the bathroom. With Joni . . . about Lizzy."

I move to the sink to clean Dottie's paints, wanting to put my back to Christine so she can no longer read my face. The sound of plastic scraping inside the metallic sink prickles the hair on my arms.

"Yeah, what about it?" I say without turning around.

"Nothing—just, I'm glad she told you. What do you make of it?" she asks like I'm supposed to know what the hell she's talking about.

I dry my hands on the paint-streaked cloth hanging from the upper cabinets. I continue to shuffle around the studio, moving things without actually cleaning.

"What do *you* make of it?" I ask, which I know sounds incredibly odd. As a general rule, I make it a point never to ask Christine for her opinion on anything.

"It's probably a phase. What do kids really know about themselves at ten?"

"A phase?" I ask. My tone has unintentionally softened with curiosity.

"I don't think Joni would know yet if she was *gay*. I'm sure she just likes spending time with Lizzy."

"*Gay*?" I repeat the word because it's the first time I'm hearing it. I stop in my tracks.

Christine makes her way over to where I've stopped, raising her head so her stare is suddenly at eye level.

"You don't remember talking with Joni . . . do you, Leah?"

I'm incapable of words as she backs away from me as if I'm wielding a weapon. She kneels to scoop up Dottie, who rests her head on Christine's shoulder. She strokes Dottie's hair, the loose coils springing back into place with each pat. It looks like she's preparing to kidnap her and bolt out of the store. If it were Joni in her arms, she definitely would.

"I remember," I say, staring past her, though I know I sound unconvincing. For good measure, I sternly add, "What are you accusing me of now?"

Her fabricated politeness will stop her from saying anything too explosive, though my body still tenses, awaiting her next blow.

"I'm worried about you. I don't know what's going on. Whatever it is, though, you're hurting your family."

I cannot contain my smugness. She is no match for me. Christine moves her gaze to my most prominent painting on the gallery wall. It's won several awards. She uses her chin to gesture toward it.

"I was always unsure about that single tree there, interrupting the unity of the other cypresses arching together. I thought maybe the eyes could get used to it, adjust and it would blend in to help support, but I just don't see a way how. I never have."

"I wish Amy were here so she could hear how you speak to me. You have her under your spell, but she'll see. One day you'll slip up around her."

Christine is shaking her head. Her eyes close like I've wounded her somehow.

"I wish you could see how it really is, Leah. But that's exactly the problem now, isn't it?"

"I think you should go." I gesture for her to hand me Dottie, but instead, she kisses the top of her head. "And before you go running to Lucas with your fake worry, please stay out of our business," I say, making my tone so caustic that my words could burst into flame.

"My son, these children," she says, using her head again to point at Dottie resting on her hip, "are my business. I will protect them at all costs."

"Protect them from what? *Me?*" I pull Dottie from her now, no longer gentle, no longer subtle. Dottie whimpers a bit but doesn't cry. I refuse to watch Christine leave but instead listen for the chime of the bell.

One morning in high school after I had finally completed a painting that would eventually earn me a partial college scholarship, I asked Madame Tessier to come critique my work. I had yet to gain the confidence of knowing when something was worth anything, so her opinion mattered more deeply than even my own. She pulled up a stool, an unlit cigarette in her left hand, her right leaning on her knee for support as she tipped forward. She was quiet, and her silence made me nervous.

"I think this is the one I will submit for the Craft Scholarship," I said just to fill the soundless air around us. I had titled it *Ache*. A blackness overtook the bottom of the canvas with streaks, like tentacles reaching upward, trying but failing to capture the light.

Madame Tessier's braid swung around and draped down between her large breasts. She put her cigarette on an empty desk, pulling her knees up as she rested her chin in her palms. She sat like that, gazing into my painting—before she threw her braid over her shoulder.

Even back then, I felt a pull of uncertainty inside me, though it had no logical origin. I was loved as a child, even if my parents were less available than others. I had Nana to fill whatever void, if any, they created. I had no real reason for disconnection to creep in, moving like smoke finding the slit underneath a closed door.

"The talent you have, Leah, can come with a price," she said, not removing her eyes from my work.

"I'm hoping at least fifteen thousand toward tuition," I said with a grin.

Unamused, Madame Tessier continued, "Sometimes the price you'll pay will cost you everything." Confused, I couldn't come up with a retort. But it didn't matter; she was speaking like she had forgotten I was even there. She continued wistfully, "The thing about being an artist, any type—poet, singer, photographer—is you create something that speaks for other people. They want to say it, to find the vision, but that's not their gift to share with the world—it's yours. Some will thank you for saying what they never could. Others will waste away in jealousy. Either way, it will consume you entirely while you try to fill the emptiness with other things."

CHAPTER 13

think about skipping Jack's birthday party and faking a headache since I've had more than my fill of the O'Connors lately, but I know I will score points with Lucas if I go. And frankly, right now, I need all the points I can get.

When we arrive at Jack and Lidy's, everyone is gathered around the table looking at one of Christine's photo books she's created using George's pictures. As photographers go, George has a very good eye. Christine is certain he could have been a professional had his investments not kept him so busy. I've always appreciated his work and displayed it around our home. He has a knack for capturing childhood innocence, almost like *The Catcher in the Rye*. I think it's because he never really grew up himself.

The photo book is almost absurdly large and labeled "Jack: Early Years." Christine insists on spending every second apart from the family compiling albums so that not one moment of their glorious togetherness is missed. I wonder if I am the only one who notices Jack's album is two-thirds the size of Paul's and one-third the size of Lucas's.

Before I can comment, Christine is motioning to Jack.

"Here you are in your orange swimming trunks and life jacket, eating carrots because you insisted that everything that day be orange." Jack looks on with feigned interest as he sips the beer in his hand. She claps her hands together. "Oh, to be back there again!"

"Yes, but now you get to be a grandmother! The best of both worlds. Reaping all the benefits without having to make any of the tough child-rearing decisions!" Lidy is speaking in her high-pitched voice that borders on shrill. She's wearing a yellow-and-white checkered apron that I know for a fact Christine got her for Christmas last year. She's such a suck-up.

"Nonsense! I feel like a trained surgeon stripped of her medical license—all my hard-earned skills are wasting away," Christine says, staring off. Paul immediately stands behind her, rubbing her shoulders before pointing down at an image.

"I remember all our beach days!" Paul grins, flipping to the next page.

"In this one, George was working. You boys were nine, eight, and five. It was one of our weekly beach trips," Christine begins. I immediately wonder how she could possibly recall their exact ages, but then I realize she has their ages chronicled in the spaces next to each picture—because of course she does. "We'd have a picnic, and, Jack, you always used to ask me, 'Mommy, if we were all out in the water and a big wave came up, who would you save first?'"

"What did you say?" Jack asks, taking another sip from his beer.

"First, I reminded you that the correct word is *whom* would you save first."

"Sounds about right." Lucas laughs, reaching into the cooler to snag a beer for himself without checking to see what I want.

"Then I explained that I would save you all, of course. Except you were so persistent. You know how you can get stuck on something." Christine looks to Lidy as if they are sharing in the same joke.

"So naturally, you'd pick the wonder boys over there," Jack says, and I witness the exaggerated creases around Christine's eyes pinch in disapproval. I am grateful for Jack's brazenness. It's a relief not to be the only one brave enough to call out Christine on her BS from time to time.

"Excuse me! I'd save you all. Moms are magical like that," Christine says, effectively ending the conversation with her tone.

"Of course you would." Amy has emerged from behind me and goes to sit down next to Christine. "If anyone could sprout an extra limb to save her children, it would be you."

"I do envy the starfish." Christine and Joni exchange a knowing look.

Lidy has taken this as her cue to bring out the cupcakes.

"Happy birthday to you," Lucas begins in a deep, throaty voice meant to mimic a bass tone. Paul raises it up an octave, and together they sound halfway decent. Even when we can't get together, which is rare, everyone is expected to call and sing the "Happy Birthday" song into the phone, even Dottie. The O'Connors have always placed an unreasonable amount of importance on birthdays in general.

When the chorus ends, Brice, Jack and Lidy's son, swipes a fingerful of icing off his sister's cupcake. Joy jabs at her brother with her elbow, and he releases a high-pitched yelp of pain. I'm relieved to witness other people's kids misbehaving in front of my in-laws.

"For my birthday, could we have, like, a minute of peace, please?" Jack says, though his tone remains playful.

"Was that what you wished for when you blew out the candles?" Joy asks, lowering her elbow. The kids have stopped fighting, momentarily awaiting his answer.

"Now, if I tell you that, it won't come true." Jack grins over at Lidy.

"Would you like one?" Lidy offers me a cupcake, and I shake my head as George pulls two off the plate. Knowing George, he'll consume both, and then in manufactured amusement, he will claim he meant to save one for Christine but just shouldn't be trusted around sweets. It's odd that I know all these details. I am not sure I could identify either of my own parents' tells so easily. We never spent nearly as much time together as I do with my in-laws.

"Hey! Da-ad! Joy stole the rest of my frosting!" Brice is crying now, big tears streaming down, cutting through the globs of icing on his face. Joy's mouth is still attached to the top of his cupcake.

"Obviously not my wish." Jack laughs, throwing his arm around George, who appears next to him. Lidy is already moving toward the children with the wet wipes.

Jack is walking us out to the car as we are set to leave when I realize I've left my purse inside. Lidy must have taken the kids upstairs to get cleaned up, because I see only George and Christine still sitting out on the patio with their backs to me, flipping through the memory book again. I try to remain as quiet as I can, not wanting to endure another round of good-byes, when I hear my name spill out of Christine's lips. I stand just behind the wall next to the sliding glass door that's open.

"I don't know how I could have, but I could have stopped him. And now something else is happening and Leah is drinking too much."

"What does that mean? Too much?" he asks.

"I don't know yet," she says. "It's completely irresponsible." I tuck myself tightly behind the wall to ensure just a sliver of my eyes peek out so I can see them but they won't see me. My fingers wrap around the strap of my purse. I'm squeezing so hard that my nails start to dig into my thumbs.

"*Leah?* You mean the girl our son accidentally got pregnant, who lived in a van for a year . . . *irresponsible?*" He chuckles at his own joke before looking at Christine, who does not seem amused. His mouth remains stuck in a grin, despite her face. George is never without a cocktail in his hand. "The Irish way," he calls it. Surely he'll go to bat for me here.

She continues, "I saw this coming. I should have—"

"What?" he interrupts. "You should have what? You and I both know trying to control Lucas would be like trying to control the tide." He pauses, motioning dramatically with his hands.

"But Leah . . . ," Christine protests.

"Leah isn't your responsibility."

Her mouth opens to speak, but then she closes it. "That's true, but what about Amy? The same can be said of her—neither girl came from me. I can take none of the responsibility. In Amy's case, none of the credit," she says wistfully. And then she adds, "In Leah's, none of the blame."

I watch George reach over to place his hand on Christine's knee.

"I know today is especially difficult and it's easier to busy yourself with worry over our daughters-in-law. But it's okay to just miss her, you know? I miss Grace too." George's voice has gone hoarse.

"I miss her. I miss her so much." Christine dabs at her eyes as George pulls her in for an embrace.

"Here, my love. Lean into me."

CHAPTER 14

Dottie is asleep for the night. The older kids are both reading books in bed. The guys are in the office working out kinks regarding The Restaurant. Amy and I are sitting on my deck, sipping hot tea. I'm relieved we've made it back out here together like this.

As a show of good faith and just to prove to Amy that I can, I'm taking a break from drinking for the next three weeks, at least until the opening. I figure I will get ahead of her next inquisition with the universal understanding that it would be completely unreasonable for anyone to stay sober the night of the opening.

"Christine is hiding something," I say, eager to metaphorically spill the tea.

"What do you mean?" Amy asks, but her level of enthusiasm doesn't reveal that she's nearly as excited as I need her to be.

"Has she ever talked to you about someone named Grace?"

Amy cocks her head to the side and pouts her lips. "No." I search her face to tell me if she's speaking the truth. But it's too dark and I'm scared to look too hard.

"I overheard a conversation between her and George about

missing Grace, 'especially today,' when they thought they were alone after Jack's party."

Amy looks the appropriate amount of puzzled. I continue to study the expression on her face to make sure she's not attempting to cover for Christine. It's not completely out of the realm of possibility that Christine would share something private during one of their walks or phone calls.

"I don't know. I mean, I've always found the ritual before dinner a little odd, given that they aren't religious. But we should probably leave it alone and wait her out." Amy goes back to blowing on her tea.

"Why are you defending her? She's clearly lying about something."

"Maybe she is." Amy shrugs like she's ready to move on when I've only just gotten started.

"Come on! How can it not bother you that she's hiding the existence of a person?" I catch myself as the words have already tumbled out of my mouth. "I mean, you know what I mean. Lucas has never spoken of a Grace before, and just the mention of her was enough to make Christine cry!"

I can sense Amy's defenses rising as she crosses her legs at the ankles, folding her arms over her belly.

"Only we can decide when we are ready to reveal the truth about something. It's up to her to decide when she's ready."

I hate how adamantly Amy is defending Christine right now. We used to be able to go jab for jab when it came to our mother-in-law.

"Sounds like you will be naming the baby Christine after all."

"Don't start that again," Amy says, but she is grinning, and therefore my jealousy is properly masked. I won't let Christine get off that easily, especially when she's been harassing me so much about Miles. Maybe Amy will come around and see my side after the baby is born.

Amy reaches between her cleavage and pulls out a stray hair that has obviously been bothering her.

"Your boobs got freaking enormous," I tell her.

"Doesn't it terrify you that Joni is going to start to sprout little boobs soon? And, like, before you know it, Dottie? I mean, don't get me wrong, I'm thrilled we are having a girl, but I hate to imagine that one day we'll be sitting at the breakfast table and they'll just appear. Then that's it. They are all little women." My heart sinks at the thought. The tumultuous time between girlhood and womanhood creeps up without warning. Joni is close to entering the eye of the storm. "Did I ever tell you about the first time I got my period?" Amy takes a tentative sip from her mug, warming her hands around the edges.

"I don't think so—but remind me to tell you one of my period stories when you're done," I say, consciously placating her now. Maybe if I let her go on a tangent, I can steer us back to Christine.

"So, I was fourteen, and most of the girls at my school had already gotten theirs. I had to wear PE clothes while I waited in the office for the nurse to get ahold of Isla. So it could have easily been an hour." She puts her cup down and her hands back on her belly. "I guess I could have gone back to class, but I was wearing white shorts when it happened, so I was too embarrassed. Isla never answered her phone at the trailer, but somehow they were able to track her down at The Nursery."

"I'm even older than you, so I'm familiar with a time of yesteryear when no one had cell phones," I interject, smiling.

Amy sticks her tongue out into a point and continues.

"When she finally arrived, she laid on her horn in the parking lot like I was keeping her from something really important. The office lady wanted Isla to sign something, but the secretary just waved me away since everyone at school was familiar with Isla's antics at that point. The nurse had given me a pad, but Isla brought a little bag with sweatpants and a tampon that she left on the armrest sitting between us. It was probably the most thoughtful thing she ever did for me." Something almost like nostalgia shows in her eyes.

Amy pauses to look out into the darkness. "'I guess you're a woman now,' she said. And that's when I realized I wasn't a little girl anymore, and I wanted to cry. But I also remember feeling a little giddy. You know?"

The pace of Amy's storytelling has sped up and I can tell she's getting excited.

"My favorite book at the time was *Are You There God? It's Me, Margaret*. It had already helped me navigate my experience with puberty, willing God to grow me boobs while struggling to understand my friendships with other girls my age." She leans into my shoulder. "I wasn't ever really good with friendships until you."

I like hearing her say this, though she's told me before. It's reassuring. My body has settled into her words now, and I'm interested to hear where the story will go. Amy is a natural storyteller, one who captivates her audience. I'm pretty sure having the ability to do that is written into her job description as a preschool teacher.

"When she drove past our turnoff, it was evident we weren't going to the trailer. I asked her to take me home so I could shower, but she said she had an idea. And with Isla, that wasn't necessarily a good thing. So we pulled up to a bakery downtown, the best one, and she said, 'Trust me—if there was ever a time in your life you needed chocolate, it's now.'"

"The woman had a point. Chocolate sounds good right about now," I say.

Amy ignores my comment, lost in thought. "I pulled the sweatpants up over my PE shorts. When we got inside, she ordered us the most decadent chocolaty treat they had, two of them, because I distinctly remember she made a point of motioning between both our pelvises to the *guy* behind the counter like he was supposed to get that we were synced up and needed chocolate. You and Isla have embarrassing me in public down to a science."

"But I hope I'll always retain the title," I say, bowing at the waist in a seated curtsy.

"Somehow the chocolate created a pillowy gooeyness around all the uncomfortable spaces between us."

"Aww, my cold, dead heart is melting," I say.

The noise of a foghorn is muffled in the distance. I can't recall Amy ever sharing a happy memory that included Isla. It feels important that she's chosen to share this so close to when she is about to become a mother. I know I should savor the rawness of the occasion, but there's a gnawing, as if something is scratching on the walls of my mind, begging to catapult us ahead to The Restaurant's opening. I'm not sitting across from Amy. I'm someplace else.

"What Isla wrote about that day is my favorite entry from her journal. You know, the ones I always take from the trailer. She wrote, 'It was the first time I felt like a mother. If I could have bottled that feeling, I'd drink it down forever,'" Amy says, reciting the words from memory.

I feel a chill run down my spine as if she has just spoken something I could have said myself. The words resonate like a memory, but from a dream.

No longer capable of sitting, I stand, picking up our mugs for a refill. Inside the kitchen, I fill Amy's with tea but mine with wine and snag some Girl Scout Cookies out of the pantry. I return, using my butt to open the slider. I make sure my mug remains in my hands, pretending it's hot by lightly tapping at the sides, though it's not steaming like hers. I can't tell if she notices.

"Okay, your turn!" Amy calls from her seat.

I place her mug in front of her as she snags a cookie off the plate and brings it up to her nose, smelling it as she does with all things these days to see if it's going to set off her stomach, before ultimately bringing it to her lips.

"M'kay, your turn," she says again, this time with her mouth full.

"I'm not sure I want to share now. That was a sweet story, and this one is definitely not that. I guess it's more funny, like 'ha ha,' in the sense that it almost aligns my mom with Christine when it comes to the importance of appearances."

"That's fine. I shared; now you share. Judy Blume says that's what matters—to have someone who can remember with you."

"Thanks, Teacher Amy. Okay, fine." I sigh before beginning, "So, my mom and I were sitting on the couch watching *Friends*. Those thirty minutes during the week belonged exclusively to us and constituted our weekly bonding time. She would use any situations that transpired between Ross and Rachel or Monica and Chandler as a ridiculously obvious attempt to pry into my personal life. However, she'd make sure to scorn how the show promoted casual sex. I could not roll my eyes hard enough when she explained that women are not that loose in the real world. She actually used that term, *loose*."

Amy chuckles a bit. I glance over at her, and she is closing her eyes as she's inhaling the steam from the tea, which allows me to raise the mug from my lap and take a sip before returning it under the table.

"I felt a surge of wetness between my legs, the unmistakable gush of blood. As a knee-jerk reaction, I shot up, leaving behind a patch of red on our beige, freshly upholstered couch. We both swore, which made me happy, right up until Mom started in on how impossible it would be to get the stain out. She wanted me to go fetch the cleaning supplies before I even had the chance to change my freaking pants. This should tell you everything you need to know about her. I skulked away to the shower with no intention of going back to be treated like a puppy who had peed on the floor only to have my nose shoved in it."

I stop talking, lifting my "tea" to my mouth but forgetting to sip. Amy eyes me strangely, patiently waiting for me to continue, but I am too deep in my head. I'm conjuring up the equal parts empty and heavy hollowness that sits on my chest. How within the shower, I made my way onto the floor and huddled into a tight little ball.

"Mom never even came to check on me," I say, pursing my lips. "It was my first period, but she couldn't be bothered to ask how I was."

"That's awful. I'm so sorry, Leah. Thanks for sharing it with me now. It's good to say these things out loud, I think."

"Yeah," I say, though I'm not entirely convinced. I'm comfortable with these conversations only when my lips are looser with wine—it makes the pain more palatable.

I decide to take Lucas to the surfing spot we went to when we first met. It also happens to be where he asked me to marry him four months into my pregnancy with Joni. We've been back many times throughout our life together. He always finds a way to remember a little detail from that first day.

Today he says, "Was I wearing a puka-shell necklace when we first met?"

I can't help but laugh. "I distinctly remember you were *not*, because if you had been, I never would have allowed you to step foot in my van."

"That checks out. But I wore puka shells for my entire senior year of high school. Was that ever a thing in Iowa, because it was huge out here on the coast," he says. And then he adds, "Glad we're finally doin' this."

"Me too." And I am. We haven't surfed together in years.

Even though my wet suit pull strip has long since been replaced, Lucas has always been the one to zip me up. After that first time, it became a part of our surfing ritual. He traces his fingers along my neck the same way he did back then.

"I always forget you have this," he says. His thumb lingers over the ink and sweeps across, back and forth.

When I got the tattoo during college, I was thrilled by its permanence. I loved that something could become a part of me that wasn't there before. The solitary wave was meant to symbolize independence, and now I can't help but blush at my childish disillusionment.

It wasn't until after I had already done the deed and looked back in the mirror to witness the indelible label of my artistic expression that I began to panic. Blotchy red hives covered the area around my neck as I struggled to catch my breath. I'd done something I couldn't escape from. The next time I felt the sensation, I was thirty-nine weeks pregnant with Joni and we were forced to watch a birthing video in Lamaze class. I tried to explain it to Lucas, but he insisted it was only nerves. *"Of course you're scared! That looked terrifying. But you are a total and complete badass. You can do this!"* It's undoubtedly how I'd feel if I ever returned to Iowa, being hopelessly landlocked and too far away from the ocean.

Lucas could never understand the sensation of being trapped inside yourself—of being a prisoner within your own body.

We stand together, looking out at the waves, with his hand still resting on my shoulders. The beach is nearly empty, with only a few people speckled along the shore. I brought Lucas here to open a conversation, hoping the echo of our emotions can revive what once was. I want surfing to cover everything we are thinking but can't say to each other.

I glance at a line of seagulls huddled together. We start to walk over and they all scatter, except for one that lingers back—either unsure what to do next or unwilling to follow the group.

We are rusty out on the water and it shows. Both of us wipe out several times before finding our groove. We give each other space to ride. At one point, we ride a wave together. His expression is that of someone entirely unencumbered. How I wish I could join him inside the freedom of just being content.

I'm so caught up in it all now, a visceral self-consciousness. I know a clock has been set, and it's counting down, but to what? My fight with Lucas . . . there are pieces of his words I can't unhear. His vitriol at The Restaurant when I brought Dottie.

Christine's acknowledgment of my memory going black. Her persistence, picking at the scab that my secrets reside under. Every so often, something will allow a flicker of doubt to ignite. I stare too hard into Joni's eyes, knowing but never accepting that they are missing Lucas's flecks of yellow. But they are no more similar to Miles's eyes either.

"Hey, you, over there." I feel the splash of salt water graze my cheek and upper lip. I open my eyes, and Lucas is waving his arms overhead.

"You totally missed that one! Where'd you go just now?" He has to shout a little as we have drifted pretty far apart.

"I was thinking about the time I went surfing while pregnant with Joni and how proud you were of me. I think your confidence in me has always been contagious," I manage to lie.

"And then I proposed," he says, grinning widely.

"And then you proposed," I repeat.

Out of nowhere, a seal pops up in the water between our boards. Its large black eyes blink back to emphasize all the darkness between us. Lucas tries to reach out his hand to touch the creature, but it dives back under the water and disappears out of sight.

Lying flat, I'm lulled into quiet while my mind refuses to stop moving. One thought stacks on another until my brain feels like a tower of Jenga blocks with only a single piece carrying the entire load. How easily everything could be pulled out from under me—how fragile the structure I've allowed to support the weight of all my worry.

Lucas paddles closer to me. We cock our heads to the side, both resting on our decks, and face each other. Rising and falling as we bob along, intentionally ignoring the swells. He reaches out and takes my hand. I let him, hoping that alone could be enough.

A wave pushes us too far apart to hang on, and I turn my neck to rest on the other cheek, knowing he could draw the truth out of me if we stayed connected for even another second. I wait a full minute until I am sure my face won't give me away.

I want to tell him that after he proposed, I allowed the ocean to help me decide how to answer—knowing there are only two ways that waves can come together. One way is when the waves meet in opposition and their momentum is halted; water blends with water and then retreats into the greater ocean. The other is when two waves meet at the exact right moment, the waters bind together in one spectacular crash, and unified, they progress farther up the shore.

Lucas had dutifully announced, *"I want to marry you, Leah."* Almost as if his proposal was a business model for our future. It was alluring. His pitch helped me shelve any dwindling doubts that Lucas should be made aware of Miles. His unyielding assurance squashed any lingering whispers of fear.

When a wave met its match, and suddenly the water was upon us, I thought, *Maybe two people can make each other stronger.* Neither of us stood; we just let the shallow bath of the water overtake us.

But now, when I go to explain all this to Lucas, he is already gone. He's up, fully standing, skimming along the top of the wake. The ocean swallows my words, and so I can discreetly murmur, "Help. I think I need help." The last part is barely audible, even to me.

We sit on the shore afterward and speak briefly about the kids. At school, Joni has tested into the "accelerated" program, which I guess is the PC term for "gifted" these days. We need better babyproofing for Dottie, which we are realizing too late after her latest spill into the coffee table. It has been too long since we've had a toddler; we forgot that we need to transform our home into one giant padded cell.

"I know you're in something. Which means *we* are in something," he says. He's dancing around whatever it is he wants to say.

I respond quickly so he won't elaborate. "I need you to trust that I'll figure it out." I dig my fingers deep into the sand until it pushes up into the base of my fingernails. I don't stop. "Enough about it now, please. Let's just sit here for a bit." He will let it go because he has always given me the benefit of the doubt, even when I haven't deserved it.

I want to let him in, to unfurl my body, exposing whatever it is I am hiding on the inside. But then I'd have to start at the very beginning with nothing but honesty. Get him to understand that I'm jealous of how he can use his creativity and fatherhood to propel his dreams forward while mine remain stagnant. How can I be envious of someone I am sharing a life with? How can I explain that, now permanently strapped into the ride of motherhood, I'm not sure it was ever the right decision for me in the first place?

I trace designs in the sand, twirls and lines. My fingers find the grooves, the sensation of finger painting. Without realizing it, I've drawn a line between us. A literal line in the sand. A divide that has been there since I made the decision to make Joni his, no matter what.

I drop off Lucas at The Restaurant, and somehow I find myself back at the Tree Tunnel. Lucas alone should have scratched whatever itch needed scratching, but here I am. I'm not up for running. Surfing has worn me out, and the thick layer of exhaustion makes me want to curl up in a blanket in the back of my minivan and wait for the sun to go down the way I used to when I drove Big Bertha.

I exit the car and start walking along the path. I can see Miles out ahead of me, working directly beneath the giant arch of the cypress trees, holding a shovel and tubing. He appears to be pulling on a sprinkler line that's protruding out of the ground. I should turn around and drive home to my family, but I know before I even approach that I'll walk over to him and examine the color of his eyes. I know it the same way I knew when I left Amy on the deck to get dessert that I wouldn't be pouring tea into my mug.

He doesn't stop working until I'm close enough that he has to crane his neck to peer up at me. I like that he must observe me from this angle. He's crouched down with a finger in the dirt; his hands are muddied, and his gloves are tucked into his mouth. The gravity of his smile forces them to fall to his feet.

"In this light, with the sunset behind you, you could be a painting. Ever paint yourself?" Miles asks in a way that's so charming I need to sit beside him rather than try to steady myself standing.

"And how do you know I'm a painter?" He must have read up on me or seen my studio.

He wipes the remainder of the wet dirt onto his pants, leaving streaks behind, before leaning over and tapping me on the nose. I wonder if he's marked me with mud. I swipe his hand away, laughing a little, recognizing it's my first genuine laugh of the day. The depth of the darkness of his irises begins to pull me in.

"It's amazing what you can discover about people on social media."

"Which is why I prefer landscapes. Human beings are far too unpredictable."

"You look good. Fresh out of a surf?" His eyes speak to me in a way that's all too familiar. His gaze washes through me, recalibrating me into a state of equilibrium. I say nothing but don't look away. Our knees are touching, though we are capable of spacing ourselves farther apart. Instead, we sit connected on the forest floor, nothing but little specks compared to the enormity of the cypress trees.

He goes to push my nose again as if it were a detonation device that could blow up my entire world. If my mind were any cloudier, I would lean into him, effectively breaking every marital rule, and that thought scares me enough to want to run back down the path. Instead, I pull his hand down and squeeze his fingers between mine. It somehow feels safer than anything else that could happen between us.

"I saw a picture of you on Instagram. You married an O'Connor?" It's a small town—they would have gone to the same high school. He'd have been the same year as Paul. "You know, your mother-in-law keeps driving by here," he says, though he's looking away from the road and out at the water. "That family is crazier than a box of snakes."

"She does?" Dread ripples through me. Immediately I release his fingers and look out toward the parking lot.

"Yeah, it's starting to creep me out a little. Why do you all keep showing up here after all this time? Not that I ever mind seeing you." Miles raises a single eyebrow.

"I can't speak for Christine, but this has always been my favorite spot to run and paint. For all I know you're the one

chasing me around," I say, still entirely unnerved by what
Miles has said about Christine. "Your office window happens
to have the best view for miles."

"I know it's been forever, but are you looking to start something?" The word *something* trickles down my spine like ice
along my vertebrae. As if it is meant to be an invitation. "I
almost called you, but your mother-in-law strikes me as the
type of woman who keeps a gun in her glove box. I mean, we
used to have a lot of fun together, didn't we?" he asks. His
arrogance is suddenly unsettling.

Did he relocate to this state beach to find me?

"Yeah, we did, but no, I'm not." Even though I answer
quickly, the idea of doing anything outside of the bubble of
the O'Connors does sound appealing. I think of reminding
him that we are both married, even tapping our ring fingers
together hard enough to send shock waves through us.

He doesn't inquire further. Men never do once their single
question has been addressed. Women want to know every detail down to the minute. He has his answer, but I'm still looking
for mine.

CHAPTER 15

Amy asked me to go with her to meet Isla at Poplar Beach. "She never asks to meet me. There is always something behind it," Amy says as we make our way there in the car. "I can't shake this sick feeling I used to get all the time when I was a kid."

"I got you, girl," I say, curious whether the spontaneous rendezvous has anything to do with the secret Isla hinted at last time we were at her trailer.

It's much too windy to be at the beach. I can tell Amy's already agitated just by the way she aggressively hauls two beach chairs out of the trunk. I remove them from her hands, tucking each under one arm. Amy carries two blankets, not necessarily for warmth but to keep the sand from whipping at any exposed skin. When we arrive, we see Isla sitting on a petrified log. Her body is buried beneath a thick blanket. Her face looks rounder and fuller somehow compared to when we last saw her.

"Well, look at you two," she says like we are all old friends. Neither of us says anything back.

She doesn't make room next to her—not that we could all sit

together that close anyway. I prop open the chairs, and when Amy and I sit down the legs quickly sink into the sand. The outside of my blanket already feels damp.

"When you were little, we'd stop here on the drive back from flower deliveries." Isla's popping a seaweed chain, squeezing the little bubbles until they are emptied of water. "Do you remember that?" She stops, turning her head to look over at Amy.

"I remember this is where you tried to teach me to ride a boogie board," Amy says, staring out like she's trying to conjure up the image. "We were fewer than twenty feet out, both on our boards. You found the ride every time, and I just bobbed around in the water, watching. You never showed me what to do; you just rode the waves until you were done. So *teach* is the wrong word."

Isla has already moved on. "I always liked the name of this beach. I had a girlfriend in high school named Poplar. Her parents were such hippies they named her after a tree." She snorts a little and squeezes the blanket tighter around her body. "My first and only girlfriend," she says, grinning. "That really pissed off my dad. Maybe that's what I should do. Go back to dating women."

I look down at my bare toes. They aren't polished, and the nails are a gross yellowish color. The last time I got a pedicure was that time I went with Amy and had mimosas.

A kite dives down out of the sky and lands a foot from where Isla is sitting. She goes to stand to retrieve it before she stops and bundles back up in the blanket. She returns to the log and ignores the kite like she doesn't see it.

"Are you seriously gonna make the pregnant woman get that?" Amy asks, frustrated by her mom's inaction.

"The exercise is good for you," Isla says. Her smile borders on snide. After only a half dozen interactions, I can see how living with someone like Isla would be impossible, never mind having her as your mother.

There was a final straw, the thing that made Amy decide she just couldn't do it anymore. She refers to it as the "drowning incident," and she told me the story once to explain why removing Isla from her life had been a necessary evil. It was harrowing enough for me to recall every detail. A chilling reminder that Isla's behavior, while often cruel and unusual, also bordered on abusive. I hate imagining Amy enduring that kind of suffering.

Amy finished out the end of high school and all of college by living with her mom's coworker Rita and Sergio, Rita's husband. It was easier on everybody. She earned a degree from the College of San Mateo and got her credentials to teach preschool. Then, on the day of her college graduation, Rita threw her a huge celebratory lunch with some friends. Isla, of course, being the deadbeat that she was, didn't show. At the time, Amy had a loser boyfriend named Brett and he, too, was a Pacifica townie, the kind that kept naked girl posters on the walls of his garage where he and his friends worked on cars and drank beer. A real winner. They decided to go out to the bars after the party, and while they were there Amy recognized her mom by her limbs, halfway to passed out on the floor in one of the bathroom stalls.

Somehow Amy got Isla out and called her a ride. But before they could get her in the car, Isla took off running down to the beach. Since Brett was a dick, he got pissed and left, and Amy ended up chasing her mom all the way down the street. One of the main parts of the story that shattered my heart into a million pieces was that along the road, Amy noticed a mom with a little girl in a yellow-and-white daisy-print swimsuit with a double French braid. The girl held a yellow pail and shovel in one hand and her mom's hand in the other as they walked down to the shore together. This was never Amy and Isla, and I tried to remind Amy that this is never really anyone. No family exists as a Norman Rockwell painting, but I get where she was coming from.

By the time Amy made it down to the beach, Isla was already wading out into the waves. Amy had to go in after her in her new graduation dress that Rita had bought for her. At first, she thought her mom was just going to splash around as she had may times throughout Amy's childhood, but when a wave overtook Isla, she went under. "She went under, and I waited." Amy whispered this part of the story to me, cupping both hands around her mouth and looking around so that I was the only person who could possibly hear the truth. "I remember I did, because I said to myself, 'Wait.' Maybe if I hadn't waited, CPR on the beach wouldn't have been necessary. Maybe she wasn't trying to die," Amy said, choking back tears.

While performing CPR, she heard a crack under all her weight, but I guess that's common with chest compressions. It's horrifying that something so violent is necessary to save someone's life. Someone offered to take over but Amy wouldn't stop. Amy is relentless in her efforts when she loves something. She kept going and going. Finally, during one of her rescue breaths, Isla coughed up salt water directly into Amy's mouth.

Amy collapsed next to Isla as they traded off coughing and gagging. She searched Isla's face for gratitude or acknowledgment, but it was blank. I'm not sure how she didn't slap her stupid like I would have.

She simply asked, "Haven't you had enough yet?" But in asking, Amy only heard her words reflected back. Hadn't *she* had enough?

She heaved herself up, her body shaking from the shock of it all. But in her head she was already plotting how to escape her old life and come here. Escape Isla, that version of herself.

Amy took my hand when she told me this last part, making her fists small so both of mine could cocoon hers, and said, "Isla didn't drown that day on the beach, and it was no longer a question of *if* something else would happen, but *when*. She would always need saving. I just knew I no longer wanted to be the one to do it."

I couldn't help but wonder, after Amy finished speaking, if the more humane thing would have been just to let Isla drown.

The owner of the kite has retrieved it, apologizing for the disruption.

"Remember the time I rescued you?" Amy asks, as if reading my mind. We both regard Isla's expression, trying to register anything on her face—anything resembling humiliation or regret. For good measure, Amy adds, "The time you drowned?"

"I couldn't have drowned. I'm sittin' right here, aren't I?" Isla is attempting humor, maybe, but knowing Amy, she won't tolerate it.

"So why did you want to see me?" Amy finally asks, ready to speed things along. The wind makes it hard for me to stop shivering.

"I just wanted to talk to you. Look at you," Isla says. "I

guess we haven't talked about your family." She uses her chin to point toward Amy's pregnant belly.

"What about my family?" Amy's tone twinges with anger.

"Do you want more kids after this?"

"Do I want more kids after this?" Amy repeats the question. "Where is this coming from? You have never taken any interest in this before. Really, in me before. What do you need?"

Isla puts her hands up as if to say, *Hold up.* Her dark hair whips around in the wind; she doesn't try to tame it as her arms hold her blanket closed. She catches me staring and offers a hopeful look, like maybe I could jump ship and join her side. I do pity her. I don't know what I would do if I ever lost Amy. Our closeness is something stronger than a familial obligation—in the way our children choose us, we were chosen for each other.

"Hey, the guys are opening a restaurant. I bet we could set up a large order with The Nursery and, if it works out, maybe make it a regular delivery." It is as much of a peace offering as I'll attempt to negotiate between them at this point.

"That's nice, thank you." Isla smiles but she doesn't inquire about The Restaurant, which strikes me as odd since, only moments ago, she was curious about Amy's life and The Restaurant will be an enormous part of it soon.

But Isla's gratitude momentarily appeases Amy, who relaxes her hands on her belly. "I still don't trust that we are having a baby."

"Mm-hmm." Isla nods reassuringly. "There'll be a baby." A sadness creeps into her eyes that is difficult to decipher, probably because she won't be invited to participate as a grandmother.

Amy gets to her feet.

"Come on. It's too windy to be out here," Amy says, motioning with her hand for Isla to get up. "We'll walk you back to your car."

It appears Isla wants to stand for a moment; the blanket loosens around her shoulders. But then she sinks farther down, shaking her head. "No, I want to stay here until the sun goes down."

Amy waves and shakes her head. We make it about twenty paces toward the cars before she says, "Typical Isla—just when I think she could meet me in the middle, she can't even be bothered to take a step."

"So Isla is a lesbian now, I guess?" Amy says once we've made it back to the car.

"Hey, so is Joni!"

"Huh?" she asks, unsure what I mean since I have yet to catch her up with the latest developments.

"Never mind. I'll explain later. Hey, do you like your therapist?"

"Yes, I love her. Why? Want to finally try therapy?"

I shake my head. I was thinking for Joni. "What could *I* gain from therapy? I have a family, a career; I have you. Isn't that all there is?"

"I dunno, you tell me. I mean it. You have three kids, your own studio. Lucas worships the ground you walk on. I'm counting on you to assure me that the 'mom life' is all I need it to be. That from here on out, everything that's thrown at me will be better than before. After just bearing witness to more of Isla's lunacy, it's gotta be, right?" Amy's shoulders are sloping down with her belly tucked almost under the steering wheel.

"Yes, it will. You get to decide what's next with Isla. She's probably just eager to meet her granddaughter. You've built such a good life with Paul and look how far you've come!" I say, attempting to sound reassuring. It's odd to be the one to nurture Amy, given her fierce independence. Despite my being older, she's often so much wiser.

She pauses thoughtfully. "I'm lucky to have gotten off the ride I was on with Isla. Breaking free from the cycle, I guess. At least that's what my shrink says. But seeing her like that still makes me feel like she's an undertow, trying to suck me back in. I need to stop answering her calls for a while. It's the best thing for me and the baby right now."

"You're an old soul—you know that?" I say, nodding in agreement with her decision.

"Mmm. Rita used to say that. But, I mean, kids tend to grow up quickly when the alternative is potentially going into the foster-care system. Hey, speaking of that, I think Paul and I will eventually adopt. I told him that's something I want to do in the future."

"Please, please, can I be there when you tell Christine you're adopting?" I laugh.

"You're an asshole, you know that?" she responds, but she is chuckling. "We don't know for sure that Christine would be against it."

"Oh, right. I'm sure she'd love to welcome your Rwandan orphan into her cookie-cutter family. She gets so uncomfortable when Lidy even mentions her ancestors who died in the Holocaust. It's not pretty and perfect. Heaven forbid! You know how I came into this family practically gave her an aneurysm. If she could have it her way, all mothers would be dedicated housewives and baby factories."

"She's not *that* bad. You give her such a hard time," she says. "When the baby comes, I'm going to need you to try harder for me with her. I can't serve as your buffer while raising a newborn."

"I only dish out what she serves me. I'm sure Christine would move in to help if you asked her—"

"See, that right there. No more of that. Maybe I would ask her to move in. I mean, of course I wouldn't, but if I did, it'd be because I have no idea what the heck I'm doing."

"I can help you."

"Can you? Because lately I'm not so sure."

Immediately, my defenses spring to attention. Why is she taking her frustrations over Isla out on me? I want to tell her she has no idea how much a woman can lose herself inside of motherhood. How at first it all sounds so gloriously appealing, reshaping your identity to include "giver of life." But then instead of being a whole person, you're chopped into a million little pieces, and all that's yours at the end of the night are whatever leftovers you can muddle together.

"I want only good things for you as a mom. I guess, for me, as I am right now . . . I'm nowhere to be found." I let out a deep, breathy sigh. "There is so much more to life than just being someone's mother." Amy hasn't learned these lessons yet, but she will soon enough. How do I even begin to explain that the time Amy pulled her mother from the water, Isla wasn't trying to die so much as escape herself by any means necessary?

Lucas is driving and I can tell he's distracted. His top teeth are hanging over his bottom lip, biting down so forcefully,

I wonder if he'll bleed. Once he's able to sit down with Paul, he'll find his way back to center. Apparently Lucas has something he can't wait until the opening to show me. Paul and Amy are meeting us at The Restaurant.

I've driven by The Restaurant hundreds of times. The property itself is stunning—located on a hill, so there is a generous view of the ocean. Nothing will ever be built in front to block the view—Lucas made sure of that by purchasing the land there as well. This is how his brain works. He could see all parts of the puzzle before the first nail was even hammered. I wonder, with all his foresight, how he could have been so completely wrong about me.

The muted numbness I've come to count on is working against me now. I know I need to be excited by whatever it is Lucas wants to show me. Plus, getting the opportunity to see what the boys have created before it's brimming over with people should make me proud, but my combined feelings of lifelessness and jealousy are not allowing me to feign enthusiasm. Hopefully Paul and Lucas want to toast their accomplishment so we can at least walk around with champagne.

As we step inside, I can sense his eyes on me. The Restaurant is elegant without being pretentious. The precise version of "nice" we discussed all those years ago around the table at the distillery. I squeeze Lucas's hand.

"It's perfect. Honestly." I lean over and kiss him. When I pull away, Amy and Paul are standing in front of us.

"Isn't it great?" Paul asks but doesn't wait for a response. "Come, come, let's walk around." He has Amy's arm wrapped in his, practically pulling her along in his excitement.

A long hallway leads us down to the restrooms. The corridor is wide and spacious. Amy lets out a little gasp, drawing a hand up to her mouth. Lucas has displayed my art. Each piece illuminated and positioned as if it were nailed to a gallery wall.

"I know you'll maybe want to order them differently, but I wanted to surprise you," he says as he turns his body so he can read my face.

The gesture is sincere, and I want to be moved more than I am. I bite the inside of my cheek until there's a metallic taste I can focus on.

"Thank you." I smile and again press my lips to his so he won't be able to decipher any coolness in my expression.

The guys slip away into the office, leaving Amy and me standing in the hallway.

"What?" she says as she reaches out to touch the frame of one of my larger pieces.

"The last time I remember seeing Lucas this giddy was when we found out Reid was a boy. I never pictured myself being jealous of my husband's passions coming to fruition. But I am."

Exhaling, she answers, "I get that."

"This is very thoughtful," I say, gesturing toward the wall. "I'm coming across as an ungrateful nitwit."

Nodding, she says, "You are, but while the boys are experiencing their dream in real time, right now, your dream of taking your art someplace bigger is still unfolding. Stalled, with all that needs to happen with three kids."

"Yes!" I am so relieved I could sob into her shoulder. "It's not a competition. Lucas and I are supposed to be a team, but even this makes me feel like the opening act to the headlining performer. A placeholder until the real talent appears onstage."

The guys decide to stick around and work out some logistics, so Amy offers to drive me home. As we walk out to the parking lot, she stops before we get to the car. The roundness of her belly consumes most of her torso at this point. Being a tall pregnant woman always worked for my body. Amy's shortness creates the illusion that she's one strong gust of wind away from being knocked flat on her face.

"Can we take a walk on the beach?" she asks, the car keys jingling in her hand.

"Yeah, that works." I was looking forward to going home to another glass of wine—but Amy looks like she has something on her mind.

In the car, I need to squeeze my fingers together to make a fist. My hand is twitching and tremors are radiating around my wrist. Amy glances over at me, her gaze gliding down the length of my body. I really don't want to go to the beach right now. We drive the few minutes to the turnoff as Amy marvels over The Restaurant.

We park at Dunes Beach, finding the least intimidating-looking entrance, though all of them are fairly steep. I remove my hands from my pockets to take Amy's, guiding her steps so she doesn't topple forward. It isn't particularly chilly, but the air is filled with the smell of rotting fish and it's making my stomach queasy.

We leave our shoes next to the cliffs as we make our way down to where the water meets our toes. Once we've stopped moving, I notice a single coffee mug abandoned next to a pet-rified log. It's distinctive in size and shape. Stouter than any-thing I've seen before, with a whale tail for a handle. I glance back at the row of houses behind us. With a deep exhale, I en-vision the unencumbered freedom the owner of this cup must have—stepping outside, sipping fresh coffee in solitude, mere steps away from their beachfront home. All I can think is someone has stolen my life. A stranger is living the way I did before we had Joni. Envy returns, and I become a boat tethered to the shore, rocking helplessly inside the tide, longing to sail.

"I need to say this to you." Amy's eyes are wide despite the glare of the sun. "I am worried about you. Officially."

"What? Why?" I'm hoping she will say something simple and straightforward. Something nondescriptive, like that I've seemed tired lately.

"You are not you. It's the way you've been drinking—it's making you depressed and I'm afraid. I'm afraid for you." Amy articulates each word like she has practiced saying them aloud. Or more likely, has already said them before.

All the blood rushes to my ears and my face starts to burn. The idea that I could be watched so intensely feels intrusive. It's offensive. I'm shaking my head back and forth, though I never signaled my brain to do so.

"It's fine. I know it's been a lot, but there is just so much going on lately," I say, wanting to explain quickly so we can move on. I need her to see that none of this is my fault. I continue, speaking even faster now, rushing to get the words out. "Christine is trying to come between Lucas and me. I know she's plotting something." I stop to see if she will accept that answer—but now she, too, is shaking her head, her hands resting within the space between her breasts and stomach. I continue, "I'm so worried about you and the baby—"

Amy puts up her hand, looks down, and sighs. "Stop. I love you, but stop." I can see that she's starting to come apart. Tears are forming in her eyes now.

I know I have gone too far. "No, I didn't mean it like that." I try honesty to see how it feels coming out of my mouth. "I don't feel anything anymore. I don't," I say, shrugging my shoulders as if this is just a casual observation.

"You are numbing it the fuck out, Leah," she says. I can't detect even a twinge of kindness in her voice. It's unusual for Amy to swear like this, let alone use the f-word.

"That's where you are wrong. It's the only time I *do* feel anything," I say, shuffling my feet in the sand. How could she suggest taking away the one thing I need to fill the unfillable holes? The putty I can swipe across the surface of motherhood to briefly stop my feelings of complete inadequacy. Now Amy has named it—called it out of me. It feels like someone is attempting to kidnap my children.

"I have done this already. I cannot do it with you," she says, still sniffling, wiping at her cheeks. "You need to get help. Please, get help."

"I'm sorry," I say, though I don't know what I mean by that. Seems I am always apologizing lately.

We continue down the shore, not speaking. The water's edge has inched up the shoreline. There is almost no beach left, just water creeping closer.

I know I'm running out of time.

CHAPTER 16

I get my hair done in Pacifica during the brief window when all three kids are in school. Since I'm already here, I decide to pop into Isla and Rita's floral shop regarding the order for The Restaurant. I checked with Paul and Lucas, and they were thrilled to have something taken off their plate for the opening.

The little bell on the door rings as I enter. I walk in with a foreign sense of purpose and head straight for the hydrangeas. The store is well kept and decorated to be quaint, with antique wheelbarrows overflowing with color. Amy said that once Rita and Sergio took on the lion's share of the work after becoming Isla's business partners, the store was really able to flourish. Rita became a life source for The Nursery just as she has been one for Amy. The thing that allowed both to survive despite Isla's destruction.

I notice Isla busying herself behind the register, trimming huge stems off giant sunflowers. I immediately think of Amy and her affinity for them since they were her wedding flowers. Rita is stationed toward the back, and she waves over to me, tucking her pruning shears inside her apron.

"Leah! What a surprise. Where's Amy?" she asks. Rita is a

small, round Hispanic woman. She has a grandmotherly face that tells a story through its creases and folds. I envy her ability to embrace aging rather than constantly fight against it.

"Just me today, I'm afraid. I was in town running errands, and I'm not sure if Isla told you, but we want to do a large order for the family restaurant here coming up."

Rita glances over in the direction of Isla, who must have disappeared into the office, because she's no longer at the register.

"I can help you with that." Rita pulls at the gold chain around her neck with a small cross.

"I'm thinking those hydrangeas in various sizes," I say, pointing toward the front of the store where I came in. "The blues and whites. Can I get three hundred delivered to Half Moon Bay?" I look at my watch for the date. There's still enough time. "We will need them for next Saturday."

"Yes, not a problem."

"Where did Isla disappear to? I wanted to say hello." I try to poke my head around the corner, but an enormous fiddle-leaf fig plant is blocking my view.

Rita glances nervously toward the office.

"What? What's going on?"

Again, she tugs at the cross on her neck. "Do you want some sunflowers for Amy?" Rita asks, seeming to purposefully avoid my question.

As if she was listening and awaiting her cue, Isla emerges from the back with an armful of sunflowers. When she places them down in front of me and stands back, it's impossible to ignore her protruding belly, rivaling Amy's in size.

I bring both hands to cover my mouth. A torrent of terror slides through me as if my insides were made of rushing water. "*This* is your big secret?"

"Ta-da," Isla says, rubbing the orb like she's just completed a requested magic trick. I look to Rita for any indication that I'm not completely losing my mind. That Amy's mother is extremely pregnant, I would say days from delivery, if not overdue. Having carried three, I consider myself an expert. And Amy has absolutely no idea. Rita can only nod in confirmation.

"Wh-why would you keep the fact that you're pregnant from Amy?" I manage to stutter. "Don't you think she has the right to know she's going to have a sibling?"

"Who says I'm keeping it?" Isla's eyes have become narrow and small.

"Uhh . . . even still, Amy should know." Again, I look to Rita for help talking some sense into Isla.

"So, then, you tell her." Isla continues to sort and arrange the stems for cutting, as if our conversation is keeping her from her busy workday.

"Why the hell are you putting this on me?" I can feel beads of sweat beginning to pool around my upper lip. I never used to get this flushed so quickly.

"You know her now better than I do—better than I ever did." Isla shrugs. Again, her demeanor is bordering on cavalier.

I have to remind myself that it would be wrong to slap a pregnant woman.

"What would I tell her exactly? That her mom is a selfish, pregnant asshole? Because that's all I know about what's happening so far," I say through gritted teeth.

"That about covers it."

"I'm serious, Isla."

She begins clipping with the shears she just pulled out of Rita's apron. Her hair has fallen around her face, and from this angle, I could swear I'm looking at Amy.

"I was never meant to be somebody's mother," Isla whispers almost under her breath. It's the first time in our interaction that she looks her version of upset.

"Except that you are and are about to be again!"

Already the sensation of doom has begun to seep in, covering all my surfaces until I'm hovering just above my body—picturing the look of devastation on Amy's face when the truth about what Isla's been hiding is inevitably revealed. I need to leave the store. I cannot bear to be complicit with Isla's duplicity for another minute.

I rush out toward my car, almost breaking into a jog.

"Leah!" I hear someone calling my name from the back entrance. I'm terrified to look up for fear it's Isla following me out to the parking lot, but the sweetness in the voice doesn't fit. I turn back to see Rita.

"I'm sorry." Rita's face is a stark contrast to Isla's; the deep folds make her appear even more remorseful about what just transpired in The Nursery.

"How could you not tell Amy?" I say, shaking my head.

"It felt like something that wasn't mine to share." Rita has her hands stuffed inside the pockets of her apron. "But I do think Isla is right about one thing: it should come from you." My head starts to spin. I climb into my car, wanting to effectively end our conversation. "She can navigate this truth with you the way she has everything else. Your friendship is the gift that Amy deserves." Her words feel heavy, like they are saddlebags she's removing from her load only to add to my own. I wonder if Rita would be saying this if she knew how badly I failed Amy when she miscarried. That I should never be in a position of authority when it comes to another person's forks in the road.

On the drive back, I recall the one and only time I was selected for jury duty. It was a criminal case in which the defendant was claiming to have performed a "physician-assisted suicide" for her wife who was already dying of cancer. She was no longer a practicing medical doctor nor in a state that even recognized this action legally. But she maintained her innocence, that her wife was the love of her life, and anyone would do whatever it takes to end the suffering of those they love most. So she had given her wife a lethal dose of morphine, killing her. Unfortunately, everyone in the jury pool I was in got dismissed when the defendant opted to change her plea. But I followed along with the trial as it became highly publicized in our area for the number of moral and ethical questions it brought up.

I've often thought about which way I ultimately would have been swayed. Where is the acceptable boundary of crossing over into someone's life to carry out their wishes because they aren't capable of literally and metaphorically pulling the trigger? Like how Amy had to make the decision when she pulled Isla from the water.

Those are the rock-and-a-hard-place kind of choices no person ever wants to make, but we women constantly find ourselves in the middle of them. The defendant had ended her testimony by saying, "Life comes down to a series of little loyalty tests that ultimately prepare us for the big ones."

Needing to seek immediate relief, I decide to stop in Moss Beach at the Tree Tunnel. I will already be passing through on the drive home. It's essentially on the way. I have to circle around a few times until I spot Miles just outside the ranger station directing another car. The expansive reach of his arm

overtakes my view of the coastline. He catches my gaze inquis-
itively as he speaks to a couple inside an SUV with two small
dogs poking their heads out the window.

"Hello?" He waves at me, so I pull up behind their car. After
petting both dogs, he taps on their roof, then makes his way
over to me. I stay seated without switching the car into Park.

When he approaches my open window, I'm practically shouting, "Want to go somewhere with me right now?" By saying it, I
recognize I'm no longer playing with fire but officially putting
my hand on the flame.

Miles snorts, which then turns into a chuckle, like I've
said something funny. His lips are cracked and dry from over-
exposure to the elements. He finally answers, "Now?" He reaches
out and his fingers tuck beneath the groove of my chin, as if he is
eager to consume my mouth.

"Yes, now, before I change my mind."

His face contorts in such a way that, for a moment, I'm no
longer seeing him hanging over my car—I'm witnessing Joni
deep in thought. Her big, brown, inquisitive eyes, down to the
scrunch of her nose, wiggled slightly to the left.

"No," I answer for him, pulling away from his look of puzzle-
ment that is so hauntingly familiar.

CHAPTER 17

I've been squirreling away cash over the past several weeks in anticipation of what I'm about to do—really, what Christine's malevolence has forced my hand to finally do. I located a paternity testing facility just over the hill that guarantees accuracy, anonymity, and speedy results. The whole process helped to alleviate some of my guilty conscience, since there evidently is an entire business model built around the idea that I'm not the only mother who lives inside the terrors of uncertainty.

The process by which I acquired Joni's and Lucas's DNA—by stealing everyone's toothbrushes—struck me as almost a form of retaliation for the domesticated servant I've been reduced to. Of course I'd be the one to replace the family toothbrushes that have gone dull with use. A task so tedious it could bore me to tears.

I've decided to go in person to pick up the results, which works in my favor. I will plan an overnight out of town before the opening. A night away will allow me the ability to drink myself into oblivion so I can't overanalyze all the ways in which things are falling apart: Discovering the truth about Joni.

Continuing to witness Amy moving farther from me. Trying to uncover the identity of Grace. Deciding how to tell Amy about Isla's pregnancy without losing her to Christine completely. All these moves are like pieces on a chessboard that has always been laid out between me and my mother-in-law.

Tonight at home I'm terrified Lucas will be able to smell every layer of deceit on my skin. While technically nothing happened with Miles, I'm fully aware of the implications of my actions and what I said—which I offered only because I'm suddenly carrying yet another entirely new secret that shouldn't belong to me in the first place. On top of the now impending results of a question I never wanted to be answered.

I'm doodling at the table, consciously not pouring myself wine for fear my lips will loosen to the point of exposing too much. Dottie and I are at the kitchen table while Lucas is at the kitchen island attempting a three-hundred-piece puzzle with the older two. Papers are stacked next to him, so for every few pieces he finds, he looks over and jots down a note or two about The Restaurant. It's the closest we have come to quality time all together in a very long time, so I keep my mouth shut.

"I got it!" Reid shouts, smiling wide to expose a fresh hole along his upper gumline. He pats down a fresh piece so it's flush with the others they have already figured out.

"Bud? When did you lose that one?" I ask. Normally he makes a whole big thing about the tooth fairy and how much more money his friends get when they lose teeth.

He tilts his head at me, appearing puzzled.

"You were there. You helped me pull it out in the bathroom last night."

Lucas looks up from his paper stack.

I try to course-correct as quickly as possible. "No, that bottom spot. Isn't that new?"

Reid uses his tongue to find the hole, which is almost halfway filled with a replacement grown-up tooth.

"Mom, that's silly. I lost this one so long ago," Reid says, appeased and ready to move on.

I refuse to make eye contact with Lucas. I am not interested in reading anything on his face.

I glance at Dottie's painting and see she's done her version of a circle.

"A circle, Dot! You did it!" How long has she been drawing her shapes? We practically threw a parade when Joni scribbled out her first square.

I'm missing it, I think. *I'm missing it all.*

Amy is the only one who knows the secret I've been hiding for more than a decade. For some reason, I decided to go all out for Dottie's first birthday. I was hoping her party would be the thing that initiated my complete metamorphosis into a Stepford wife. I thought if I ordered the special cake with Dottie's face on it and hosted the family, I could prove something to the O'Connors. I could belong with them if I wanted to—if I chose to, on my terms. I could compete with Christine for Mother of the Year and prove that it was possible to have it all: the ultimate work-life balance.

The party started at noon, which was my first mistake since that was Dottie's nap time. I started drinking champagne at breakfast to make the preparations less stressful. I even made a dozen little goody bags with candy and Elmo stickers for the kids.

Halfway through the party, Amy found me hiding in the pantry.

"And here I thought I was the only one who sought comfort in confined spaces," she said, whispering so as not to reveal my location to any of the other guests. She closed the door behind her, tossing me a goody bag before sitting down and opening one for herself. Her hair was done in those big loose curls that make her look like a Disney princess. "I don't want to be a buzzkill, but Dots are a major choking hazard for one-year-olds. Really for everyone." She laughed a little and pinched the bell-shaped candy between two fingers.

"Come on! Little Dot's nickname? The one *you* came up with. How cute is that?" I asked defensively. I thought it was very clever.

"Cute in theory, yes," Amy said as she popped a yellow one in her mouth. Her fingernails rooted around the edge of her gumline as she pried the gummy off her teeth, all while scrunching her nose in irritation.

I let out an exaggerated sigh and reached for the wine bottle I had opened and brought into the pantry. There was something so soothing about having wine to fall back on whenever I was overwhelmed, which at that point seemed to be happening constantly.

"There are too many people in my house. What the hell was I thinking?" I said, taking a drink directly from the bottle.

She shrugged. "This is very un-you-like, I must say," Amy said, pointing toward the party. "What were you thinking?"

"I seriously have no idea," I told her, sticking out my lower lip in a pout.

Sometimes when my mind gets fuzzy, it does this thing where I envision myself speaking something aloud, knowing I should stop, but it's as if I've teleported through time: it's too late. I already know I'm going to say it. I'm powerless to stop myself.

"I wish there was a way to have my kids but lose this version of myself propped up alongside them," I started in, pointing as if someone else was in the pantry with us. "After they were born, my heart exploded into an infinite number of pieces, and I saw the appeal of placing each of those pieces directly back into them. I believed my children could be at the center of my universe, just like Christine did. Well, she still does. But it's not enough. And now, every day, it just feels like I've become a hostage inside my own life—forced to choose between them or myself."

There, I said it.

Amy's big eyes blinked at me in confusion. She was the last person I should have been saying this to after she lost Elijah. I knew that, but again, my voice seemed to have taken on a life of its own. I needed to try hearing what it sounded like out loud—the booze enabled me to let the feelings drip off my body, like a fever finally breaking. But the look on Amy's face made me want to suck in as much air as possible, inhaling the words back up into my mouth.

I tried another approach. One that would bond Amy to me forever so she would know how much I trusted her. Maybe, I thought, it would even help me gain her sympathy or under-standing since she, too, knew what it was like to carry the weight of a secret.

"I want to tell you something I've never said out loud. To anyone." I paused and then barreled forward, ready to un-burden myself. "I don't know for sure if Lucas is Joni's dad. I mean, he probably is. I mean, it's very unlikely it could be someone else. But not impossible."

Amy's reaction was unreadable, but it wasn't one of shock or disgust, though her body noticeably unstiffened as she waited to see if I wanted to say more.

"It could be this other guy. His name is Miles. We slept together only a few times, but it overlapped with Lucas." I stopped to bite at the skin around my fingernails, unsatisfied, then continued, "I didn't know what I wanted back then. I was too scared to commit to Lucas, and I felt like I needed to actively fight against becoming . . . well, this." I motioned with my hands out toward the party. "We had only known each other for a few months. I wasn't even going to have her. I swear, I even went to the appointment . . ." I faded off. My face burned; saying out loud that Lucas might not be Joni's dad was one thing, but imagining a world where Joni didn't exist was quite another.

While I felt notably lighter, our closeness seemed muted somehow. It all began to blur with the confinement of the pantry and the haze of alcohol. I needed to change the subject.

"There was a study I read back in college where, if given the chance, rats would tap levers that put dopamine directly into their little brains, choosing the pleasure feeling even over food and water. The scientists eventually had to unhook them, or they'd die of starvation or dehydration," I told her, knowing I probably sounded crazy. It had been on my mind lately. There was something hauntingly reminiscent between the study and my decision to have three children when I wasn't even sure about having one. Just like there was something familiar about not wanting to bring a bottle of wine into the pantry, while at the same time knowing I was still going to. "Maybe it was mice."

"I'm going to take this now, thanks." Amy pulled the bottle away from me and brought it outside the pantry. When she closed the door, the mirrored glass rattled. I assumed she would come back in and join me, but she never did.

I sat there alone for another twenty minutes or so—it could have been longer—thinking about how deeply unprepared I was for the sacrifice of what I'd done, realizing that the narrative of motherhood reads mostly about all that's given and nothing about what's taken away.

My wish for Amy is for her to experience only the good parts. The sensation of her children lying with their heads somewhere on her body. When no one is moving or speaking, and it's just limbs intertwined and draped across the bed. With someone tucked inside the space between her shoulder and ear, nuzzled into these toddler-size nooks—the synchronization of breaths.

I wish that version of being a mom could exist like that for Amy, always. The simplicity of heartbeat on top of heartbeat—how in those first few moments after their birth, there isn't anything but endless possibilities before them.

If Amy had returned to the pantry, I would have told her all that. But she never came back.

We are at the last Sunday dinner before the soft opening. Tensions are running high, and the air is thick with misery inside my in-laws' house. I've managed to completely avoid Amy until now. After trying several times but failing to get ahold of Isla, I need to understand what Amy can expect moving forward—so I'm not presenting her with only half the story. At least this is the excuse I'm giving myself for not telling her right away. I finally left Isla a message demanding she do nothing until we speak again. I will be the one to come up with a way to break the news to Amy.

Dottie is potty training, so she asked to use the bathroom during grace, and things have only gone downhill since. As retaliation, Christine commented on how Joni should be eating protein-rich foods to put some "meat on her bones" before remarking on Reid's need for a haircut. Of course, she would be happy to take him. All these superficial little things to keep from addressing our run-in at my studio.

The adults are seated around the table while Dory has the kids upstairs. We are attempting to numb out the palpable stress the guys seem to be under.

"Bad news, I'm afraid—Joy has an orchestra concert the night of the soft opening at her school," Jack says, inhaling a full swig of whiskey before setting it down on the table.

"Orchestra? Since when is she in the orchestra?" Christine asks. Normally she's the first to be informed and consulted on such news about her grandchildren.

"It's brand-new. They let them pick instruments, so they're doing a mini performance for the parents to show off what they've learned," Lidy chimes in, beaming a little. "Joy picked the violin!"

"Frankly, it sounds like she's dragging a dying cat across a chalkboard." Jack chuckles, missing the daggers his mother is shooting him from across the table.

"You cannot miss the opening!" Christine looks at Paul incredulously, nodding her head as if to say, *Do something about him, will you?*

"There is another opening for families they can attend. Aren't you always saying our kids should come first?" Lucas says, shrugging it off.

"Our family should come first! What about all the work you put in for the soft opening? We all need to be there together to support what you've done!"

"I'm sure it's not a big deal if we miss the concert. I can reach out to her music teacher and explain. Maybe we could even get them to change it since so many other parents may be impacted by the opening as well," Lidy says, sucking up as always.

"You sure, babe? I'd hate for you to go through all that trouble." Jack eyes her in a way that suggests maybe this whole thing was staged to get out of going to the opening.

"It's settled then. We will all be there!" Christine claps her hands together.

"What time am I getting you for lunch tomorrow, Mom?" Jack asks Christine.

"Tomorrow? No, I'm riding in the afternoon with Paul tomorrow. Surely our plans are for the following day."

Jack lets out an irritated huff as he pulls up his calendar on his phone, scrolling through until his statement is confirmed. He shoves it almost a little too close to her face, victoriously stating, "See. Lunch with Mom."

"Oh dear." Christine glances in Paul's direction.

"We can reschedule riding for later in the week," Paul offers.

"Nonsense, you and Lucas are in the homestretch now. I

don't know how you managed to fit me into your schedule at all! Jack?"

Rarely have we witnessed such a display of Christine's favoritism and almost never twice in a row. The deliciousness of the drama is nearly as sweet as the limoncello I've poured for myself. I savor both, leaning back in my chair.

Overhead we can hear the thundering of little footsteps. The children must be playing chase in the house, which is strictly forbidden.

George stands, tapping Jack on the shoulder, and says, "Come on, boys—let's go get these kids outside to burn off their energy before they destroy your mother's display shelves."

Paul, Lucas, and Jack stand as Jack downs the rest of his drink, which inspires me to do the same, especially if Amy and I are going to be left here with Lidy and Christine.

Later, when I return from the bathroom, somehow we have gotten on the topic of discussing the sizes of our individual families.

"Two is just the perfect number for us," Lidy says, glancing over at her kids playing tag with Paul just outside the window. "Disneyland passes only come in family four packs, and I'm just not brave enough to go for another. I don't know how you and Christine manage."

I hide my grin by raising my mug to my lips. I love every time I get lumped in with Christine regarding motherhood. If she were an animal, all her hair would be standing on end as her claws extend.

"Mmm," is all Christine can manage to get out before adding, "If Leah can do it, I'm certain you could, Lidy."

I try to catch Amy's gaze after Christine's unsubtle insult, but her eyes seem to have glazed over. I hate when the

O'Connors talk over Amy's struggles to have children. Like it is just assumed women can snap their fingers and the von Trapp family could waltz right out of their vaginas upon request. As if conceiving a child was something that happened easily for everyone. I feel territorial, wanting to protect Amy from their ignorance.

"Let's stop pretending anything about motherhood happens in a straight line," I say. Lidy glances back at Amy, who is polishing a dish that is too delicate for the dishwasher. She moves in a manner that's stiff and robotic. I want to say more to reassure her that everything will be fine with her pregnancy. I consider bringing up her latest prenatal appointment and how great everything looked, but I hate to allow the tone to be shifted once again to sunshine and rainbows that fit neatly into a pristine Christine-size package. Suddenly I want to blow up the fairy tale completely.

"Really, it isn't everything we pretend it is. It's not always magical or transformative, because still, everywhere you look there you are. Now just with children." I'm speaking to Amy specifically, as a way of nudging her across the finish line. I hope she understands that imperfections can be part of a spectrum. But she will do it well. I know she will.

"I disagree. Motherhood brings out the best version of ourselves," Christine says, squeezing Amy's arm.

CHAPTER 18

I decide to take Joni out for milkshakes after dinner one night when Lucas is home with Reid and Dottie. I am hoping to get more information out of her regarding her feelings for Lizzy. I don't trust Christine's account to be free from any implicit biases.

We sit inside an old-fashioned red booth at the HMB Creamery on Main Street. The floors are checkered black and white, and there's a jukebox in the back left corner. The staff even wear roller skates to serve customers.

"Have you ever tried a malt?" I ask as Joni sips her strawberry milkshake with extra whipped cream.

"What's a malt?" A layer of pink coats her lips like lipstick, and I have a flash of her as a teenager and all the destruction her beauty will cause the world.

"It's like a milkshake, but they add malted milk."

She sticks out her tongue in protest. "Why would anyone try to improve something that's already perfect?"

I pull out my straw from my Diet Coke to use it as a pointer. "You make a valid point." Small droplets of brown drip onto the table between us as Joni pulls at the napkins from the metal dispenser next to the bottles of ketchup and mustard.

She continues to drink at a regulated pace, my guess is to avoid getting a brain freeze. Unable to wait any longer, I finally ask, "How are things going with your friend at school?" I intentionally leave out her name in case Joni has already moved on.

She swallows and answers, "Lizzy's good. We made the mutual decision to stop caring what the boys are sayin' about us. It's more fun that way." She uses her tongue to guide the straw into her mouth as it twirls around, until finally it makes its way up to her pursed lips.

"What are the boys saying exactly?" I hate the idea of anyone mistreating her.

"Just dumb stuff, but boys are dumb a lot. 'Specially when it comes to feelings," Joni says, shrugging off what she's declared to be universal knowledge. As if she recognizes in her youth something I'm still discovering myself.

"Agreed. Boys can be dumb sometimes, except for Daddy and Reid."

"And Grandpa and Uncle Paul."

"Yes, all the boys in our family."

She ponders this for a minute and grins a milky smile. I hold up my finger, recognizing that she's about to make a joke at Uncle Jack's expense. Sometimes I forget that Joni will always be my ally in this family. Not in the same way that Amy is, but more like the way coming home smells.

I'm not sure I can get her to say more about Lizzy without being painfully obvious.

"Want a sip, Mom? You can use my straw." Joni's combination of innocence and sweetness could almost break me in half.

"Love one," I say, misjudging the viscosity of the shake. I sip too vigorously and wind up with a brain freeze. I pinch my temples, sucking in air. "You're right. I would never try to improve upon perfection."

It's only a few days before the soft opening. The kids and I arrive at my studio. Dory is meeting me at the house in less than an hour so I can go pick up the paternity results.

Near where I parked, a few men are gathered around a makeshift fire created out of a trash can. They acknowledge us with nods before returning their gazes to the flames. I take notice of their brown paper bags, and immediately my throat goes dry. I sip from the Starbucks coffee I snagged at the drive-through on our way here. Slamming the door of my minivan, I miss the force required to close one of Big Bertha's doors properly.

"We'll be here for only five minutes. I'm just grabbin' something, then we're leaving," I tell the kids.

"Mom, is this your dream? Like, would you say you're livin' it right now?" Reid asks from his designated location on one of the oversize beanbag chairs. He's facing the wall and staring into one of my paintings as if he has never seen it before.

I'm caught off guard, but there's something wholesome about his question. Adults are constantly asking kids, "What do you want to be when you grow up?" Now the tables have been turned on me.

"Our dreams are always shifting as grown-ups. But I can say without a doubt that the love I have for you and your sisters surpasses any original plan I had for myself." I mean it as much as I can right now. I know I haven't answered him, so I add, "Are you livin' your best life, bud?"

"I will be when I'm playing baseball in the MLB." He stops to smile and picture it before continuing. "I know Dad's thing is The Restaurant and yours is painting. I like this one a lot," Reid says, and with that he pivots his body away from the wall and buries his face in his handheld gaming device.

The girls have already settled in. Dottie has flopped her little body down on the smaller of the two pink beanbag chairs and is scrolling through the iPad to a preloaded cartoon. Joni sits on a barstool reading her book.

Letting my bag fall from my shoulder onto the floor, I stand in front of my latest collection. I have completed four pieces, but I am not satisfied with any of them. Not one. I haven't been able to determine a theme that translates as well as my collection *The Fluidity of Sexuality* did. The truth is, without Lucas's success, I know I wouldn't be able to continue as an artist. I have sold pieces and had successful shows, but there is no way we'd survive on my work alone. I certainly couldn't support our family. Twelve years ago, I was happy to be painting by the coast and living out of my van.

My cell phone rings, and I kneel to pull it from my bag. I look to see that it's Nana calling.

"Hey, how's El Paso? Or did you guys make it to Austin yet?" I ask, still frowning, staring back at my collection.

"New Orleans! Or NAW-lins as they say in these parts. Ha! What a hoot," Nana says. I can picture her inside their RV, "Big B II" as she calls it, slapping at the dash.

"I hope you're keeping your top on. I'll overnight you some plastic beads if you don't feel like you can control yourself!" Joni and Reid look up at me, confused. Joni raises one of her eyebrows. I wave my hand out in front of me, indicating they should return to minding their own business. Nana's chuckles turn into a deep throaty cough she's had since I was little from being a chain-smoker back in the '60s and '70s.

"How are the kids and Lucas? Your mom says she hasn't heard from you in a while." Nana, my mother's mother, has always served as our go-between.

"Fine. All fine. I hope you're gonna circle back to California soon; we miss you in these parts," I tell her. I really do. I wish she were here to give it to me straight: *These pieces are total crap.* Those would be her exact words. I hear Ricky calling for her in the background. There's music and the buzz of excitement. "Sounds like fun there. Go, go."

"I'm sensing some uncertainty. Breathe into the phone."

"No time for an aura reading today, Nan." While she is convinced she's a level of clairvoyant that could have made her rich and famous, she chose to limit the use of her gifts to within our immediate family or for my personal entertainment. My parents lack the patience for it, but I usually play along.

"Party pooper! We'll be out there in six weeks, my darling. The jazz music is calling my name. Off to see a man about a saxophone!" With that, she's gone.

Usually the sound of her voice with any snippet from life on the road brings me happiness. It reminds me of our drive together from Iowa to California, and I welcome swimming inside the nostalgia. But my lack of passion is painfully displayed all over the work in front of me. I can't seem to sink into that groove where creativity streaks through my fingertips, like opening a vein at the wrist, infiltrating the innate splatter of color from the deepest channel within. My work is noticeably lacking because I am noticeably not myself.

Suddenly Reid is in front of me, frantically flailing his arms in front of my face, but he appears staticky. Like I haven't turned the dial to the correct station.

"Mom, I think Dottie peed through her diaper," Reid repeats, his face growing red in exasperation.

Have I changed her since she woke up this morning? I have no idea. Reid already has a fresh diaper and wipes in his hand.

"Thanks, bud. I owe you."

I strip her down, though she's protesting because she wants to keep watching the iPad while I do it. I keep her standing since it's the only way she will allow me to change her and has been since she was one and already full of opinions about her bodily autonomy. On her back, she'll scream and fling her body around, and poop or Desitin will go flying everywhere. I didn't bring extra pants, so she'll just have to wear a diaper and her shirt until Dory can bathe her at home. I doubt anyone will come in, but I don't care either way. Once Dottie is back on the beanbag chair, I throw my coat over her bare legs and crank up the heat.

I stand, cocking my head sideways, hoping the small canvases will somehow become more impressive from that angle. Normally I work with much bigger prints, but I've lost the confidence to do so. It has taken me three months to create these four. With the dirty diaper in one hand, I tuck the entire collection under my arm.

"Joni B., Reid, watch your sister for a minute. I need to take this diaper to the trash in the alley." No one looks up, but Joni nods, indicating she's heard me.

On the night of my last art show, Amy stayed afterward to help me clean up. The sensation of pride, as I'd sold out almost completely, swelled within my body. I grabbed a bottle of water and joined Amy on the studio floor, lying down flat on our backs, head-to-head.

"You're amazing, you know that?" I couldn't see her face, but I could tell by the sound of her words that she was smiling.

"Aww, stop. You'll give me a big head. But don't stop," I said with a laugh.

"I mean it. I don't think I liked art before you. Actually, I know I didn't. I mean, I guess I didn't get it. Or maybe that's not true. It never made me feel anything. Does that make sense?" Amy was rambling, which she does whenever she gets lost in thought.

"Mm-hmm." I turned my head and looked at a piece on the wall—a red dot on the corner, marking it sold.

"How can you paint something that I can feel?" Amy asked. She had flipped over and was kneeling next to my face.

"Now you have to stop. You'll make me cry." I swatted at her knee, uncomfortable with the vulnerability of her words.

"I'm serious."

"I've never had that protective layer of skin between me and the outside world. So when I paint, I take the hurt or the love and put it there. Sometimes I don't see how anyone can understand it, but they must." I paused to look around at all the red dots.

We didn't speak again for a long time, and she put her head back down beside me. I wished I could stay there, sober in my contentment, in the safe space we had created together, surrounded by proof that I was understood.

I am immediately cold when I get outside. I throw the soiled diaper in the dumpster. The men stop talking as I approach them.

"Any chance I can throw these in there?" I raise my shoulders slightly, indicating I'm referencing putting the canvases into the open flame.

"That bad, huh?" one of them says. I realize I initially mistook her for a man. She is young, no older than her early twenties; her fingers are wrapped around a fifth of vodka that is out in the open instead of hidden inside a paper bag. I recognize the brand I drank in college because it was cheap. The cap is black because they filter it through charcoal.

"That bad," I repeat.

She says nothing but tilts her head toward the fire. I like that she's in charge of decisions made among grown men. One by one, I put them in. I feel nothing, only that I am acutely aware of the lingering smell of vodka wafting around me.

CHAPTER 19

Amy unapologetically heaves herself into the passenger
side of my minivan.

"I feel like you're too pregnant to travel," I say,
keeping my eyes forward, and by doing so, I want her to know
I'm salty she is crashing my top-secret trip out of town.

"The doctor said it's fine. I'm not under house arrest. It's not
like we're going to Mexico . . . right?" She lets out a little grunt
as the weight of her pelvis pushes up into her chest. I vividly
remember the sensation of breathlessness at the very end of
pregnancy. As if the baby was greedily consuming the last tiny
pockets of air in my lungs. "Plus, if I've learned one thing, it's that
sitting around never actually wills anything good into existence."

"I kinda think I should be alone." I continue to stare
straight ahead, watching a bird I don't recognize swoop down
and narrowly miss crashing into another bird.

"Nonsense. Being alone is overrated. Take it from me—I
haven't been alone for almost forty weeks now." She points at
her enormous stomach. "Whatever you need to do, you can do
in front of me," she says in a voice so convincing that it sur-
prises me a little. "Now, where we goin'?"

"I guess you'll see when we get there," I say, making my way onto the road. We pass over the hill and then stall in traffic. The busyness of this side of the freeway and the manic energy of Bay Area drivers are furthering the tension in the car and only exacerbating my bad mood. I don't like being this far away from the ocean. The driver in front of us has a bumper sticker that reads *I'd Rather Be at Summer Camp*. I keep reading it and rereading it every time we inch closer.

"I remember I went to this one camp when I was a kid. It was supposed to teach us about teamwork or unity or something, but in reality it was an excuse for horny teenagers to grope each other in the woods," I say, pointing at the sticker on the little red Honda we are stuck behind. "We'd play this game, I think it was called Nervous, where a girl would slide her hand up a guy's leg while asking, 'Does this make you nervous?' Then they'd take turns flirting in various ways, and if you got the other person to crack a smile, you won." I roll down the window to circulate more air since we've stopped moving completely.

As a tendril of hair falls onto her sunglasses, Amy turns to me and asks, "What exactly would you win?"

"A raging boner, evidently. I was the reigning champion, naturally."

"You have always been skilled at making people . . . uh, happy." She sweeps the hair back up, tucking it behind her ear. "But thanks for officially sealing my daughter's fate of never, ever going away to summer camp," she says, laughing.

The light drops down suddenly in front of us, and the sunshine warms my cheeks.

"Do you remember when I first told you about Isla? When we were at the preschool's playground?"

"Yeah, that's when you asked me to be your maid of honor.

Or I guess I was the 'matron of honor,' since I'm married and the patriarchy is bullshit." I make a face of disgust.

She ignores me and continues, "I thought by sharing what I considered a big secret, I would solidify us as a safe space. The place we could go and be there for each other. But you and I were written in the stars. I've never felt as close to anyone as I do with you. I imagine it's what having a sister must be like."

The fog outside the car has completely dissipated and morphed into a cloudless sky. I let out a long, slow exhale, wanting to offer her a nugget of truth before blindsiding her completely with Isla's. Maybe it will help put things in perspective.

"I did a paternity test for Joni. Christine is about to go nuclear; I can just feel it. I'm going to collect the results so they don't come in the mail. It cost most of Joni's college fund, and just the process of getting it . . ." I let myself trail off. "It is impossible to imagine a world where Joni isn't an O'Connor by blood."

"Okay. What are you gonna do with the results?"

"I snagged their toothbrushes. No one even noticed," I say, purposefully ignoring her question. "I've been getting cash back at the grocery store so as not to leave a paper trail. I feel like a drug dealer."

I can't help but think of the number of lies my single lie has fractured into—what it means to start a chain of events that affects not only your own life but the lives of almost everyone around you. Somehow I've become a wife who hides money to keep my husband in the dark about a secret even more massive than wads of unaccounted-for cash.

"I can feel you judging me over there," I say, though I'm not even looking over at her.

"I wouldn't dream of it. I just know the amount of effort it takes to perpetuate a ruse. It's exhausting," she says, shaking her head.

"I am really tired," I admit so sincerely that she reaches over to rub my arm. I want to pull her hand away. I don't deserve her sympathies. I can't bring myself to tell her now.

"I'm taking us to the bell tower room. I can't help but feel like something there is going to tell us everything we need to know about the mysteries of the universe," I explain ominously. "Plus, as punishment for tagging along, I'm finally going to get around to painting your maternity portrait," I say, grinning. "But first, I need to make a pit stop."

I pull into a gas station while Amy waits in the car with the envelope containing the DNA results. There isn't a world in which she would open it, but there is an appeal to leaving it with her, allowing her to carry the weight of my secret while I carry the weight of hers, made heavier still now that Isla is secretly pregnant. If only we could do things like that for each other and it would be enough to get by. But we can't, so I ask the clerk to pull down a fifth of vodka from behind where he's standing. I ask for the cheap brand from earlier, for the sake of nostalgia. He packages it away in a brown paper bag. I know I promised Amy I'd wait until the opening, but it seems that the only logical solution for living in a world that now holds an answer about Joni is the promise of fading into complete blackness.

I slip back into the car, attempting to tuck the bag into the space next to Amy's feet and use my large purse to try to cover it. Once I start the car, she picks it up, grunting a little as she reaches around her belly.

She turns the bag around in her hands. "We made 3D Mother's Day cards like this"—she nods to the way the paper bag is pinched and puckered around the neck of the bottle—"by twirling the eraser part of the pencil around tissue paper and dabbing it in glue. Remember those?"

I nod but say nothing, embarrassed she's drawn so much attention to the bottle.

When we arrive at the building, I open the door for Amy to walk through first. Her movements are tentative, each slow step stretching my nerves, and I fight the urge to nudge her forward, willing her to cross the threshold faster.

The office manager looks at us strangely when we ask to go up and check out the room with the bell tower.

"I'm an old college friend of Beth's—she's the building owner. We won't be long," I say, purring like a kitten to get my way. I don't have to wonder what Miles would have said had I given him the chance to respond to my pseudo-proposition. "I brought my paints to do a portrait." I shrug the shoulder that's carrying my materials, though he's already waving us up.

The bell tower room is almost identical to before. The bedspread is still a horrible floral print that's a deep brownish red, like it was explicitly picked to conceal blood splatter. We stand gazing up at the drum of the bell. I scratch a single fingernail along the braided brown rope.

"How much do you want to pull it?" I ask Amy.

"A shockingly large amount," she says, but stops when she notices that I've only said it as a distraction tactic to get her to look away. I crack the bottle's lid, twisting too zealously as the plastic cuts a perfect ring into my inner thumb. I try to hide the blood by squeezing my hand into a fist, not wanting to examine the gash. Amy reaches out and cups both hands over my single injured one, sucking air into her mouth. She's maternal even in her innate gestures.

I have brought my own cup for the occasion. "Is that the whale mug from our walk on the beach the other day?" Amy asks when I pull it out of my bag.

It is unnecessary for me to respond. She can see whatever she wants to see.

I had intentionally hidden the mug, draping my coat over my arm like a waiter to sneak it off the shore. It was an act of defiance after Amy had scolded me like a child. I thought if I stole a relic from my phantom self, maybe I could embody that version somehow.

On the bed, I wipe my bloodied finger on the comforter, and as I suspected, the blood stain disappears. I pour myself at least two shots. My movements are as ritualized as a baptism, though I'm clumsier now since I must work around my injury. Amy unabashedly watches. She stops me before I put it up to my mouth—inflicting a pause more pregnant than she is.

"Wait!" she says. "If you're going to read the results, shouldn't you be sober?"

"Oh, I'm not gonna open it," I explain as if that were somehow obvious. Then I lift the whale tail high in the air. "To being temporarily untethered." I toast even though Amy raises nothing, despite the water in front of her. I interpret her lack of participation as disapproval, and so I take all the liquid down in a single swallow. "You insisted on coming along, so it's only fair that I get to paint you here. This will be perfect—you'll see."

I unfold the easel and the briefcase containing my paints and brushes even before I allow her the chance to answer.

I sense her watching my movements as I begin to uncap the colors I will need. Maybe she's waiting to see if there's an upset in my composure because of what I've consumed. There won't be. I'll make sure of it.

"Where do you want me?"

"Do you mind standing, or do you want to sit? I'll get a better angle of the bump if you're standing, but I know that's not really comfortable."

"I'm fine to stand," she says, though her tone has gone neutral, as if she's lost interest in us suddenly. She clears her throat. "I remember playing a game alone on the shore as a kid: I'd outrun the waves as they crept closer to my toes. The unspoken rule between us was that I had to come within a single inch of contact or I'd have to declare myself a cheater." Amy is removing her jacket so she's in only her long-sleeved, form-fitting dress. She pulls her hair out of the clip that is holding it together, letting it fall wildly around her shoulders. "It was tempting to watch for the frothy water at my feet, but I was best able to predict what was coming by the wave itself out in front of me. My playmate showed its hand in the size of the wave, the ratio of blue to green to white. Only by watching could I gauge what I should do next."

Her words are distracting me from my mission. I know I need to tell her before I lose my resolve.

"If it weren't for my childhood with Isla, I could have easily misinterpreted what is happening to you, Leah. Lightning is never supposed to strike twice, after all. But it's all too painfully familiar. These days with you, I'm transported back to the trailer with Isla. I was too young to notice if there was a shift in Isla's descent. Without having watched the shape and colors of Isla's waves, I easily would have missed yours."

I hear her and yet my head is so far underwater that I can't make my way to the surface. I pretend to be lost in thought with each stroke of my brush. As if I'm so consumed by my work, it would be impossible for me to interpret yet another Amy metaphor, especially one brazen enough to compare me to Isla. And so I paint her. Stroke after stroke of my brush. The movement comes so easily I could paint her blindfolded.

Again, I pour more. I don't want to drink; I need to. Similar to our bodies' repetition of taking in air. An inhale and exhale. Inside I am screaming to stop. Knowing that if I speak again aloud, it will all spill out horribly wrong.

I return to the canvas and work frantically without looking up to determine the proportions of her face, since I memorized them long ago. She isn't smiling, but I depict her as though she is because it's what I need right now—the warmth of her sunny smile.

"This is good. I'm happy with this," I say aloud. It's true. Maybe it's the rush of adrenaline or something else, but I'm uncharacteristically inspired because Amy is my anchor and I want to do her beauty justice. "Finally! The start of my next collection!"

But she's lost interest, in the way a child grows bored when adults are talking. She turns and begins pulling on the rope. Its weight disturbs her already unstable equilibrium. Not until her third attempt does the bell finally toll. Deep and jarring, the sound echoes into the silence.

I'm finishing the piece while Amy puts her feet up on the bed. Eventually I'm satisfied, and I wander over toward the bell.

"In my dream, I saw the rope as a noose." I am craning my neck as if trying to calculate an equation in my head. It's been more than an hour, if not longer, and the hum of alcohol has made me suddenly fearless.

"And you saw Joni before you even knew there would be a Joni," Amy says, like it's a story she's heard a million times.

"It marked the beginning or the end—can never quite decide which." I stand now, leaning over the railing like I'm going to toll the bell. Instead, I try to make a circle by flipping the extra slack over the railing and knotting a loop in the middle of the rope.

"What the hell are you doing? That's not funny," Amy says from the bed, though now she's sitting erect.

I like her attention. It's what I've felt like I've been missing from her all day. So I climb the circular metal bars that encapsulate the rope and slip my head into the loop I've created.

"Please, Leah. Stop."

At first, I'm stoic, determined almost, but the knot is flimsy; the coarse rope is too thick to remain taut. I try to laugh it off, as if it were all a funny joke. The noose easily breaks and slides down one shoulder, so that I appear like Rapunzel offering my golden hair for the prince to climb. Except no one is coming to rescue me.

"I am not taking you to get more alcohol; I'm taking you to a meeting," Amy tells me once I'm buckled into the passenger seat and look behind me to see our bags are neatly tucked into the back. We were supposed to spend the night, or at least that was my original plan, but suddenly it's dusk with only the dwindling light left in the sky. Amy has tricked me into getting back into the car.

"What meeting? You said you were craving Flamin' Hot Cheetos." I frown. "Does that mean we aren't getting any Cheetos?"

"No, we aren't going to the store. We are going to a twelve-step meeting."

"Are you serious right now?" I'm trying my best to be silly, fun Leah. Make it obvious that Amy is overreacting because of everything that happened with Isla.

"You are overreacting because of everything that happened with Isla. News flash: I'm not your mother."

"Okay, tough guy. You want to not be my mother? Go to this meeting with me." Then she adds, as if it were a dare, "Isla never went."

"Fine." After a pause, I repeat, "Fine." It's not the worst idea because then she can hear for herself why I don't belong in a group with people who are alcoholics.

We arrive outside a large Catholic church a few miles before we hit the outskirts of Half Moon Bay. Inside, the room is well lit, but the smell of burned coffee turns my stomach. I'm grateful that the chairs are not in a circle. I would have stormed out in protest if they were.

We sit near the back. We haven't spoken since I agreed to sit through this with her. A man with salt-and-pepper hair and round glasses stands at the podium in the front of the room. He has a large, rotund belly and rosy cheeks. Luckily, I don't recognize a single person here, although I guess it's supposed to be anonymous.

"Hi, I'm Ray, and I'm an alcoholic," the gray-haired man says. An echo of "Hi, Ray" is sprinkled around the room, like we're in a play and everyone else is already familiar with the script. Ray continues, "I'd like to start off the meeting with a moment of silence followed by the Serenity Prayer."

The room goes silent.

After a few seconds, the other attendees recite in unison, "God, grant me the serenity to accept the things I cannot change; courage to change the things I can; and wisdom to know the difference."

Okay, this is clearly a cult. They've already mentioned God within the first minute of our arrival.

There's a lot more reading, and I'm already almost sober. A woman makes her way to the podium.

"Hi, I'm Julie, and I'm an alcoholic."

"Hi, Julie," the room answers, again in unison.

Julie is a Caucasian woman in her late sixties or early seventies. You can tell that she was attractive in her heyday, though she hasn't aged well. She's put together, wearing a necklace with a turquoise pendant that matches the color of her eyes, and her hair is a silvery gray.

"I have a sobriety date of August 28, 2020. I just celebrated three years sober." She takes a deep breath and begins. "Originally, I drank to feel better than my 'factory settings' allowed. Whatever my baseline feeling is, it's just not enough." She stops to acknowledge the nods around the room and then continues, "I got married, and we had our kids young. I drank through both of my pregnancies but, by the grace of God, somehow have two healthy kids. I took that as a sign that I could get away with drinking through their childhoods too."

A sick feeling pools inside my chest, like Julie is pointing at me in front of everyone, shaming me in front of Amy so I'll finally have to admit that I drank during my last pregnancy.

"When my oldest was two, I left him in his car seat overnight in the garage. I was in a blackout, and I forgot he was with me. I came out the next morning to pick up more booze and saw him there. You hear about mothers leaving their kids in hot cars for an hour . . ." She stops and starts sniffling but isn't crying. The room is waiting, sitting in a calm stillness—like what she is saying isn't entirely insane. I realize I've been holding my breath. "And these babies don't live, but somehow he lived. My son lived. He survived, so I decided I could keep drinking, and maybe things would get better if I had another baby."

Coming here was a mistake. The dread seeps up my fingertips like drops of dye onto a coffee filter. This woman is demonic. She and Isla could be drinking buddies with their callous cruelty and child abuse. I don't belong in this room with these people. But something, an ineffable force, keeps me firmly planted in my seat.

Julie continues, "These are the types of lies we tell. The half-truths we need to patchwork together to convince ourselves and the people in our lives that everything is fine. To keep up this charade. I started having more and more problems. I'd create rules surrounding my drinking only to break them. No more hard stuff. Beer only. Okay, wine is fine. Sometimes vodka, but I'd have to mark the number of shots on my arm. Until I couldn't drink the way I wanted to around other people. So my world got smaller and smaller. I'd cross the line over and over again. I had no moral compass. Alcohol was the sun, the moon, and all my stars." I hate that Julie has spoken aloud something I thought only hours earlier.

She takes a sip of water. I don't dare glance over at Amy because she'll read the fear on my face. My best course of action is just to sit and continue to pretend to pay attention. Just get through the next twenty minutes, and then I'll have served my time. I won't yawn because that would be rude. But staying for Julie's speech should appease Amy. Clearly this woman has mental health problems and everyone can hear that. When it's over, Amy will have to admit this was a waste of our time.

"The consequences of my drinking weren't a DUI or prison, like I thought were a requirement for me to be deemed 'an alcoholic.' No, they were so much worse. I got a failed marriage, which I guess many people do. But my husband was one of the good ones. He is still. What hurt the most was losing my kids—and not, like, by having them go live with their dad. I missed out on witnessing who they were becoming. I was convinced motherhood was the problem; I was wired wrong because somehow I was the only miserable woman in the role. I didn't realize it was the alcohol poisoning my perception of reality. I couldn't function as a mom when I was drinking." I hate that I know exactly what she's talking about. That, to me, is more terrifying than anything else she could possibly say. *Is it the alcohol that's making me miserable?* Another thought I need to purge from my head. No one just gives up drinking. What about New Year's? Every single O'Connor dinner and event is centered around alcohol. My husband is opening a restaurant with a full bar, for heaven's sake!

Julie is still sharing. "I couldn't connect with other people because booze served as our barrier when I swore up and down it was the very thing that brought us closer. I so badly wanted to be different—I'd witness my friends who could have wine with dinner without finishing the entire bottle. Somehow when they put their kids to bed at night, they would remember doing so. Other people could go to open-bar weddings and not end up blacking out before the cake was served. But I couldn't. And I was angry and resentful over this for years. Years."

She picks up her water bottle again but doesn't put it to her mouth. I look around the room at heads bobbing in agreement, like what she's said is perfectly normal. No one appears shocked or disgusted, simply content to listen, as if doing so allows them to collectively absolve one another of their sins.

"I sacrificed my relationship with my son and daughter to worship at the feet of Addiction. Everyone, including them, begged me to stop. They even staged an intervention, but all I wanted was for them to leave so I could continue drinking, the way I wanted to, alone." Julie is crying now; large tears slide down each of her cheeks. She brushes them away with her fingertips. "I got my wish. I woke up one morning only to realize I *was* completely alone. My children were grown and had separate lives from me, which I knew nothing about. I no longer wanted to live. I went to the supermarket to buy enough alcohol to drink myself to death. I was checking out and a clerk about my kids' age asked to see my ID. Now, I don't want to shock anyone, but I'm looooong past twenty-one." The group chuckles a bit. "I told her so, and she asked again. I went to reach for it, and my hands were shaking with DTs already. I know I looked like death warmed up and reeked of stale booze. I couldn't find my license in my bag. She told me she couldn't sell to me now that she'd asked and I couldn't provide it—claiming it was the law—but I saw her watching my hands shake. I saw her looking at me, not with pity but with familiarity. Before I left in a huff of humiliation and anger, she told me about this meeting."

Julie uses her hand to point toward the ground at her feet. "She said it was the same one her mom attends. I'll give you one guess who wound up becoming my sponsor. Now, you can chalk all that up to coincidence, but here in this room, we call that clerk from Safeway my 'God shot.' I hope you pay attention"—I swear she's looking at me when she says this last part—"because you don't want to miss yours."

I find myself staring at the age spots on her hands. The discoloration of her flesh, the wrinkled folds around her fingers. Julie takes a deep breath.

"There are only two options for people like us: recovery or death. There is no easier, softer way, as they say. The Program has given me many gifts—one of the greatest, along with my sobriety, is my relationship with my granddaughter, Lacey. She reminds me so much of myself at seventeen—rebellious and wild, with purple hair and a nose ring. Except she's selfless and kind. She's generous with her love and gives it to me so freely. I think about how I could have missed getting to know this beautiful soul. I could have missed it all." Everyone claps and cheers loudly.

Ray is back up front because evidently there is more torture to come.

"We will now open up our meeting for discussion. Please limit your share to the topic of issues related to alcohol."

I motion to Amy that I have had enough for one night. I stand without looking to see if she is following me. On our walk back to the parking lot, we are both quiet. I continually look down at my feet as if I'm afraid I'm going to trip over something. Inside the car, Amy waits to push the Start button.

"I'm going to say something to you. Please try to hear what I mean," she begins, and already I hate where this is going. "You can do what you're doing for your whole life if you want. That's exactly what Isla did, and I hate her for it. I hate her so much; she's literally dead to me. And I hate that I cannot let her go completely because part of me keeps believing that by some miracle she'll change. Is that what you want for Joni? For Reid and Dottie? Eventually they'll need to escape you to the point that they will create a life for themselves where you no longer exist. Where they could be days away from making you a grandmother and they'd rather cut you off completely than have you around to share in their joy. Because that is where the road you are on eventually goes."

She uses her finger to point at me, then pulls it back hesitantly. She places her hand on the center console and lets out a slow exhale. "You can try to fool everyone but me, Leah. And I think you know that. You started to realize it when you called me to drive you to your son's baseball game because you were too wasted to take him yourself. Some part of you knew I would recognize that as a literal call for help. I know better than anyone that I can't do this for you. I love you too much to ignore or pretend, or just hope it goes away. You're missing everything. Do you know what I would give to have three healthy children? And you are missing it all."

How could she echo my exact words from the other night?

"Everyone, including you, is boxing me out," I say. "You put me on the outside. Since when do I sit on the outside looking in at you and Christine? You invited her over and then acted like I wasn't even there, in my own house."

"That's because you weren't there. Don't you get it? Sometimes you are there, but you really aren't. Pay attention to all that's happening around you," she says, looking so sad I'm scared she's going to burst into tears. But then she continues more forcefully, "I won't apologize for building a relationship with my mother-in-law while you are busy destroying yourself."

CHAPTER 20

The entire drive home I think about Julie's words. Over and over.

"I couldn't function as a mom when I was drinking."

Aren't I functioning? I have a husband, a career, a family, Amy. Yes, my husband is angry with me, and my career is stalled, and Christine definitely hates me, and now Amy is disappointed in me. But all of those circumstances are coming from powers outside of my control. The drinking isn't necessarily the problem.

We get home late and for some reason Lucas lets me sleep and takes the kids to school in the morning. His side of the bed is too ambiguous to know whether he slept there in the night. I make my way into our closet, where I have stored the portrait I did of Amy. After showering and getting dressed, somehow it's already time to pick up Dottie. I am anxious to appreciate my creation and certain it will get me back on track for the collection I destroyed. When I bring it out into the bathroom, standing it up against the mirror, and step back, I'm baffled by what I see. The sloppiness of my brushstrokes and misrepresentation of Amy's beauty are jarring. She should be a glow of maternal radiance, but all I've managed to capture are her shadows, as if I painted her within a room that was absent of light.

This can't be right.

But Amy was insistent I bring it home before gifting it to her officially. When she dropped me off, I went to put it in the back seat of her car, and she shook her head.

"You take it inside. Look at it when you're sober," she said. Now I see why.

After I've picked up all three kids from school, Joni asks if Lizzy can come over and "hang out." I've placed myself strategically at the window seat, pretending to read so I can spy on them without being too obvious. I'm drinking wine out of one of the kids' sports water bottles because nothing else seems to be settling my stomach. There's a small, imperceptible *tap* at the front door before Christine lets herself in. She's carrying a casserole in her hand and places it on the kitchen island along with a Post-it. I watch her from my position, holding my breath. If I lie very still, I wonder if I could somehow blend into the cushions without being spotted. I pull the blanket up to my chin. Even though I know she's seen me, we both pretend not to notice each other as she heads to the kitchen table.

"Hey, Grandma," Joni says. I notice a hint of trepidation in her voice. "This is Lizzy."

Lizzy has a round face with short brown hair and is wearing a T-shirt that says *The Future Is Female*. The girls are cocooned together under a blanket, sharing AirPods.

"Pleasure to meet you, Lizzy," Christine says. The shape of Lizzy's face changes into more of a heart as her smile grows.

"Hi," Lizzy says, beaming over at Joni.

Christine pulls over a chair and situates herself so she's facing Joni, close enough for their knees to be touching. She doesn't seem to concern herself with her close proximity to Lizzy, and Joni raises her eyebrows in questioning. Lizzy leans away from them, unsure what's happening. Again, they are able to sequester themselves inside a bubble in which only they exist. Lizzy and I have been cast away as temporary outsiders.

"I need to tell you a secret," Christine says in a soft, low voice as she removes Joni's earbud, and Lizzy nods and walks to the sink. Somehow in her youth, she recognizes their need for privacy, though I will not be offering any. Christine tucks Joni's hair behind her ear and leans in so her lips are almost touching her skin.

"I love you." She whispers loud enough and with such a pronounced exaggeration in her facial expressions that I can understand her very clearly from where I'm sitting. Then she pulls away so she can look into Joni's eyes. She grips Joni's forearms in her long, spindly fingers and releases them slowly, nodding her head as if confirming her message. Neither of them moves. "You are the girl I was waiting for." There's a tugging inside my chest as my breathing begins to hurt. I stand, bringing the blanket along with me. It drags behind me, even as I wrap it around my shoulders. I trip a little over the kitchen rug, which has come off its rubber runner.

Dottie is in her crib as I make my way up the stairs, wondering whether it's possible to understand matters of attraction at Joni's age. I have no idea if Joni's closeness with Lizzy is because they have feelings of friendship or of love. Or if Lizzy fills something within her life that she needs, the way Amy does within mine. I know that eventually I'll want to have a reckoning with my daughter similar to the one I already attempted over milkshakes, though less shallow and surface level. Of course, I'll accept her exactly as she is, but much like the one I've been avoiding with

Amy regarding Isla's pregnancy, the need for future conversations is piling up around me. I'm not even sure where to begin. I am so overwhelmed by it all.

When I reach the bedroom closest to ours, Dottie is standing in her crib, not napping as she should be. I lift her up, cradling her to my chest—my favorite sensation of motherhood. All the senses are set ablaze at once with the smell from the top of her head, a chemical blend more potent than any drug—as if trust bears a weight that says, *I belong to you because I came from you*.

Feeling the need to busy myself, I pull Dottie onto my lap as I sit in the rocking chair that once belonged to Christine. I open a book and begin to read, and she snuggles closer to my neck, draping the blanket around us both.

I've pulled *Love You Forever*, knowing Christine will interrupt us long before I reach the part of the story when the son sneaks into his mother's room at her nursing home and rocks her in the way she did for him when he was a baby. I have never gotten through the book without crying.

"I wish I had a camera. I'd take a picture," Christine says as she appears standing in the doorway exactly as she did before. Dottie wiggles her way off my lap and runs over to Christine. "I put a casserole in your fridge and left the instructions on the island. Let me know if you can't manage it," she explains, as if heating up a casserole were complicated. She kneels to hug Dottie.

"Thanks, you didn't need to," I offer, signaling for Dottie to come back on my lap. Dottie plops her little body down between us, clearly not interested in picking sides, and starts picking through a pile of dolls on the floor.

"Leah, I'm worried about you." Christine is still within the doorframe but has returned to a standing position.

I exhale loudly. Amy's worry has been tolerable because hers comes from a place of love. Christine's feels like more of a performance piece that stems from judgment and criticism. A calculated attack on the way I choose to live my life and parent my children.

"Everything is fine," I say, rubbing my temples, trying to ward off an incoming headache.

"I know you and I aren't exactly close. I know that. But you hold things that are more precious to me than I can ever explain, which makes *you* precious to me," she says, refusing to let up. Her eyes dart down the hallway to Joni's room, where they stay. I wonder if she practiced this speech on Amy before delivering it to me now. It feels overly rehearsed, even for Christine.

"I'm just stressed about work. I'm not able to get anything done. I see now why you didn't work," I say, hoping to annoy her just enough that she'll want to leave.

"Then you and I have very different definitions of work."

"Yes, well." I walk over and scoop up Dottie. "Thank you for the casserole. I'll have Lucas call you if we have any issues heating it." I suddenly want her to believe that I'm an idiot in the kitchen because it would help drive home the point that I'm nothing like her and never will be.

I'm about to pass her in the doorway when she puts her hand on the outside of my elbow. Dottie wiggles loose from my arms, removing our last barrier of protection. Christine takes both my arms now.

"Christine, it's fine," I say, frozen in the doorway.

After witnessing an entire conversation transpire between Joni and Christine almost exclusively with eye contact, I wonder how we have managed to build and maintain our own fortresses, protecting ourselves from each other. I try to escape her, but she only grips me tighter.

"Your children need you. Your family needs you." I wonder if she can smell the wine on my breath.

I want to lean my head back and scream up at the ceiling that the stress of Isla's secret pregnancy and Christine's obsession with Miles are completely valid excuses for my actions. My behavior is a direct result of her twisted implications and the impact of knowing and holding on to these things. I want so much to protect Amy from all the hurt that's headed her way, and Christine doesn't know the half of it. If only Christine cared for Amy the way I do.

If only she knew how lonely it is to carry around the weight of these secrets.

"Whatever is happening with your drinking . . . ," she begins. My blood runs cold. *What does she mean?* I scramble to play the only trump card I own.

"Who is Grace?"

Christine immediately releases her grip and steps back into the hallway.

"How do you know about Grace?"

"That's not important," I say smugly, thrilled to have turned the spotlight back on her.

"You don't know what you're talking about."

"And neither do you. So let's both agree to drop it."

I can already taste how well the remaining sips of wine will pair with the sweetness of this victory.

CHAPTER 21

The evening of the opening, I decide to go all out with my outfit and makeup. I remember the sexy version of myself from back in college and how she existed as both an entity and a state of mind. How feeling desired as a woman was somehow wrapped up into my self-worth. I haven't been able to tap into the same sense of radical sexuality since I birthed my children. I know Lucas still looks at me all the time with want in his eyes, but it's difficult to look at my body and not see the places it's been pulled and stretched and torn raw. How it suddenly became imperfect the second I permanently marked it with a tattoo.

I wish I were appearing in the mirror as a blank canvas so I could paint myself into a version of me that's more palatable. I shouldn't ache in all the ways I do. As Amy said in the car after we met Isla at Poplar, I have it all. All of the ingredients for a happy life but nothing in the correct measurements.

Even with all the unnecessary drama, Dory was happy to stay with the kids during the opening. She had invited her nephew and his band over the previous night for dinner and much preferred the quality one-on-one time with them to watching them perform at the opening.

I sweep my hair up in loose curls, exposing my neck with a necklace Nana sent over from her travels. The shape of my dress hugs every curve. I know it's asking too much for Lucas to comment on my appearance, but I am hoping to have a little acknowledgment of my efforts. When I make my way downstairs, he's busy muttering to himself and pacing around in circles.

Christine enters The Restaurant with Paul and Lucas on either side of her. As if the queen herself were being escorted into the grand ballroom. The sun is only just setting, and the orange light is spilling out into the dining room. The second they separate from Christine, there is a low rumble of manic energy radiating off the guys. It matches the pace of the dining room. The music that's playing overhead is a touch too loud, which forces everyone to speak at an almost unreasonable volume. The scraping of silverware on porcelain competes in the background. Whatever buzz I entered with has been replaced with an assault on my senses.

The boys lead us around while Paul points out every detail they've copied from the original. I'm pleased to see the hydrangeas add just the right something to the room, though their presence serves as a nagging reminder of Isla.

The boys get called into the kitchen for a moment. I'm greeted by another mom, Dawn, from Reid's baseball team. She has a goblet of wine in her hand, and she, too, has dressed up for the occasion. She goes on and on, practically giddy with excitement over the outcome of The Restaurant. As if it were *her* husband who has slaved over its creation all these years.

"I'm just so excited to have a night out away from the kids. Cheers! Am I right?" she says, lifting her glass. There's a waiter circulating with champagne, and I lift one off his tray and manage to meet her midair.

"Cheers!" I bring the drink to my lips, and she does the same. She's one of the team moms who always provides the snacks in prepackaged labeled baggies for everyone. I wonder what she means by "night out away from the kids." How that translates for her and whether a single evening recharges her enough to feel excited about racing out in her minivan to go buy more SunnyD and pretzels.

"You must be so proud of Lucas!" Her cheeks flush a little when she says his name. It's oddly arousing to have another woman lust after your husband. I wonder if Lucas will want to de-stress in the powder room with me later.

"So proud," I manage to get out. "'Scuse me. I'm gonna sneak off to the bathroom before dinner begins."

The noise and the bustle are more than I'm prepared for. Lucas warned us all during Sunday dinner that the nature of the soft opening was meant to challenge the waitstaff and the kitchen, to work out all the kinks as a dry run. They've packed the dining room with patrons, requesting only the most nit-picky of customers. This must be why they invited Dawn.

My walk to the bathroom takes me down the corridor displaying my art. Lucas's act of inclusion, bringing me inside his dream in this way, should be more than enough. A gesture of thoughtfulness so profound. And while I know that to be true, why can't I feel it?

I enter the powder room, where Christine and Amy are sitting next to each other on a velvet love seat. My gaze stops on Amy. Looking at her, all I can see is a pregnant Isla. She's sitting beneath a golden-framed still life of black-and-white roses. The gold is meant to offset the colorless flowers, but it's not working.

"I'm glad you're both in here," I say, walking over to the only other chair in the room.

I rummage through my bag, carefully avoiding the flask I've stored away for emergency use, and pull out the envelope containing the DNA results for Joni's paternity. I'm incapable of allowing Christine to have the last word when it comes to Joni. When she finally turns to face me, I shove the results into her hands.

"What is this?" Christine asks. She seems genuinely baffled as to the envelope's contents.

"I know you think something is going on, but it's not what you've imagined. Miles, the park ranger from the Tree Tunnel, was a fling I had long ago when I first moved here and then never again. This is a paternity test for Joni. I haven't opened it, and I don't want to. I don't need to. Joni is Lucas's daughter. She has been since I told him I was pregnant. There is a possibility the results will say otherwise, and if that's the case, I hope for Joni's sake you'll realize I only want what's best for her. That's all I've ever wanted. If you need to know, well then, you'll know."

I can tell by Amy's face that she's just as stunned as Christine. After she ambushed me with that twelve-step meeting, I wasn't able to share my decision to give the results to Christine. The truth is, I'm not entirely sure what I'm doing or how I arrived here.

"Why wouldn't Lucas be Joni's dad?" Christine asks.

"Isn't this what you wanted?" But before Christine can answer, Lidy comes in. "What are you all doing in here? We're supposed to be seated now—together." She's holding the door open and tapping her foot in agitation.

I want to tell Lidy to leave us alone. But I know Paul and Lucas have us on a strict schedule, and it's important we follow through.

Lidy leads the way, with the three of us trailing behind her single file. I stand in the back and watch Amy and Christine walk arm in arm to the dining room. Somehow Christine has found a way to replace my role for Amy. For so long, Amy and I could endure the ridiculous nature of the O'Connor family and their codependent enmeshment because we had each other to depend on. But now they are up there and I'm back here. I put the flask up to my lips and manage two swallows without anyone turning around. As we step into the hallway, Christine's attention is immediately drawn to a framed newspaper article about The Cove's success forty years ago. She intentionally keeps her back to me, reaching out to touch the face of a woman who I assume is her mother in the picture.

Our large circular table is in the very center of the room. George and Christine are seated across from Jack and Lidy. Amy is next to Christine, and Lucas and I are next to George. Each of the tables surrounding ours is filled with nicely dressed couples or groups of friends and family. Already the smells wafting out from the kitchen are incredible. I will need to eat soon to absorb the amount of liquor I've already consumed.

"I love the touch of the centerpieces. Paul, that must have been you," Christine comments. Each table has a magnificently large bowl filled with sea glass and shells like the original.

"Yes, with a lot of help from Joni." It's an exclusive interaction between the three of them, the way Christine, Paul, and Lucas all gush over Joni. Christine's attempt to punish me for our earlier encounter.

There are more shouts from the kitchen, though neither Paul nor Lucas looks particularly alarmed. I've watched enough episodes of *The Bear* to know that a chef's intensity isn't something mere mortals should mess with.

"Mom, you look radiant this evening," Lucas says as Christine looks to George, who gently kisses her fist as he cups it in his own hand.

"Stunning," he says, grinning.

The waiter walks around the table, handing each of us a menu. Paul and Lucas watch Christine intently—like they are in on a joke and looking for the punch line written somewhere on her face. I bring my eyes back to the menu. Until this moment, they have managed to keep the name a secret. They even kept the sign covered out front. But now the restaurant's name is printed at the top in a regal, stylish font: *Say Grace*.

Christine puts her hand to her mouth as, one by one, the family tries to read her response. What should be a delight registers as a version of distress I've only ever witnessed in Christine that day I inquired about Grace in the doorway of Dottie's bedroom.

George reaches for her hand again. She puts the menu to her chest, finally allowing her gaze to meet her sons'. Paul and Lucas are still watching her intently.

Her eyes fill with tears. She goes to reach for her napkin but keeps her other hand clutching George's. She carefully dabs around her eyes, paying mind to her makeup.

"It's no secret that being your mother is the best thing I could've done with my life. With each of you, my heart's capacity swelled, and I became fulfilled in a way that only a parent can understand. But it's time I told you something," she says, her voice becoming a hoarse whisper. "Boys, I need to tell you something. Well, all of you—it's important that everyone in our family knows the truth finally, as you are all a part of who we are now. I need to tell you why we say grace," she says again, but this time with more strength behind it. "Boys, you had a sister. Jack, you had a twin, Grace. She died the day you were born, and I decided to keep her from you." The noise in the room is considerable. There's a crash from within the kitchen, but no one at the table can move.

"We kept her death from you—to protect you," George adds. It's perhaps the first time I've ever witnessed him being stoic. Even his smile lines appear confused in their grooves, deep and pitted from overuse.

"I'm so sorry, Mom, truly. Losing a baby . . ." Paul's visible burden of grief is evident in the welling of his eyes. He turns to Amy, and she nods. She is crying softly but is not drawing attention to herself. Everyone is blurry, as if I've used my finger to smudge at a stroke that's too defined on one of my paintings. The once jovial tone of the evening has been muddied. What's out in front of me is all wrong. I look away before I, too, get swept up by the sadness.

"I'm sorry too," Jack says. He's touching the condensation on his water glass, swiping at it with his index finger. Like his dad, Jack isn't his typical shade—he's showing no signs of anger, and it's deeply unsettling. "What happened? How did it happen?" There is a catch in his voice as he audibly tries to inhale.

"The doctor said it sometimes happens with twins. One is just stronger while they are growing. It was all okay until it wasn't in the end. Grace was stillborn," George answers, trying to explain in a way that delicately dances around blame being directed anywhere.

"One was stronger? So, what, that was me? It was my fault?" Jack's face has turned red. He reaches for his glass and takes several swallows. Lidy is rubbing his arm that's resting on the table. I follow his lead and down the rest of my wine.

"It wasn't anyone's fault at all. Losing Grace was a tragedy that felt bigger than what your mother and I wanted to burden you with. You were only children when it happened." George is serving as their spokesperson.

"But we are all adults now and have been for some time. Since when do we have secrets in our family?" Jack asks. I sense his temperature rising.

"That's fair. No, that's fair," Christine says, nodding.

"Hold up, Jack. Let's all stay calm." Lucas puts his hands up as if to protect Christine. I can sense he wants to placate Jack, to ease his brother's volatility.

Our waiter has returned and starts to refill water glasses and my wine. There is a nervousness to his face, his lips pinched together like a fist, and yet he still could have been pulled directly from the audition tapes for *Love Island*. Scott selected only aspiring models and actors as staff, claiming their allure was as essential as the restaurant's aesthetic. You can tell "Hunter," as his name tag reads, is eager to begin announcing the specials; no doubt Paul and Lucas have given him strict orders. We are all relieved for the break to collect our thoughts.

Scott approaches the table and whispers something into Lucas's ear. There's louder, more aggressive shouting coming from the kitchen. Immediately Lucas and Paul stand. The timing is either impeccable or disastrous.

"Excuse us, please," Paul says. They move briskly toward the sound of the noise.

"It's fine, Mom. It's all fine." Jack's eyes are squinting like he's troubled by his own words. "Makes sense." He nods solemnly. "No wonder you never . . ." He drifts off, his words spilling into the glass at his lips.

"It's okay if it's not fine, Jack," Christine says, pausing to look over at George, who is attempting to divert the remaining women's attention by discussing the appetizers. I ignore George to eavesdrop on Jack and Christine's conversation.

"The thing about men, about raising sons, is in many ways, I've been let off the hook," Christine continues in a hushed whisper. "I should have looked harder at the inequity. I never meant to create a divide. But I can see now that I did." The warmth of the wine has left me with a relieved satisfaction that the perfect mother is far from it. She is just as tragically flawed as the rest of us.

The waiter places some appetizers on the table. No one makes a move to begin eating. My eyes dart to the kitchen as I will Lucas to return to the table.

Jack has pushed away from the table with his shoulders slumped so far over they could tumble directly down and be poured into the drink in his lap. Christine makes her way over to Lucas's empty chair and drags it next to Jack. I can't look away. I'm watching her every movement.

"It wasn't balanced or evenly distributed," she tells Jack, refusing to name the "it" because that would be an admission of fault. "All those times you asked whom I would rescue, you were questioning what you were feeling. The unevenness I was showing you." She tilts her head back, trying to keep the tears inside her eyes. Jack stares off into the distance like he is trying to picture it too. "Now that you're a father, I know you understand you could never choose a favorite. Of course, each child stands out at times and phases—glowing during their moment in the sun. But they make their own light, the kind that has absolutely nothing to do with us. You could never single out just one to save. We'd sacrifice ourselves as parents never to have to make that choice." Her explanation cannot possibly be enough for Jack after a lifetime of inequity and misplaced anger.

Once Christine returns to her seat next to George, she repeats aloud to Jack for the benefit of the table, "I never meant to keep secrets from you. Please know that."

I scoff, making sure she knows I'm not buying it. I reach for the scallops at the center of the table and drop two onto my plate, then aggressively scrape the sauce off the porcelain, purposefully drawing attention to myself. After I've stuffed both scallops in my mouth, butter drips down one side of my chin. I chew for several seconds before wiping it away with the back of one of my hands, suddenly preoccupied by the primal act of eating.

"These scallops are *really* good," I announce, needing to contribute my two cents.

I catch Christine's eyes squinting in my direction as if *I'm* the embarrassing person at this table. She removes the envelope from her purse and holds it in her hand as menacingly as if she were holding a loaded weapon between her fingers.

I swallow what's left in my mouth and again reach for my wine, gulping it down as if it's water. When I return the empty glass to the table, I lift one of my eyebrows, daring her to push it further. The alcohol has stripped away my fear and replaced it with a cold smugness.

"What's that?" Lidy asks, using her chin to point toward Christine's hand.

A game of Russian roulette, I want to say.

While the envelope is still pinched between her two fingers, Lucas and Paul return to the table, their cheeks flush with color.

"Sorry about that," Paul says, apologizing on their behalf. Amy and Paul exchange a strained look.

"Everything okay?" Amy asks Paul.

"Some kinks to work out before the real opening, unfortunately, but hopefully we've sorted the major ones." Paul dabs at his brow with his napkin. "Everything here all right?"

Lucas whispers to the waiter and then turns his body toward me. The skin between his brows is puckered. He uses his napkin to dab at my chin. I recoil from his attempt, swatting at his hand.

Christine returns the envelope to her purse.

"Let's get someone to take our photo." George reaches for his camera bag hanging off the back of his chair.

"We've hired someone for that. James, can you take our picture?" Lucas waves over the photographer dressed in all black, who is standing beneath the most magnificent chandelier.

"At least have him use my camera," George says.

"Dad, I'm sure he can manage with what he's got. We'll get copies of all these to share."

"I insist." George is uncharacteristically firm. "What are you working with—looks like you've gone for the newer model of the classic that I have," George tells James as he hands him his Canon, draping the strap over the other man's neck the way he has always done whenever Joni asks to use it.

They all lean into one another around the table. I refuse to smile as I sit among the O'Connors and participate in such a ridiculously contrived moment.

"How were the apps?" Lucas asks after we've taken our seats again. Suddenly he sounds like a small boy seeking his mother's approval.

"Everything is simply wonderful," Christine answers before anyone else.

"You know, if it's too painful, Mom, we can change the name," Paul offers.

"Oh, for fuck's sake," I echo into my wineglass, just loud enough that I'm certain everyone will hear. It's Lucas's turn to draw in a breath.

"Leah!" he scolds, like I'm a child at the kids' table.

But I continue, unbothered by his warning. "I'm sorry, but I've played along pretty well, I think. We all have. We get that you must continue to do whatever it takes to impress this woman"—I gesture toward Christine and then the rest of the table—"since she needs to be at the center of your universe." Then I address Lucas. I can hear my words are slurred and rage filled. "You've killed yourself over this place, spent almost every waking moment away from the kids and me to create what can only be seen as a shrine to your mother." The drink in my hand splashes out as I make a dramatic circle, no longer sure of the glass's weight and contents. "She just admitted she lied to you for more than thirty years, and now you're worried about how *she* feels about the name? The mama's boy bit was cute for a while. We all played along. Some better than others"—I point my fingers at Lidy now, wanting to single her out for being such a kiss-ass—"but jeez. It's, like, enough already!" I recognize only after I've finished my speech that all the booze has hit me at once, and I'm drunk.

"Leah, stop." Amy attempts to pull away from the table, but Christine reaches for her. The maternal stroke of her hand on Amy's forearm, guiding her back down to be seated, is the final strike along the matchbook's edge.

I am on fire.

I might be shouting, but I need to compete with the ambient chatter surrounding us. "I dunno what type of spell she's got you under," I say, directing my frustration toward Amy. "Maybe you can't see 'cause of Isla." My words are swimming around the table.

"Let's go to the bathroom." Amy is standing, rushing to my side. Her legs are hidden beneath her bulbous shape, making her movements mysterious, like how a snail uses its mucus to propel itself forward. I launch myself up, ready to receive her. Happy that she chose me.

My tight dress limits my mobility and my heel catches on the corner of the chair. I tumble while managing to stay on my feet, though, in my missteps, my back collides into the front of Amy, forcing her off-kilter, and she lands directly on her butt. She remains there on the perfectly polished hardwood, stunned. The gnarled detail of the flooring reminds me of driftwood, and I am certain that choice was intentional. Paul shoves past me and kneels, reaching for Amy's hands.

"Baby, you okay? Here." He drapes himself on top of her as if allowing his own body to become a protective shield. Despite Paul's theatrical movements, Amy's eyes haven't left mine.

"What happened?" I ask, wanting to lean down and pull her up, but instead, I place my hands on my knees and lean over.

"What happened?" she repeats my words back to me as if she can't quite hear despite the buzz in the dining room having died out completely.

"You okay?" It comes out more flippant than I mean it, but I can't understand why she's still on the floor.

I shove off my knees in hopes my action will inspire her upward. Though awkwardly, Paul is guiding her, and the O'Connors have circled around as if she were a toddler launched off the bottom of a slide.

She's made it to her feet, finally, pressing hard into Paul—meandering back in the direction of their seats.

I could apologize, but it wasn't on purpose, and it wouldn't do any good to draw more attention to the situation.

"Dinner and a show, lucky us," Jack says into his drink, shaking his head snidely.

He's such an asshole. I pretend to curtsy with my arms outstretched since my body has again found the chair.

"Always happy to fulfill my role and serve as the entertainment for this family," I say, but I want to cry. Why do I have to act as the official circus performer to the O'Connor clan?

Voices return to the other tables and the hum of activity drowns out our silence. I can see Christine desperately trying to seize hold of the moment, to pivot the limelight back on her in a way that paints her as the victim in all this—instead of the villain.

"Amy, you sure you're all right?" Christine asks, and Amy responds by pursing her lips together and bowing her head in a slow nod.

As if Amy's exaggerated choreography served as a signal they had prepared together before our arrival at the opening, Christine holds up her glass, pausing to gather her words. "I'm so proud. I wish Grace were sitting with us at this table. I'm sorry I kept her from you all until now."

"But she's here. She's always been here," George adds with his quiet yet remarkable kindness.

"Yes. Well, now, let's say grace," Christine says.

Four of us are standing in the parking lot. I think about going on all fours, crawling like Dottie when she and Reid pretend to be animals on the floor.

The tunnel I am currently inside feels dark and damp. I have to move my shoulders back and forth in exaggerated motions to get to the other side. I can't stop my body from shivering as Lucas shouts words next to me.

"What exactly is happening here? You know what tonight meant to me!"

I can't blame him for being mad. I enjoy anger—it feels purposeful.

"I dunno what's happening," I whisper at first in response to Lucas, and then I try shouting it to match his volume. "I don't know!"

"Lower your damn voice." I can't focus on his face, but I can mentally replicate his look of defeat and confusion. I've seen it before. Thankfully, Amy has come to my rescue. I don't hear her car pull up next to us, but suddenly she is dragging me into her open passenger side door.

"We are leaving. Leah, get in the car."

I am looking at her, but her shape isn't Amy.

"Seriously, this is your night. I want you and your brothers to stay here and celebrate. It's your last chance." I hear Amy speaking, but she sounds like she's underwater.

"Are you going to take her home? She's too much for you to handle right now."

"I wish I could show you snippets from my childhood so you'd know what I've already survived. This is nothing. She'll just pass out and might puke. Like taking care of a baby. So it will be good practice for me."

Lucas is trying to help get me in the car, but I swat at his arm, still angry with him for treating me like a child.

"I will check in with you later. Go. And take your brother with you," Amy says.

"Thank you. Thank you." Paul walks around behind the car, putting his arm around Lucas's shoulder. "Amy has her."

While I'm struggling to focus on his face, I can tell Lucas is furious, practically combustible, with his fists clenched at his sides.

"Hey, I got her."

I roll my body around in the seat, feeling like a caged animal that needs to escape.

"I got her, Am. You shouldn't have to deal with this," Lucas says.

"Well, clearly you aren't dealing with what's happening!" When Amy yells there is a scathing edge to her voice.

"You tell him, girl!" I'm thrilled to have Amy back on my team.

"What does that mean?"

"Your wife, my best friend, is an alcoholic, Lucas. She has a problem. We need to help her," she says, and again her words sound like they are happening inside a vacuum. "It doesn't just go away if we ignore it. That's not how these things work."

"Are you the expert now? Suddenly you're an expert on all things Leah?"

Paul grabs Lucas by both his arms.

"Don't talk to my wife like that. Don't." I love that I'm the cause of Paul's maniacal tone. I've never heard them shout at each other before, even during the most stressful phases of opening the restaurant. It's as if Christine raised them to be well-behaved robots—and now, finally! Some emotion out of these boys. Lucas throws his hands in the air in defeat.

I manage to relax my body into the passenger seat of the car. I am alone, but I can hear the voices ping-ponging as echoes just outside. I curl forward, pulling my legs up onto the dashboard, and hug my knees toward my chest.

"I'm not doing this. We are all on the same side here."

Wait, why does Amy sound like she's crying?

"I'm so damn grateful to just have one, to be loved and be a part of something. You all have no idea what it's like not to have a family. But this family, our family, is not exempt from tragedy—that truth became evident tonight when Christine told us about Grace. Just because we pretend something doesn't exist doesn't mean the pain stops. Look at Leah!"

"Sorry, I'm sorry." I don't know what Lucas is apologizing for.

"Can't you see it now—that she needs help? Or do you just not want to see? Look! Look at her!"

I do my best to position myself so I'm sitting up in the seat, but my arms begin to flail around for no reason at all. Paul and Lucas are embracing.

"You haven't said anything that I haven't said to myself before. I see it." Lucas backs away, closing the car door with Paul's hand still offering him support.

"You and Lucas go to our house when you're done. I'll figure something out for us. Everyone can just cool off. You both deserve to enjoy the rest of the evening. I have it covered, but come tomorrow, everyone gets behind her. Let's just hope she wants tonight to be the end of the road."

"I love you. Thank you. You're amazing." Paul bends over to kiss Amy. Lucas starts making his way back toward Say Grace.

"Oh, I know," Amy tells Paul. "You relieve Dory at their house with Lucas. I'll call to check in. Leah will be fine with me. Nothing good will come from them being in the same house tonight. Maybe tomorrow things will look different."

I know we are driving because objects outside the window are moving. The warmth that's pooling within has penetrated my protective shell. I wonder how it passed through the barrier when nothing else, not my husband, my friendship with Amy, or even my children can break in. It shouldn't be like this, and I'm scared because contentment never used to be so hard to achieve. And I have no concrete reasons—when I go to hold on, they all slip through my fingers. I got on the ride willingly, just not knowingly. I said yes to motherhood, and Lucas, and the O'Connor way, without having any of the necessary foresight to recognize that despite an entire forest full of people, I'd still feel like the single tree standing alone inside the arch of the other cypresses.

I want to go to the Tree Tunnel. My body's limbs are too long and spindly in this space meant for a much smaller person. Amy is speaking in the melodic cadence she reserves only for my children, but it is far from her patronizing preschool teacher tone. I'm so grateful for her kindness I could weep. I want her to experience what I am, to envelop her inside this space with me so I am no longer in it alone.

After the meeting, inside Amy's car, I knew my time had run out. Since then I've felt like Alice in Wonderland trying to escape the Queen of Hearts, only to look through the keyhole and find that I've spent this whole time sleeping it all away.

"Oh, Leah. Please. Please get off the ride." Amy's voice is miles away.

I must help Amy wade through the clouds, using my arms as oars. I never realized how glorious it feels to swim through fog. Streaks of white barrel toward us, but I'm unable to propel forward fast enough. It is becoming too much too quickly. I need to unbury myself. Or maybe I'm waving my arms to draw attention to the version of me that exists just out of reach.

"I can't escape. I'm trapped!" I scream, turning my head from side to side. Then it all goes dark.

CHAPTER 22

I come to on Christine and George's couch in their living room that's closest to the kitchen. The twilight between awake and asleep has become a vessel for dread. My mouth feels dry and sour.

I turn my head slightly to the left. Christine is sitting in the chair next to the bay window. She's looking outside and hasn't yet noticed that I'm awake. Every ounce of me wants to run for the door, but I've been dragged under the wave and left to die. For a minute, dying sounds easier.

Amy stands somewhere in my peripheral vision and the two of them walk over to the kitchen together. They are speaking at a normal volume as if they are alone and have forgotten anyone else is in the room. I decide to remain quiet in hopes of piecing together the events that led me here at the end of the night. I can't help feeling betrayed that Amy brought me here for Christine to see me at my lowest point.

"No one tells you that when your baby dies, you have to decide between a tiny coffin or cremation. It isn't something people talk about." Amy is speaking to Christine. Her back is to me as she sits on one of the barstools lining the kitchen island. "When the social worker came in to discuss Elijah's *remains*, the word was so offensive I almost spat at her."

I can hear the clanging of a teapot.

"What did you choose?" Christine asks.

"Cremation. What about you, with Grace?"

"Same."

Grace. The revelation of her identity is my last solid memory from last night.

"I know it's morbid to talk like this while I'm pregnant, tempting fate, but I haven't had anyone to say these words to before. Nobody I can trust who understands besides Paul, but even he can't comprehend fully. And just saying that aloud to you now helped me more than a year of therapy. I am so sorry you lost Grace, Mom. I am so very sorry."

There is more opening and closing of drawers in the kitchen. Of course, Christine won't know how to respond to Amy, to something that vulnerable. I wouldn't be surprised to look out and see a Christine-shaped hole in the wall. But instead, I hear the scraping of a barstool on the wood flooring as she pulls up next to where Amy is seated.

"It's miraculous what women can endure. Grief bleeds into the marrow of a mother's bones when she loses a child; the loss is forever a part of her. A baby who only exists in memory becomes all the things they could have been, all they never got a chance to experience," Christine says.

"Exactly." Amy is no longer holding back her sobs. "It felt as if I was drowning in my pain. Living a nightmare. A fate worse than death. Will you tell me about the night Grace was born?" I am unable to fathom that this is the conversation Amy and Christine are having right now. My head is throbbing like someone is attempting to cut out sections of my frontal lobe.

At the end of the night, I must have swallowed rocks filled with putrid, rotting apples, because a sweetness has coated my tongue, creating a filmy layer throughout my mouth. I'm meant to sit in it, soberly, and suffer for my sins.

After a minute of hesitation, Christine begins speaking from her place at the counter.

"We didn't yet know the sex of the twins, so the opportunity to finally have a girl left me hopeful with possibility."

I peek through my blanket and see both of them at the barstools sipping from their teacups, their backs hunched. I really don't want to throw up. I swallow what's in my throat and the bile tastes like wine, which means I probably haven't gotten sick yet.

Christine continues, "There were unforeseeable circumstances surrounding the birth of the twins. Jack came first, angry but focused. He was quickly swept away, since it appeared that he may have swallowed meconium in the birth canal. With all the attention largely on him, I sent George to be with Jack. Grace happened suddenly, an entanglement of flesh and blood. She was immediately placed on me. *Of course*, I thought, *our family ends with a daughter*. A baby sister for her big brothers to adore."

I picture Christine cradling Grace in her arms the way she did Joni when she was born, all the pieces finally clicking into place. Her words echo like the sounds from the bell tower. *"You, my girl, are exactly who I've been waiting for."*

"Suddenly a flood of people entered the room. The noises were jarring—going from perfect stillness to a cacophony of scraping metal and machines. All at once the room was full, when just moments before we were perfectly at peace on our own. The way they carried her body away from me, I knew she wasn't alive. There are things a mother just knows." Christine allows only a single hitch in her voice. The force of her restraint shows in the way she's clenching her hands into fists at her sides.

"Yes." Amy finally speaks in an achingly soft whisper. I sneak a small sip of water from the table and no one detects my movement. I know to take small sips from the times my children have vomited up large quantities of water after drinking too much when they had the stomach flu.

"Jack took too many nutrients away from Grace, and while he grew healthy and strong, she simply couldn't survive. It must have happened shortly before birth; otherwise her death would have stimulated early labor. Stillborn." For some reason, I think of the child left in his car seat in the garage overnight. I want to cry out and beg Christine to stop talking. The sadness of her story in my current state makes me want to rip off my own ears to keep from listening. But she won't stop. I can tell by the way Amy is crying that she needs to absorb every word Christine will offer. Which is the only reason I remain silent.

"Maybe if I had held her there forever . . . Knowing George, he would have welcomed every ounce of blame I hurled in his direction. But his kindness only made me angrier." I close my eyes and picture Lucas. His inherited goodness and my sensation of impending doom that I somehow ruined all that he had worked for last night. "As I stood there a week later, holding Jack in one arm and my suitcase instead of my daughter in the other, I realized I could never explain Grace to her brothers. Toddlers' minds are all questions without filters. No, we'd say it was only ever Jack inside. At their age, I could tell them the sky was green, point up at it and say, 'We call this color green now,' and they'd nod along, devouring our words as gospel. In their eyes, we were only capable of the truth. Misery overpowered

all my judgment, and maybe George could have convinced me
to make a different decision, but then he would have had to be
a completely different man. I told him there and then that we'd
keep her existence from the boys. There and then I decided to
drown the lie, allow it to be swallowed up within the cesspool
of my despair." There it is again. Common ground. This time
not from the speaker in the meeting but from the last person
on earth I ever thought I'd relate to.

"That type of tragedy defines someone forever. It would be
impossible to be seen as anyone other than a mother who lost
her child. I've tried—I've tried so hard to always regard you as
a mother first, Amy, and never someone who is defined by her
loss."

It's Amy's turn to speak now. "You have. It was always you
who understood without words somehow. You made it so I felt
less alone in my grief." Their connection is suddenly broken
down in black and white while I am perched atop the ceiling,
an insect swaddled within a spider's web. "I've never looked
at Elijah's ashes. I've avoided opening the urn. The meager
ashes contained inside would be too much to witness. A grown
body, the volume of it in ash, contains a lifetime worthy of its
weight. A newborn's is just not enough. It could never possibly
be enough," Amy says.

"Exactly." They reach out and cling to each other's hands,
unabashedly intertwining fingers. They linger there long
enough that I need to rest my eyes.

When I open them, Christine is reaching over the teacups
to hold up a photograph left out on the counter.

"George took this picture of me at the beach on Grace and
Jack's birthday. I told him it was silly to capture an image of
just me without the kids. You'll come to discover one day that

you exist for them as the sun, the moon, and all their stars, and then the next day you'll wake up and have to settle for being a lantern outside their windows. But George reminded me that I exist even when they aren't with me. I needed that reminder. And you reminded me too," Christine says, her tone smooth and gentle, "when you asked to call me 'Mom.' Called me over to Leah's . . . You opened a doorway into a new space for us. There's a sixth sense I've always had about my sons, being an extension of me. Now you've gifted me something. I needed our relationship to remind me that my role as a mother hasn't ended. In a lot of ways, it's just beginning."

"You have no idea how much I've needed you, Mom. What our relationship has meant to me . . . because, um, the truth is, my mother, Isla, is still alive. I only said that she died because I wanted a fresh start. She's an alcoholic and a liar, a manipulator, and what you've gifted me with the O'Connors . . . it has been the happiest version of family I never thought I was worthy of."

"Your mother is alive?" Christine's confusion is evident, and I'm suddenly grateful that maybe now I can be the one to rescue Amy from Christine's wrath.

Except when Amy finds out I didn't immediately tell her Isla is pregnant, Christine will finally be able to replace my role in Amy's life for good.

"I'm so sorry I lied to you." I'm struck by a cloud of envy that I'm no longer the harborer of her secret. What should be relief, one less burden to carry, means now Amy will need me less. It is impossible to interpret Christine's body language from behind.

I can tell only that she hasn't released Amy's hand.

Their affection, Christine's capacity for forgiveness, is

what causes me to shoot upward and reach for the bowl that's been placed next to the glass of water. Both women leave the counter and descend upon me. Moving my feet to the floor sloshes the contents of my stomach even further. Amy is beside me, helping to clutch the bowl just below my mouth as my tears of shame begin to fall.

I haven't even had the chance to wonder how I got here as I'm hit with more humiliation, though my stomach is immediately settled. I have small glimpses from dinner.

"The kids . . . Lucas?" His name catches in my throat. I wish they'd taken me to my own house, although maybe I'm no longer allowed in.

"Everyone is good. Lucas is home with the kids." Amy adjusts the pillows behind my back as Christine sits across from us, leaning in and then scooting back before finally settling on an awkward hunch. I'm slowly recalling some of the words I shouted during dinner.

I lift my eyes to meet Christine's. I've never looked at her this closely. We haven't ever sat together and tried to truly see each other. I notice what I did not see before: she is just a woman. What a strange thing that we could love the same people so deeply and yet so differently.

Christine takes the bowl and leaves the room momentarily. I'm hoping she'll let Amy tend to me in peace, but when she returns, she's holding the envelope with the paternity results I gave her in the powder room. I notice none of the edges are ripped; it is still sealed. She puts it in my sequined purse near my coat that's slung over a chair—something Amy must have done since I have no recollection of walking into the house. She faces me and pulls her chair even closer.

"I had no idea this was even a question. I'm furious you

would keep something like this from my son. All this time."
She's shaking her head in contempt reserved solely for my
omissions. I could have just let sleeping dogs lie. But instead,
seeing Miles, the fallout from all my internalized worry that
maybe Joni wasn't really an O'Connor . . . I drank because I
needed to numb out the noise when it all could have just as easily remained quiet. As dormant as it's been in Christine's mind
this entire time.

"As for me . . ." She lets out a breath that's so heavy I can feel
it touch the skin on my face. "Joni is as much a part of my heart
as my own children have ever been. A piece of paper isn't going
to give me an answer to a question I don't have."

There's a long, weighty pause. I want to cry in relief that the
envelope is back in my possession. While I recall the brazenness with which I presented it to her in the powder room, giving
it to her was a huge risk I never would have taken if I had been
sober.

Amy finally speaks. "Do you want me to call Lucas? I'm
sure he will want to know you're awake."

I shake my head. I'm not ready to face him just yet. Amy
rubs the skin atop her right wrist. A horrifying memory comes
flooding back to me from the opening.

"Amy, did I make you fall? I can't believe—I'm so sorry."

"I'm good—we're good," she says, patting her stomach without formally accepting my apology.

The room feels cold. I'm still wearing my dress, with the
blanket draped over my legs, which, again, I'm sure was Amy's
doing. Dread continues to rattle the door of my brain. I'm too
tired to rally my defenses to fight against it. I open my mouth
and then close it.

Christine speaks again. "If you were my child, I'd punish

you for your behavior. But you're neither mine nor a child, and I can see you're going to punish yourself enough, which will only further hurt your children."

I start to speak. "I—"

"Let me say this, Leah," she interjects. "There isn't a better, softer option when it comes to being a mother. These decisions we have to make—as it turns out, all the ways ache. That's just what happens. We've exposed our hearts completely to love them that much. There isn't a less painful way."

"All the ways ache," I repeat aloud, turning the words over. I never imagined someone like Christine could suffer within the walls of motherhood.

I'm unsure where to put this or why she would want to share it with me after everything. We've only ever sparred back and forth—a blow for a blow. We've never talked like this. She's lowered her defenses not in retreat but in acknowledgment. I want to bend down and match her. I know I'm not strong enough to do so yet, but for the first time, I want to.

After I get home and I've showered off only a single layer of my shame, I ask Lucas if we can go for a drive.

"You have every right to be angry with me. I'm so embarrassed with myself it hurts to even look at you. But please, can we take a beat and bring the kids to the beach?" I'm standing in my towel, speaking to his reflection in the mirror. I want to reach out and pull him into me so he can be reminded of how my body becomes a comma in his. But I won't allow myself to attempt any manipulation tactics.

"I'm not sure you are in a position to be asking me for anything right now."

"I know, you're right. But can we do it for the kids?"

He reluctantly agrees. We stop to get gas on the way, and I
can tell he is hesitant to leave me in the car while he uses the
restroom.

"I'm okay, really," I lie.

I left okay a while ago. I take note of the unusual line of men
snaking around the building, waiting their turn. I can't physically stay in the car. My body is a betrayal of organs, thudding
against the walls of my insides—provoking me to seek a remedy
for my discomfort.

"Joni and Reid, can you watch your sister while I go in for
a sec?"

"Candy?" Reid says. The childish implication of his ask is
so simple I have to swallow the lump in my throat to keep from
welling up.

"Sure."

I left the house without a sweatshirt, so I locate a zip-up
Cowboy Surf Shop hoodie in the shop and immediately put
it on.

At the refrigerator case, I grab a carbonated drink with
caffeine. The ooze lining my stomach feels like it's in the critical stage immediately preceding an uprising. I look up to see
my reflection in the mirrors they use to catch people stealing.
From this angle, I can't see any version of myself that feels
real. I grab each child's favorite candy—Sour Patch Kids for
Joni, Reese's for Reid, and I think about getting Dots for Dottie
but recognize they are still considered a choking hazard for a
toddler, so I snag a Kit Kat Bar instead.

As I am paying for my items, I immediately locate the alcohol behind the counter. Of course, that was why I came inside—to sneak something into my bag. I knew I couldn't stop myself from buying it. I physically can't, not after the utter humiliation of last night. I need something to destroy this concoction of feelings; no sane person could handle my current reality.

"Anything else?" the teenage girl behind the counter asks. Her hair is streaked with purple, and she has a ring in her nose like a bull. Her eyes are marked black with too much eyeliner, but they are a shade of green that is complemented by the color in her hair. Her name tag reads *Lacey*. We are the only ones in the store.

My voice sounds chalky, like it's being pulled out by a string. "I want to buy some booze . . . but please don't sell me any. Please." I don't need to look up at the mirrors on the ceiling to know how desperate I must seem.

Lacey stops chewing her gum, and her eyes meet mine. She nods casually, as if my request didn't sound completely insane—like I'd asked to borrow a penny from the tiny red tray between us.

"Don't worry, I got you," she says before she goes back to chewing her gum.

I pull cash out of my sequined purse I used last night; its fanciness mocks me. As I hand over the bills, my fingers aren't steady enough to be able to count them out. I go to scrape the money off the counter, and Lacey rests her hand on top of mine, covering it the way you would at a blackjack table, indicating *stand*. Her face is sincere and reassuring. If she is uncomfortable, she doesn't show it. After she counts the dollars and hands me my change, I nod in gratitude, crumpling it all back inside my purse next to the envelope Christine returned to me.

I make it outside. I look toward the pumps, hoping to see that Lucas is already waiting for me at the car so we can leave. Maybe I will even tell him what I almost purchased, revealing a sliver of honesty a little at a time. If I saw him standing there, I'd have gone to him. But he isn't there. I can't bring myself to make eye contact with my children within the car. That would break me.

I don't want to turn around and go back inside. I don't want to, but I know I am going to. Lacey has soundlessly followed me and is standing on the other side of the glass door. Her face is neutral, still giving nothing away. I go to reach for the door handle, looking beyond her, behind the register, then back. She shakes her head no, her green eyes greeting me with forceful empathy. I unfurl my fingers, releasing the handle, but leave my forehead pressed against the pane.

Lucas doesn't acknowledge that I've switched over to the driver's seat. I can tell he doesn't care where we are going. When I pull up to the Tree Tunnel parking lot, I'm relieved to see the ranger station is closed, though I already knew it would be on a Sunday. The kids tumble out of the car, familiar with the spot and all their favorite trees to climb.

It's completely deserted as we meander the path until I find the spot I'm looking for. The location of my most recognizable painting with the centralized singular tree claimed by neither side of the forest. Reid has Dottie on his back, and they are weaving between the cypress trees. Joni is a few paces back, hunting for something on the ground.

I sit with my back against the trunk of the lone tree, hoping but not expecting that Lucas will do the same. He positions himself so he's facing away from me while still using the base for support. I can't help but believe it's strategic on his part. I wouldn't want to look at me either.

He finally says, "I found a stash of empty bottles hidden inside our suitcases in the closet. Leah, why didn't I see this for what it is?"

"I couldn't—so how could you?" I can't meet his eyes. Even the branches overhead are completely soundless. Normally there's a creaking of the spindly branches' raw wood rubbing together as they weave into one another to form the archway.

"I'm so angry with you. But I've been looking into what to do, like, what is happening. Everything I've read says you should get help—the sooner the better." He sucks in a lot of air in preparation for what comes next. "You can't drink anymore. Ever. In our situation, it works best for people like you when there isn't time to waste in the in-between, trying to moderate. Lingering in this gray area."

People like me. I turn it over in my mind. *Lingering*—like I did at the gas station.

If it wasn't for Lacey . . . Lacey with the purple hair and nose ring. I realize suddenly I know who she is. It's my turn to speak.

"Amy took me to a meeting—like a twelve-step meeting, for alcohol, for people whose drinking is maybe a problem—the other day. I didn't tell you because I didn't want to belong with those people. But I think I met one of the women there—or I met her granddaughter just now when we stopped at the gas station. Which I guess is like some insane coincidence the universe is attempting to smack me over the head with. A God shot, I guess it's called. She helped me—turns out I need all the help I can get," I say, smiling a little, even though it hurts. It feels like the most honest thing I've said to him in years. It didn't kill me though, telling him this. Somehow it didn't kill me.

I draw a wavy line in the dirt before rubbing it away. I look up, out toward the water, which we can see from where we are sitting. Almost like the tunnel of trees is a kaleidoscope lens and the ocean is the focal point.

I rest my head on top of my bent knees and turn so I can search for answers in Lucas's face.

"You have no idea how badly I want to say, 'Fuck it, let's go surfing.'" I laugh a little, swiping away the pools of tears that have collected within the corners of my eyes. "You're right, though. I'm scared that if I don't try to stop now, I won't ever be able to." I don't know if Lucas wants to say something, but I need to keep going. "I don't know how to live like this anymore."

"I'm sorry. I don't want it to be like this for you. To be going through this. I would give anything. I . . ." Lucas strokes my hair as he desperately tries to understand, to meet me where I am. I stop him from trying to take on more of my pain.

"No, please." I'm no longer catching my tears as they stream down my face.

I stand; sitting no longer feels comfortable. Lucas does the same and brushes the combination of dirt and leaves off his pants.

"Fair enough. I'm tryna understand," he says, stopping to point his body in the direction of the beach. But he doesn't understand, and I know he can't. Some things are ours alone to keep. "Last night, what you said, the way you've been—we don't deserve any of that," he says, still wiping away dirt even though there is none left on him. The kids are almost to the sand out ahead of us. "All of your good parts, all that magic that exists within you, the light that radiates and draws everyone in—the things we all love, all of us: me, the kids, Amy, my mom—when you drink, it disappears."

How could he possibly still have any kind words to say about me at this point? I don't deserve his goodness. I want to apologize, tell him I'm sorry a hundred times over, but we'd have to start back at my very first lie, the one inside the envelope in my bag, and right now the best I can offer him is "You're right. You are a good man, the best husband. An even better dad. How do you do it? You know what, never mind." I shake my head. "Hey, let's make a date for surfing. No matter what happens, we will always have surfing. Deal?" I begin to unzip my purse, feeling for the envelope. I know the answer belongs with him.

"Deal." He takes off, moving at a brisk pace along the path until we are both running. There's something perfect about the way he's leading me toward the horizon line until he lets me pull ahead. My toes are sinking, disappearing beneath the wet sand as I make my way closer to the surf, pausing then to inhale the mist. My sweatshirt slips down my shoulder, exposing my bare skin. Lucas runs his fingers up and down, making his way up my back as he rubs his thumb along the ink between my shoulders.

I take off again until my toes are numb and tingling in the frothy surf.

"Watch me reappear," I hear myself calling back to him. Lucas is beside me; we are almost in step, content simply in the knowledge that I'm here, inside, underneath all this hurt.

I call Rita the following week.

"A healthy baby girl, Eve Marie," she announces as if she were a proud grandma.

"I'm telling Amy."

"Good. Good," Rita says and hangs up as if I was done talking.

Amy appears to be twice as pregnant as she was only a few days before. The courage required to have this conversation with her feels cruel without the ease of alcohol. But I've managed to go to a meeting every day and not drink in between them. All of my emotions feel as if they've been lit on fire. I cannot speak without crying. I cannot sleep no matter how hard I try. But now that I know Amy's sister has safely arrived, it's time she knew. Amy's past due at this point, but I know that I will continue to find excuses for why I shouldn't tell her.

"Can we sit?" I ask. "Don't worry, I'm still sober," I add, since I know it is where her mind will immediately go. "I have to tell you something, but before I do, I want you to know that whatever happens, I'm here for you—in a way I haven't been lately."

Her hands are folded in her lap, and I reach out to grip them tightly in mine.

"You're scaring me. Just say it." Her deep brown eyes are so dark they look like giant holes.

"Isla had a baby. This whole time she's been pregnant. I know it sounds impossible, but she had a baby girl."

CHAPTER 23

During the drive to the trailer, all I want to do is unburden myself of my decision to tell Amy. I need absolution for my terrible timing and to confirm that I've made the right decision by telling her about Isla having a baby girl. I want to reassure her that we will handle whatever comes our way as we move forward.

I open my mouth to speak but stop. She's gone the color of ash—after the fire has long burned out and the wood's charred surface has been beaten and turned over until it's white. She's deep within a hell all her own, and I've been directed in The Program that all I can do is reach across the center console and stroke the exposed skin between her hand and her wrist as it prickles into gooseflesh. It's the next right thing.

I've been so selfish. Everything always about me and my needs.

"This can't be happening," she says under her breath as if maybe we could turn around and forget the whole thing. As if she wishes she could go back in time and leave Isla and that life for good back in Pacifica—never have visited, truly severed ties the way she's implied she should have but just couldn't bring herself to. Then maybe she could continue the life meant for only her and her new family.

"I know," I whisper. "But I'm here."

"How could I not have seen it? There were signs in her face, her healthy cheeks I mistook for the color of sobriety—it was so foreign in her skin. I just assumed—at Poplar, when she refused to stand and retrieve the kite . . ." She's fitting it all together as I did when I learned what Isla was really hiding. I remain silent, letting her put the pieces wherever they need to go. "I should've known that the blanket she kept glued to her lap was all part of her disguise. Shouldn't I be fluent in her language of deceit by now?" She is shaking her head back and forth at a pace so rapid, I add my second hand to try to slow her movements, but it does nothing.

I scratch at the San Francisco Zoo sticker that's been left on the window from the time Paul and Amy took Dottie there. Afterward, Amy explained the story of their outing in tremendous detail, the way people do when they have a real affinity for children. No detail is spared because everything is precious. It's how I would have described stories about my own kids if I were a different version of myself.

"It was freezing," Amy explained. *"Dottie wanted to stop to get a churro, so of course Paul bought her one and she needed to eat it in the car because her hands were numb and she couldn't hold it up. Probably the weight of the thing too."* Amy laughed in her remembering. *"She sat on my lap because at the time I still had one. Sugar and cinnamon rained down all over the seats and I just shook my head at Paul for succumbing to her giant eyes and pouty lip when we passed the churro stand. He was for sure powerless over her cuteness. We are in so much trouble when our daughter gets here,"* she told me. I recall specifically because she never spoke about the future with such certainty.

I begin to pick and peel at the Z in *Zoo*. Some of the sticker gets tucked too deep beneath my nail beds, and my brain receives a quick message of pain. I resist the urge to drive it deeper. That's not going to help anything.

Isla had a baby. The tears find the creases next to Amy's eyes now. They slide down, and I notice that some have pooled into the small canals of her ears.

"I'm here," I tell her as we navigate the uneven pavement and I lift my head from the window to stop it from banging into the glass. I want to continually remind her, even if I have nothing of any value to say. Back when we were in the kitchen, before she called Christine, I disappeared. I ran away because my fear was stronger than anything else, and when I look at Amy now, I know that's simply not the case. My love for her is what's strongest.

"I have a sister," she says as a whisper. "I have a baby sister named Eve Marie."

I wonder what Amy having a sibling could mean for her life moving forward. The intricacies of family have very little to do with blood and biology and everything to do with whom we welcome into our hearts—those worthy of earning keys to certain chambers within. Looking over at Amy, I know this to be true. "We will figure it all out," I say, though I'm not entirely confident how. I want to ensure she heard me use the word *we*.

"Up ahead. Look!" Amy says, urgently thrusting her finger toward the windshield, pointing a few hundred yards toward the double-wide out in front of us. Up on the bluff is a silhouette of gauzy blackness, like a kite powerless before the fluid force of the wind. She's there only a second before disappearing, descending the bluff that falls into dunes, rolling into sand that succumbs to the sea. "Did you see her too?" Amy asks, almost as if she can't trust any of her senses.

"Yes." I point at the spot where Isla stood before being swallowed up.

Amy pulls in next to the trailer, so close that the bumper taps the pole Isla is using as a clothesline. Half a dozen pink and yellow onesies pinned all in a row sway as the line strains when it's jostled, but nothing falls. I consider the care that must have gone into securing each tiny article of clothing.

"Go look in the trailer. Go!" Amy shouts over to me as she rushes toward the bluff.

My palms are sweaty on the railing, almost slick. I swallow a lump that's caught in my throat, but I'm too scared to cough. Inside, there are burp cloths and baby clothes on the couch and floor, with diapers folded into small triangles littering the ground. My body recognizes the smell almost instantly, the unmistakable musk of newborn baby poop that isn't foul or putrid but has almost a sweet, vinegary tang.

Within the mess, my eyes find what they shouldn't: liquor bottles upon liquor bottles. I pick up one at my feet and notice there isn't so much as a drop left inside. Here within the double-wide, I'm presented with my phantom life. The confinement of being enclosed within this graveyard of empties, no sign of anything remotely human around. Panic ensues. All this horror is available to me if I succumb to the darkness.

I hear the smack of the door behind me. The dirt has turned into sand, and I realize I'm running, using my hand to shield the light. My eyes scour the water and see Amy charging toward the shoreline. Her movements are pronounced because of her shape and the unevenness of the sand.

From where I stand, the wind has funneled the sounds of the waves into an echo chamber of white noise. I follow Amy down, recognizing suddenly that Isla's feet are being swallowed up by the surf, and she's holding her baby low in her arms. Almost like she's cradling it against the residual mound of her belly instead of up within the safety of her chest. I understand Amy's urgency, knowing I can outpace her to get there first. My decades of running on the beach have prepared me for the speed required to get to Isla faster. Just then Isla turns, and she sees us coming—our movements appear to have spooked her.

"Wait, stop!" I call to her, though the volume of the waves is drowning out my voice. I'm struck by the superficiality of her body, like she's attached to her limbs by accident—her tether to her newborn like a toddler dragging a rag doll. I've bypassed Amy, and I can hear calls behind me that could be mistaken for panicky, primitive seagull squawks.

Isla moves farther out and turns to reveal vacant, lifeless eyes. Shivering, I can see that luckily, Eve is swaddled, so the awkward positioning of her being so low on Isla's torso is slightly less terrifying. All of her limbs are confined, with only her head protected by the bump that remains in Isla's belly. I keep my arms extended in case that's the signal Isla is waiting for.

"Please!" I manage to shout above the waves. My tone is forceful and familiar, reminding me of all the times Lucas has needed to coax me back, when I've crossed over the threshold too far to be bothered with any way but my own. Another snapshot of a shadow life in an image so jarring it shouldn't be real: one portraying the magnitude of selfishness.

I feel Amy's presence. She, too, has her arms extended, and she's begging Isla not to go any farther.

"Gimme the baby. I'll take her, please," Amy cries, but Isla only steps back, deeper into the waves. "Stop!"

There's a familiar craze on Isla's face, the kind that only a mother who's been on the brink can recognize in another mother. It's an imperceptible wavelength of hopelessness that I can channel because I've stood at the railing inside the bell tower. I've been the rat who has chosen the high over survival. Paradise lost. There's been an underlying hum that has lingered for a while now. I've been prepared for what's on the other side if I don't choose to change. Maybe all the versions of me have existed all along, all at once. But maybe there is a way to merge and weave the strongest pieces together.

It's not so much a question of Isla's motives or desperation as it is a certainty of inescapable doom that warrants my next explosive action. I lunge for the baby as I would for one of my own, knowing the roughness of any transfer will be far less perilous than the fate Isla has in store for them. When I touch the unmistakable warmth of new life, I secure Eve into the space beneath my neck. Isla continues to retreat deeper into the break, faster now that I've unburdened her of Eve. The constant churning of white, frothy foam is like a spin cycle; the disorientation of it all makes me acutely, painfully aware of both Amy's and Isla's lack of equilibrium.

"Come back," I hear Amy call out. But Isla's so far gone now.

I turn and fold the baby's fragile frame into Amy's open arms. Amy's eyes are pleading with mine.

"Go—I'll get her," I promise, even though I, too, am desperate to retreat from Isla, to allow a wide berth for her self-destruction. But I won't. I follow her into the shadowy depths as she leans into the wave, using the sea as a worthy playmate, an equally cunning enchantress. Isla's playfulness switches effortlessly between emotions that cannot be trusted at the hands of obliteration.

I'm trudging through wall after wall of water until Isla leans back, arms out as if she were attempting a snow angel, and everything goes eerily still. A temporary flatness presides

over the ocean, now suddenly satiated by the consumption of
Isla's body. I'm on all fours feeling for a limb to tug upward. By
the time she's surfaced she's choking on water, inhaling huge
gulps, and it's impossible to make out her garbled jumble of
words, but I'm sure they are "Help me. I need help." A bigger
wall of water hits and she's pulled backward, farther and farther from my reach. I turn to see Amy has Eve safely onshore.
Isla has become solely my responsibility.

Amy is pacing, calling out to us both, but her words are
swallowed up incoherent, only decipherable as an octave that's
frantic. So I heave and swim until I've made contact with one of
Isla's limbs, which has succumbed in a lifeless way that's reminiscent of what I saw when I first met her eyes in the water.

If only. If only. If only I could save her from herself.

I pull and pull while two men descend on us and help drag
Isla out of the water. I didn't even feel them coming. Without
their help, I never would have been able to manage her water-
logged body; I am too exhausted. They get her up into the drier
sand as I tumble toward her.

Amy tries to hand me back the baby, but I refuse to let her
strain her body in such a way, to risk her pregnancy in any capacity by performing CPR. However illogical my thinking,
I kneel beside Isla and listen for breath. The two men have
backed off. One of them is calling for help on a cell phone.

I can save her.

Amy is directing my movement, shouting out the pattern
I am meant to follow. Laid out on the sand, Isla is a version of
pale blue that I know will haunt me—haunt me in the way Julie's
words were meant to. A siren song I'll carry as a reminder.

I know she's not breathing when I begin compressions. I
place one hand on top of the other, interlocking my fingers.

Amy drops down, tapping the location where I need to put the heel of my palm. My loyalty will be reflected with every beat.

I'm sorry. I'm so sorry. I'm sorry.

Amy tries again to relieve me by rotating Eve closer to me. I shake my head. I'm too wet to hold the baby. The stickiness of my hair slaps at my cheeks as I will Isla back to life. I refuse to give in.

"Keep her. Hold her. Come on, Isla," I say, sucking up the salty sea air around us, hopelessly trying to inhale all of Amy's unyielding determination from the time before, when Amy brought her mother back from the dead. Was it all just borrowed time?

"Breathe!" I'm shouting, my face stinging while the wind whips sand into my eyes. I don't want to wipe them, to have to stop, because I can sense that I've hit the proper depth in the center of her chest. All I can be is here. Some moments are bigger than everything we are or will ever understand. All my fears are instantly rightsized as another mother's life hangs in the balance. *I* want to survive, while all of me knows that Isla never truly wanted to die. She just no longer knew how to live.

When the paramedics arrive, I wait for them to make the official call.

We need to make our way up the bluff. The baby needs milk, though Amy has managed to use her pinky to temporarily appease Eve's sobs. The paramedics confirmed the baby's vitals and we will bring her into the hospital for a full checkup. Her sounds are growing louder now that we've moved away from the ocean—a combination of cries and hushed cooing.

As we carefully move up the dunes, I'm unable to gauge my steps in the sinking sand. I steady my pace so I won't fall and place my hands up to steady Amy's movements. My arms are like jelly. Exhausted by the hike, we need to stop to rest. I witness Amy examining the baby's little face, pressing their cheeks together and smelling the scent at the very top of her head. She hugs the baby into her.

"It's okay, little one. I've got you. We've got you now." Her voice comes out as a soft, buttery whisper. The urgency behind the rush and explosion of movements that brought us here has dissipated.

Time stands still. Again, we look out into the sea. Maybe there is a disturbance in the waves a hundred yards out—a movement like a seal, but the darkness of the crests makes it impossible to interpret.

I curl my arm around Amy's belly, matching my steps to hers as we descend the dune. She has the baby tucked away, safely resting inside the shelf between her belly and her breasts. Smiling in recognition that every part of her body is now finally filled with children.

The wind has stopped as we walk beyond the rhythmic hum, the siren song propelling us away, lifting one leg after another: all of us moving forward together.

EPILOGUE

Christine insisted that all the grandchildren be dressed in white. All seven of them. She's requested that George capture the day, not so we can live in the past but so Grace's first family outing is forever memorialized.

Paul is wearing baby Chrissy—she looks like a Chrissy, all cheeks and hair—and Amy has Eve in her arms. She is forceful in her need for freedom.

When Amy and I returned to the trailer, she found Isla's journal. The final entry, Amy said, she didn't need to read because there was a knowing in her bones that had existed since the long-ago day she pulled Isla from the water. That it could always end this way.

If I just wasn't here.

It has been an all-hands-on-deck situation for Paul and Amy with two newborn baby girls. I've gotten to witness Amy in her element. We've sat out on my deck, our hands spilling over with children. It isn't perfect or pretty because no mother anywhere, even Christine, ever claimed it was.

I no longer need to wave to my shadow self because I am able to pull from all components I swore were once lost forever.

Turns out I never needed to look for ways to escape the scariest, darkest corners of who I am. Amy has shown me this as she's charged forward in the throes of grief and fear while still surviving within those hellish feelings.

I've gone half a year without drinking, 180 days. Christine was insistent that we come out to scatter Grace's ashes after I received my six-month chip in that same Catholic church where Amy first took me to a meeting back when I was a wisp of what I now recognize to be my shadow self. The family offered to come support me, but I'm still getting used to a sober identity, and blurring all my worlds together is a step I'm not quite ready for, though maybe I will be someday. Reid has Dottie on his back and Lucas is holding Reid's hand for balance along the shoreline. We all make our way out into the tide pools.

I presented Lucas with the envelope along with my recognition that my actions were unforgivable. The DNA confirmed Joni as Lucas's biological child. While the relief is visceral, the bittersweetness of all this unnecessary suffering has been a cruel pill to swallow. My sponsor assures me that every road, no matter which fork taken, could have dead-ended with us becoming alcoholics. I was certain that my uncertainty of Joni's paternity was the culprit behind my need to drink away my feelings of deep-rooted discomfort. But it helps to hear stories inside the walls of my twelve-step meetings that, when I listen closely, have nothing to do with similar tragedies and everything to do with similar sensations from within. The nodding along that I so detested from that first meeting isn't an indication of absolution but of solidarity and understanding.

Lucas and I are in a newer place. A more honest one. Yesterday we even went surfing.

I've started to discover that motherhood is not a confined

space but a wide-open one made for exploration. So I've begun doing just that with each of my three children, often failing, but doing so while present with them.

One morning in sobriety, I was walking alongside Dottie as she pedaled her pink bike with clunky training wheels that stabilized her enough to make her believe she was a "big girl." She had us stop among a collection of fallen flowers that were also pink because that is the only acceptable color these days—besides purple and rainbow, and unicorn if that were a color, and polka dots in a pinch—and I pointed out how it looked as if they were doing "handstands" because their petals created a kind of weighted corset so the stem could stick straight up in the air. We laughed and laughed until our cheeks hurt, and I couldn't help but think, *This is the joy I thought existed only outside of myself.*

Christine is, of course, walking in step with Joni. They have divided Grace's ashes into the boxes that lined Christine's hallway, which contained their most precious shells. I was there when they determined which boxes would be worthy of such a momentous occasion. Christine began to remove each shell and display them in their nakedness along the wall.

"No, Grandma," Joni said, shaking her head. "*Let's return them to the sea. To be with Grace.*"

I stood in the hallway beside them, in awe—I had witnessed my daughter's ability to selflessly navigate the challenging and often intimidating world around her with such limited time in it. Instead of retreating from the enormity of the moment, I stepped forward, placing my hand on Joni's with Christine doing the same. That became the first image I painted for a brand-new collection.

There's a participation I'm conscious of now that I wasn't

before. The one I swore up, down, and sideways was happening all around me while I was excluded from the O'Connors. But as we step from rock to rock among the tide pools, I'm here with them in a way I wasn't able to be before.

Joni passes out the boxes to each member of our family. We've all found a patch of rocks that forms a complete circle as if it's been waiting for us. The light pokes through two clouds that have begun to repel each other in the fogless sky. As the sun casts its final light, the shaded phantom stretches across the rippled canvas of sand behind us. I lean in closer so that our shadows will meld and merge. I can predict what Christine is going to say even before she does. There's a knowing that you have when you are a part of something.

A NOTE FROM
THE AUTHOR

Dear Reader,

Thank you for reading my debut novel, *Between the Devil and the Deep Blue Sea*. As a person in recovery, my intention was to expose the harrowing experience of being a mother in active addiction while ultimately conveying a message of hope.

Recently, I sat in the jury box for a criminal trial involving the use of illicit drugs. It was during the jury selection process, known as voir dire questioning. I was shocked by the level of personal details they were allowed to ask in front of a courtroom full of strangers. Over the span of twelve hours across three days, I spoke openly about being a survivor of sexual assault and my history with substance abuse. The district attorney representing the state was a well-dressed man with square glasses who might once have been described as GQ.

I was the only potential juror he asked, "Are people who have been found guilty of past offenses more likely to repeat the same types of crimes in the future?"

I proudly responded, "Sure, people can show patterns of behavior, but as someone in long-term recovery, I am living proof that people are capable of change."

Later, when the DA pulled a Post-it note off his board and held it up, I knew my name was on it, even before he made eye contact. His shoulders drooped with an air of defeat, as if he carried some private knowledge that I was too naïve to understand. With his microphone, glasses, and position of power, he seemed certain that he had seen more of the world than I ever could. Yet, in the way he spoke my name, I sensed a hope that maybe, in this case or the next, someone would surprise him with their ability to reform. Not because the system works (we both knew it was broken), but because I have witnessed firsthand the resilience of the human spirit. The DA may have seen more than I have, but I have lived more like a "criminal" than he ever will.

Although I have learned to silence my inner demons, I feel called to advocate for those who have yet to find peace with theirs. I have been given the gift of articulating our tortured descent, which is why I created the character of Leah. There are far too many of us who never make it safely to the other side. In my addiction, I was never a bad person trying to be good; I was a sick person trying to be well.

Given my healing, lived experiences, and survival, I understand why I was thanked and dismissed in this case. However, this does not mark the end of my service to the community. It is only the beginning.

In gratitude,
Jessica

ACKNOWLEDGMENTS

I'd first like to thank my literary agent, Ismita Hussain, and the Great Dog Literary team. I feel so lucky to have you championing my career. None of this would have been possible without you. Laura Wheeler for having the type of enthusiasm for my novel and for me that a writer can only dream of; my line editor, Whitney Bak; and Margaret Kercher, Kerri Potts, Taylor Ward, Caitlin Halstead, and the entire team at Harper Muse.

My family: My husband, whose faith in me never faltered—thank you for being my partner and doing whatever it takes to make all our dreams come true. My daughters—Charlotte, Maddie, and Joey. I wrote about my love for you three in a way that can now be permanent. My surfer sister, Cara, for being such an honest, thoughtful editor and knower of me—I'd pick you as my sister every time. My mom, for reading to Cara and me every night and fostering a love of literature in our home. Books have been how we connected from the moment we all cried together during *Where the Red Fern Grows*. Thank you to my stepmom, Peggy, for being such a genuinely loving and supportive person. To my stepdad, Toni, for your devotion to my mom. And to my dad, the magic of my love for you is endless.

Bono may have been the one to say, "Love is a temple. Love, a higher law," but you were who showed me how to love with my whole heart.

For the Guerrieri family: I hit the marriage jackpot with you all! My sister-in-law, Michele, who was my first reader and brainstormer—we are definitely not Leah and Amy, but I like to believe the best parts of us sure are. My mother-in-law, Maureen, the matriarch of all matriarchs. You were our family's heartbeat and North Star. Grammy, thank you for welcoming me with open arms into your big, beautiful family. Thank you to my wonderful father-in-law, Dennis. My sisters-in-law, Sharron and Lauren, and their husbands, Martin and Jay. I'm listening closely to all my nieces and nephews when you tell me what you want to be when you grow up because I always said, "I want to write books." Never stop believing in yourself. I love you all and cannot wait for our country adventure.

For my grandparents, Norma and Jim, with seven children, you both set the stage for the beauty and complexity of what it means to be part of a large, close-knit family. For showing me that family is the greatest gift there is. All the members of the Cutter, Clark, and McCarthy families. For my auntie Berni for walking the path and showing me the way so I knew exactly where to go. My cousin Eden for your love and support. My uncle Gary, thank you for your belief in me and too many lunches to count—in your retirement, I promise to be the one to treat you to meals.

For all the women in The Program who helped to save my life, specifically my first sponsor, Meg: You showed me that humor was never lost in sobriety. And look what happened when I ceased fighting! The women of the Wednesday 5:30 p.m. meeting in Woodland and in Davis, my home groups. Each of you helped me in more ways than I could ever express. Thank you to my incredible sponsor, Mary Sue. Thank you to my first principal and remarkable friend, Michelle.

To my closest friends: Allie, I never would have survived the darkest days of motherhood without you—your friendship continually serves as my oxygen mask. Cristina, thank you for listening and participating in every phase of this roller coaster and for pushing me to complete Spartans and achieve my strongest, most authentic self. Thank you to my first best friend, Katie, whose best traits and big heart I borrowed for the character of Amy.

The Good Vibe Gals, specifically Laura, Sara, Anais, Molly, Heather, and Breidi, you always treated my writing career as a foregone conclusion and believed in me when I struggled to believe in myself. Thank you also to Nora and Jess. I'm lucky to call you my dear friends. Thank you, Christina Menze, for telling me back in 2019 to just start writing my book.

For my early readers: my mom, Cara, Peggy, my dad, my aunt Karen, Molly, Nina, Amanda, and Devon. Thank you for not cringing too hard at those first drafts. I had no idea what I was doing, and it showed, but without your feedback, *Between the Devil and the Deep Blue Sea* never would have evolved the way it was meant to.

To my favorite high school English teacher, Mr. Joey Jill: you helped to foster my love of literature, and I'm forever grateful for your tutelage.

To Lori Galvin: thank you for being the first in the industry to take a chance on me and for giving me an entire year of your precious time.

Thank you to the many people behind the scenes who made this book possible, including Emily Dilbeck, for so generously being my artistic muse so I could get into the headspace of what it means to be a painter. Rose Chloewinski at SwimAmerica-Davis for allowing me to use an office as a designated writing space during the pandemic so I could write in peace during a time when there was none. Thank you, Gaby and Kathy, for your French translations. A special thank-you to the Peloton Moms Book Club for supporting and encouraging my literary journey and to my early readers from this fabulous group. Thank you to the community of Half Moon Bay, California. I spent my youth on your glorious shores. Thank you to my cousin, Justin, for helping me with the surfing imagery. To Jamin, for showing me that young love can be as formative as the sea. Aunt Karen, thank you for coming in as my cheerleader. And Fit4Mom Davis-Woodland, thank you for providing me with endless mental and emotional strength, a book club, and a sisterhood in motherhood.

Thank you to Dr. Andrea Sherman, Dr. Sam Siegel, Christina Stokke, R.N., and Dr. Vi Ha. Thank you to Julia Aue, Jennifer Hatch, and Heather Elizabeth. Thank you to Carmen Isais. Remember, back in 2012, I came in wanting to be "cured" of my phobia of bridges, which planted the seed that alcohol was only exacerbating my symptoms of anxiety. Thank you, truly.

Thank you to all the writers who so graciously offered me support, especially Lara Love Hardin and Sara Goodman Confino. Thank you, Barbara O'Neal, Ann Napolitano, Claire Lombardo, LL Kirchner, Courtney Maum, Daniel Quigley, Margot Douaihy, Hannah Sward, Jeffrey Dale Lofton, and Leah Elson. Thank you, Celeste Ng. Your novels and breathtaking prose are what inspired me to aim for the sweet spot between book club and literary fiction.

Thank you, Lisa Didio, for taking the time to show me the ropes of what it means to be a writer. Thank you, John Lescroart, for your guidance. Thank you, UC Davis and the College of Letters and Sciences, for awarding me the Maurice Prize for Fiction in 2023 for *Between the Devil and the Deep Blue Sea*.

Finally, thank you to *The Shit No One Tells You About Writing* podcast: Bianca Marais, CeCe Lyra, and Carly Watters. The opportunity to be on your show kickstarted a series of most fortunate events. All the WFWA Conference Babes, specifically Beth, who brought me into the fold, and Nicole, for your friendship and for being such a great hype woman. Thank you, Kym, Meredith, Alexis, Gina, and Harper. Thank you to the IG sober community, specifically Kat from @no.wine.in.the .carpool.line.

If I left anyone off the list, thank you. They say it takes a village to raise a child (and it does!), but it also took a village to get me to this point in my career and in my recovery. I have become one of those people who claims to be a "grateful alcoholic," which, in my early days of meetings, always sounded completely insane. It has become perfectly clear to me that I was meant to use all my challenges with addiction to share my message of hope. Mothers are being sold a lie in this alcohol-obsessed world that glorifies drinking as the solution to the maternal load. Don't believe it for one second. *You* are the magic. Recovery is possible.

DISCUSSION QUESTIONS

1. How does Leah demonstrate that she is an unreliable narrator?

2. Is Christine genuinely as monstrous as Leah portrays her to be? What are Christine's character flaws, if any?

3. How does the author use ocean imagery throughout the novel to enhance the themes and emotional experiences of the characters? Can you provide specific examples where this imagery deepens your understanding of the characters' internal struggles or the overall narrative?

4. The phrase "between the devil and the deep blue sea" describes a predicament where one must choose between two equally undesirable options. What dilemmas do Leah, Christine, and Amy face that put them in such situations?

5. At the beginning of the novel, Leah expresses a deep longing for her "shadow self." What resolution does she reach by the end, and why is this message significant for all mothers?

6. How does Christine's secret loss affect her relationships with her family members, particularly Leah and

Amy? How does Amy's relationship with her mother, Isla, affect her relationships with the O'Connor family, specifically Leah and Christine?

7. Leah often mentions using wine to take the edge off. How does this narrative reflect on the controversial issue of "mommy wine culture"?

8. A prominent theme of the novel is the exploration of "escapism within motherhood." Are healthy forms of escape available to mothers? Which characters in the novel, if any, utilize these healthy escapes?

9. List the support systems available to Leah by the end of the novel. Which one do you believe was most instrumental in helping her shift her mindset toward sobriety?

10. Compare Leah's journey with alcoholism to Isla's. How does Isla ultimately help Leah with hers?

LOOKING FOR MORE GREAT READS? LOOK NO FURTHER!

HARPER MUSE

Illuminating minds and captivating hearts through story.

Visit us online to learn more:
harpermuse.com

Or scan the below code and sign up to receive email updates on new releases, giveaways, book deals, and more:

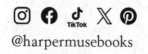

@harpermusebooks

ABOUT THE AUTHOR

Julia Aue Photography

JESSICA GUERRIERI's debut novel, *Between the Devil and the Deep Blue Sea*, won the Maurice Prize for Fiction from her alma mater, UC Davis, in 2023. Originally from the Bay Area, Jessica lives in Davis, California, with her husband and three daughters. She has a background teaching special education but left the field to pursue a career in writing while raising her daughters. With more than a decade of sobriety, Jessica is a fierce advocate for addiction recovery.